55

Boy, the things I do for my dad. He and his partner, Paul, are feuding, and he won't tell me why. It seems really unusual, because Dad and Paul are a comedy team who have been together forever, and I can't remember ever hearing a cross word between them.

Not like between Paul's son, Alex, and me. Alex and I can't talk to each other without barbs flying through the air like flinty arrows. It's been that way for over twenty years.

Which is why this charade that Alex and I are engaged is going to be so hard to carry off. But I can't think of any other way to get Dad and Paul speaking again. If he thinks they're going to be in-laws, Dad will have to talk to Paul. He has to do that for me. After all, look what *I'm* doing for *him*.

Paula Stewart

Reluctant Grooms

1. Lazarus Rising
   Anne Stuart
2. A Million Reasons Why
   Ruth Jean Dale
3. Designs on Love
   Gina Wilkins
4. The Nesting Instinct
   Elizabeth August
5. Best Man for the Job
   Dixie Browning
6. Not *His* Wedding!
   Suzanne Simms

Western Weddings

7. The Bridal Price
   Barbara Boswell
8. McCade's Woman
   Rita Rainville
9. Cactus Rose
   Stella Bagwell
10. The Cowboy and the Chauffeur
    Elizabeth August
11. Marriage-Go-Round
    Katherine Ransom
12. September Morning
    Diana Palmer

Instant Families

13. Circumstantial Evidence
    Annette Broadrick
14. Bundle of Joy
    Barbara Bretton
15. McConnell's Bride
    Naomi Horton
16. A Practical Marriage
    Dallas Schulze
17. Love Counts
    Karen Percy
18. Angel and the Saint
    Emilie Richards

Marriage, Inc.

19. Father of the Bride
    Cathy Gillen Thacker
20. Wedding of the Year
    Elda Minger
21. Wedding Eve
    Betsy Johnson
22. Taking a Chance on Love
    Gina Wilkins
23. This Day Forward
    Elizabeth Morris
24. The Perfect Wedding
    Arlene James

Make-Believe Matrimony

25. The Marriage Project
    Lynn Patrick
26. It Happened One Night
    Marie Ferrarella
27. Married?!
    Annette Broadrick
28. In the Line of Duty
    Doreen Roberts
29. Outback Nights
    Emilie Richards
30. Love for Hire
    Jasmine Cresswell

Wanted: Spouse

31. Annie in the Morning
    Curtiss Ann Matlock
32. Mail-Order Mate
    Louella Nelson
33. A Business Arrangement
    Kate Denton
34. Mail Order Man
    Roseanne Williams
35. Silent Sam's Salvation
    Myrna Temte
36. Marry Sunshine
    Anne McAllister

Runaway Brides

37. Runaway Bride
    Karen Leabo
38. Easy Lovin'
    Candace Schuler
39. Madeline's Song
    Stella Bagwell
40. Temporary Temptress
    Christine Rimmer
41. Almost a Bride
    Raye Morgan
42. Strangers No More
    Naomi Horton

Solution: Wedding

43. To Choose a Wife
    Phyllis Halldorson
44. A Most Convenient Marriage
    Suzanne Carey
45. First Comes Marriage
    Debbie Macomber
46. Make-believe Marriage
    Carole Buck
47. Once Upon a Time
    Lucy Gordon
48. Taking Savanah
    Pepper Adams

Please address questions and book requests to: Silhouette Reader Service
U.S.: 3010 Walden Ave., P.O. Box 1325, Buffalo, NY 14269
Canadian: P.O. Box 609, Fort Erie, Ont. L2A 5X3

Make-Believe Matrimony

MARIE FERRARELLA

IT HAPPENED ONE NIGHT

Silhouette Books

Published by Silhouette Books
America's Publisher of Contemporary Romance

SILHOUETTE BOOKS
300 East 42nd St.,
New York, N.Y. 10017

ISBN 0-373-30126-X

IT HAPPENED ONE NIGHT

Copyright © 1990 by Marie Rydzynski-Ferrarella

Celebrity Wedding Certificates published by permission of Donald Ray Pounders from *Celebrity Wedding Ceremonies*.

A Letter from the Author

Dear Reader,

You have before you one of my very favorite books. *It Happened One Night* was my first Special Edition and a milestone for me. But more than that, it had two of my all-time favorite characters in it. Paula and Alex's banter took form in my head long before I could get to a computer. It was as if they couldn't wait to be written about.

The idea was actually conceived while I was reading an article about a legendary comedy team. I started wondering how they managed to maintain private lives and an ongoing, lifelong friendship under stressful conditions. What if, as happens all too often, something split them up? Could their family bring them back together again, and how far would they go to do it?

For me, the plot thickened and got better when that family took the form of a perpetually squabbling hero and heroine who harbored a long-standing attraction they weren't conscious of. Caught in a well-meaning web of deception intended to bring their feuding fathers together, Paula and Alex found themselves thrown together time and again—more than enough to make them aware of just how strongly attracted to each other they were. How they dealt with this twist, and how they managed to maintain the charade of being engaged, was the fun part for me. I hope it is for you, as well.

Love,

Marie Ferrarella

To Jaclyn Brilliant,
the answer to a prayer,
and more

Chapter One

The bannister beneath her hand shook as a door on the first floor was slammed. Paula Stewart stopped on the staircase and listened. Another slam, this time less emphatic, resounded. She dragged a hand through her hair. What was this, day number four? And there didn't seem to be an end in sight.

Shaking her head, she made her way down the stairs and into the living room. On her way to the kitchen, and the center of the hurricane, she picked up a sweater from the floor that had been carelessly thrown toward the sofa and had missed its mark. Her father didn't need a cleaning lady; he needed a keeper. Preferably a deaf one.

The cupboard door banged mightily as Paula approached the kitchen. The slamming and banging had been going on ever since she had arrived at her father's house last week. It was quickly getting to be more than Paula could stand. She had temporarily moved in with her father while major surgery was being performed on the water pipes of her two-bedroom condo. She was beginning to think that perhaps she had made a mistake in coming here. Taking sponge baths with bottled water was preferable to an enduring headache any day.

Braving the storm, she walked into the kitchen and found her father there, puttering around the tile counter with its ultra-modern features like an overage Pillsbury Doughboy. Her father, Wally Stewart, known as the funnier half of the comedy team of Stewart and Hamilton, had a round beach-ball face that was given to rubbery smiles and innocent, befuddled looks. The only time she had ever seen her father look annoyed or troubled was when he and her mother had gotten a divorce. And even that episode seemed to pale in comparison to this. He was wearing a scowl this morning. It was the same scowl he had been wearing for the past week, ever since he and Paul Hamilton had broken up because of an argument, the details of which he refused to give her except for making strange, guttural noises each time she asked.

At the moment he was in the midst of making breakfast, or creating havoc, she thought, depending on one's point of view. Cautiously she entered the kitchen, not unlike a soldier approaching the line of fire. She kept a wary eye on the man she had always adored.

"Good morning." She draped the sweater over the back of one of the four stools that faced the breakfast counter and made for the coffee maker.

Wally spared her a glance as he laid out utensils on the counter. "For some."

She kept her eyes on the coffee as she poured. It was going to be another one of those days. Filling her mug to the rim, she perched on the stool farthest away from him. For a moment she sat there mulling over the situation, scrutinizing her father. This was so out-of-character for him. It had to be stressful, although not as stressful for him as it was for her. She had never seen her father quite like this. He was usually good-humored to an irritating fault. If he *had* a fault, it was his cheery enthusiasm, which threatened to get out of hand each time he and Paul went on the road, or had a new act to break in. He had been entertaining since the age of twelve. Life on the road and comedy were all Wallace Stewart knew or truly loved, besides his only daughter and, up to seven days ago, his partner.

She knew the story of their first meeting by heart, but never tired of hearing it. Her father had run into Paul Hamilton when they were both down-and-out entertainers working the Catskill resort circuit in upstate New York. At the time Wally had been a hapless comedian searching for the right niche and Paul had been a hopeful actor with a stunning profile that was chiseled in granite and, unfortunately, an emotional range to match. An hour into their first conversation, Wally had seen his chance to change his act and utilize both Paul's looks and his lack of verve. The comedy team of Stewart and Hamilton had been born. It was a match, Wally had often told Paula, that had been made in heaven. It was Wally who brought the energy or zip to the act and Paul who provided the stability. The two men worked well together and cared for each other like brothers.

Given their temperaments, Paula felt that if there was anyone to blame for this argument that her father refused to elaborate on, it was most probably him.

Swirling her coffee in her mug, Paula made the decision to interfere. She wasn't going to stand by and see her father go on this way. He was suffering. She only had to look at his eyes to tell. Knowing it was bordering on insanity, she still risked the suggestion. "Why don't you just apologize to Uncle Paul?"

Wally, carton of milk in hand, slammed the refrigerator door with his elbow. An incredulous look filtered across the wide, almost childlike face. The carton met the tile countertop in slow motion as he stared at his daughter.

Paula winced, grateful that he hadn't slammed the carton down. She scrunched down in an unconscious and utterly fruitless effort to hide behind her coffee mug. The sprinkling of freckles on his face seemed to stand out on his pale face in indignation.

"Me?"

Not her father's daughter for nothing, she knew just how to play it. "I don't see anyone else here."

"Apologize?"

Another sip wound down her throat before she answered. "That was the word."

He reached for a bowl and cracked four eggs into it as he shook his head. "How is it," he wanted to know, applying a fork to the eggs and beating them mercilessly, "that I raised you for twenty-six years and never noticed that you were feeble-minded before?"

Paula pretended to peruse the newspaper next to her on the counter. "Well for the first fifteen years, you were on the road."

Wally nodded his head sagely, his words addressed to the eggs. "I should have never let her mother keep her. That's when the damage happened."

Paula gave up the charade and put down the paper. "The only damage that's going to happen is to your house, if you don't stop slamming things."

He raised his head, a mincing expression purposely flittering across his cherubic face. "I'm only acting out my feelings, the way psychologists like your mother are always accusing men of not doing."

It took her a minute to play the sentence back in her head before she could make sense out of it. She knew exactly what her father thought of psychology, in general, and her mother's opinions, in particular. Although he and her mother had eventually parted as friends, there was a wound there that never quite healed. Whenever he hurt, his humor had a bite to it. With all the tenderness she felt for him coming to the surface, Paula leaned over the counter and put her hand on her father's thick wrist. He stopped working to look at her.

"Face it, Pop, you need Uncle Paul."

Shaggy rust-colored eyebrows that had once been a bright red drew together. "I don't need Paul."

Paula removed her hand and shrugged. Lovable though he was, he could be the most stubborn of men when he wanted to be. "All right, have it your way. Let's just say you make less noise when you're on speaking terms with Uncle Paul." She looked over at the coffee machine and debated having a second cup. Today she needed all the boost she could get. Another dose of caffeine wouldn't hurt.

"Look," she said, half filling her cup, "Gilbert and Sullivan worked for ten years without speaking to each other. Couldn't you and Uncle Paul come to some kind of an arrangement?" She knew if they worked together, the cause of the argument would have to evaporate. They cared too much about each other to carry a grudge.

He pulled a package of bacon out of the depths of a refrigerator that brought tears to the eyes of his cleaning lady. "We could," he tossed the package on the counter with a thud, "if he weren't so pigheaded."

Paula worked hard not to laugh out loud at his pronouncement. "Said the levelheaded, calm, collected member of the partnership."

Wally raised a pudgy finger. "Ex-partnership. Besides that," he shrugged humbly, "you got everything right." He bent down, throwing open a cupboard door. It banged against the other door.

Paula threw up her hands in semidespair. "There's no arguing with you!"

He spared her a recriminating look over his shoulder before he went on pushing pots aside. "Then why do you bother to try?"

"I have a suicide complex." She looked down at him as he rummaged. Sliding off the stool, she rounded the counter and came to crouch down next to him. "What *are* you looking for?"

"Another pan. Wanda straightened everything out and I can't find anything around here anymore."

Paula elbowed him aside. He always blamed his inability to find things on his cleaning lady. It took Paula one try before she came up with a suitable pan.

"Beginner's luck," Wally grumbled, taking it from her.

"You're welcome," she answered cheerfully.

Bacon sizzled as Paula threw herself back into the subject under discussion. He wasn't about to get away that easily. "You and Uncle Paul have to make up. You just can't throw all those years away."

Her argument fell on deaf ears. "Never tell your father what he can't do."

"But you've got all that time invested. You've been 'married' to Uncle Paul longer than you were to Mother." She reached over to turn down the flame beneath the frying pan as her father poured the eggs into another pan.

The bowl clattered into the sink, empty. "Paul never tried to analyze me. Until last week," he muttered under his breath.

But Paula heard him. Her eyes grew wide. "Is *that* what this is all about? What was Uncle Paul doing, analyzing the act?"

But her father wasn't about to expound on the cause of the problem. "No, it's over. Finished. *Finita le comedia.*"

She could feel herself losing ground. "Stop babbling in Latin, Pop. It is not finished. You even named me after Uncle Paul!" It was her last-ditch attempt—for the moment.

Wally stopped tending the bacon and let out a heavy sigh. "I've been meaning to talk to you about that."

"About what?"

"How do you like the name Rebecca?"

She scrunched up her face, as if the action would help her absorb his meaning better. It didn't. "What?"

"It's never too late to get a name change," he told her innocently.

Paula closed her eyes. This was far worse than she thought. "Pop, be reasonable."

Spatula in one hand, Wally put the other to his chest, and said in his best dramatic voice, "I am the soul of reason."

Paula pursed her lips. "Hardly."

"Leave the wisecracks for the paying customers."

Because the eggs threatened to turn black, matching the bacon, Paula saw her father elaborately turn his attention to what was happening on the stovetop.

Paula had had enough. Her father and Paul belonged together. They were still funny, still playing to big crowds, and she knew that without each other they were miserable. Without comedy, each would wither on the vine. If he wasn't going to be big enough to put an end to it—and she had no idea why he was suddenly acting so strangely—then she would.

Draining her mug, she put it on the counter and marched over to the wall phone. "If you won't call Uncle Paul," she said, lifting the receiver, "I will."

The devastating look he gave her only succeeding in looking comical. "Don't touch that phone."

She kept the receiver in her hand and looked at him defiantly. "And why not?"

Coming from her father, the voice was unbelievably calm. "Does the word *death* mean anything to you?"

She wasn't going to move him this morning. Resigned, Paula hung up. "You don't want me to call Uncle Paul."

For a minute the smile that could infectiously light up a room at a moment's notice was back. "The brains you got from me. The looks, from your mother." And then the smile faded again.

Tactfully Paula refrained from reminding him that he had just called her feebleminded a few minutes earlier. "What are you scowling at now?"

He arranged the bacon on the plate, while the eggs dried out in the pan. "I was just thinking what if it had been reversed— if you got my looks and your mother's brains." He shuddered rather elaborately.

Paula decided to give it one more try. "About Uncle Paul—"

"The subject is closed." He frowned at the eggs that were stuck to the pan and refused to surrender to his spatula. Muttering under his breath, he took out four more eggs from the carton he had forgotten to put away. "How do you want your eggs?"

Paula glanced at the kitchen clock. "In the car." She picked up a piece of bacon and took a bite. "I'm late."

"Something else to blame on Paul."

Paula halted in the doorway of the kitchen. This she had to hear. "How, pray tell?"

"If you weren't so busy taking his side, you would have had time to eat a hot meal."

She crossed back into the room and kissed his cheek. Standing side by side, they were almost the same height. She always marveled how such a funny, little man could attract so many women. They were always there at his side, every club date. It was the goodness inside that spoke to them, she had decided. She had never met anyone who didn't love him.

"I wasn't taking his side, Pop, and I love cold eggs—even yours." To prove it, she scraped them off the pan onto a paper plate, threw aluminum foil over them and tucked the package into the cavernous interior of her gaping purse. She could always throw them into the trash at work, she told herself. "And now I'm off." She took three steps, then turned around again. "Pop?"

"Yeah?"

"Do me a favor."

"Anything but call Paul."

Paula sighed and turned back to the doorway. "Never mind."

"Whatever you say, baby." Pulling himself onto a stool, her father began to eat his breakfast.

Irritated wasn't the best frame of mind to be in when she was going into work, Paula mused. Not when work involved writing for a weekly situation comedy. This morning she didn't feel very creative or witty. Pushing her mood aside, she flashed a quick smile as she walked into the Burbank studio office that she shared with Marty Sorensen and Ted Hammerstein. The two men nodded in response.

Paula sat down before the computer and switched it on. It was her turn to keyboard their combined thoughts onto the data disk. Mechanically she called up yesterday's work and scrolled to a fresh screen.

Up until this morning although the rift between her father and his partner had surprised her, it hadn't worried her. She had assumed—naturally enough, she thought—that whatever problem existed between the two old friends would blow over. She had never known her father to let a single day go by without talking to Paul, much less seven days. This, she had to admit, was obviously getting serious. It spoke not only of the end of a long business association, but more importantly, of a twenty-seven-year friendship. Those, she thought as she stared off into space, were hard to come by.

"Paulie, where are you today?" Marty's voice broke through her haze.

She blinked and realized that he was standing over her, and that she hadn't heard a word that had been said. "Sorry."

Marty reached for another doughnut, his fourth of the morning. "Not half so sorry as we'll all be if we don't get this episode of *Hayley's House* in the bag."

Paula gave the head writer an apologetic smile. "My mind was elsewhere."

"So will our paychecks be." The doughnut disappeared behind satisfied lips.

"Your dad still feuding with his partner?" Ted positioned himself on the side by her chair.

He could make a person feel surrounded all by himself, Paula thought, shifting in her chair. "'fraid so."

"Look," the tall man continued, perching on the arm of her chair and putting his arm on Paula's shoulder, "if you need a place to crash, my offer still holds." The smile he gave her came under the heading of lascivious.

Lifting his hand from her shoulder as if it were a separate entity, she let it drop to the side. His seductive attempts had become a standing joke between them, even though there was more than a hint of truth behind them. "Thanks, Ted, but I can always stay at the Y."

Marty sighed, running his hand through the little hair he had left. "Why don't we take a fifteen-minute break and start fresh?"

"Fine with me." Paula rose. "But Hammerstein's already as fresh as the civilized world can stand." She patted Ted's baby-smooth cheek as she left the room.

She went as far as the soda machine in the hall before she made up her mind. It wasn't a decision she was crazy about, but it was the only option she had left. She had promised her father, in effect, not to talk to Paul about the rift. But she had said nothing to him about Paul's son, Alex. That was mainly because, she knew, her father felt secure that she *wouldn't* contact Alex. It wasn't that she and Alex were hostile toward each other, it was just that they no longer existed on the same planet. She was too capricious, he maintained, and she thought he was far too conservative. Oil and water.

Paula had known Alex all of her life. There were even pictures in her mother's album of him holding her, all swaddled in blankets, on his lap when she was six-months old and he was a proud four. As children they had played together. In later years their families tried to get together whenever the two men were in town for any length of time or, barring that, at least twice a year. But somewhere along the line, Alex had gone straitlaced on her. It had happened during his first year in college, when he had decided to become an estate lawyer. While Paula had been growing up, she had had a fierce crush on Alex that no one knew about. But it faded in the face of his premature sternness, his desire to "make something of himself" at the cost of his spirit.

Eventually the crush had been forgotten. She had never really been able to warm up to the new Alex. Oh, he was a fine, upstanding lawyer, handsome in an Ivy League, clean-cut sort of way, but he just didn't have a spark anymore. She couldn't remember when she had last seen him with his hair mussed or wearing a pair of jeans. He had become all work and no play. She doubted if he even remembered how to laugh. She didn't relish the thought of calling him and asking a favor, but it was for her father's sake, not hers, she reminded herself. Her father's and Uncle Paul's, who she guessed was probably just as miserable as his partner—just not as noisy.

The Los Angeles skyline was clear for a change, but Alex hardly saw it as he stared out the window of his twentieth-floor office.

His father was driving him crazy.

Alex didn't know what had gotten into him. The man was definitely behaving strangely. Incoherent. Bereft. All the words that Alex would have sworn had no place in Paul Hamilton's life—until last week. His father would call him at odd times of the day. Or worse show up at his apartment in the evening, looking like a lost waif with nowhere to go. It just wasn't like him. Alex hadn't thought that his father had *ever* been affected by anything in this way. Even his mother's death hadn't elicited such bizarre behavior. He wondered if the senior Hamilton was suddenly coming unhinged. Probably it was a result of all those chaotic years on the road. Alex frowned, remembering how he had resented his father's absences when he had been growing up. Paul Hamilton had led the life of a nomad who just happened to hang his hat in a particular closet several times a year. And now it was apparently all coming to a head.

It was a sad thing to face.

The intercom on his desk buzzed. Alex sat down again, bracing himself for yet another call from his father. Today, they seemed to be coming at ninety-minute intervals.

"Yes?"

His secretary's very British voice came on the line. "There's a Ms. Stewart on line two."

Alex frowned slightly. "*Ms.* Stewart?"

"Yes."

Probably just another new client. After all, Stewart was not that unusual a name. "Did she give a first name?"

"Paula."

He paused, confused. Why would Paula be calling him? Paula never called him. He and Paula had an unspoken agreement at "family" gatherings to interact as little as possible. Ever since he had become a lawyer and she a comedy writer, they had found very little they could agree on.

"You're joking."

There was silence for a moment, then a very clipped, "I never joke, Mr. Hamilton."

"No, of course not, Bianca." As far as he knew, the woman didn't even smile, but then, he didn't require smiling, just efficiency, an area where his secretary excelled. "I'll take the call." Alex pressed the flashing red button down. "Hamilton here."

Paula leaned back in her chair, twirling the coiled phone wire around her finger. Same old Alex, formal to a fault. "Alex, we used to go skinny-dipping together. I know your last name."

Trust Paula to find a way to embarrass him in the first ten seconds of a conversation. A fragment of a memory, blurred with time, flashed through his mind. Paula, lean and lanky, leaping into the water, her long red-gold hair whipping about her in the wind. He straightened in his chair. "That was twenty years ago, Paula."

"Gone, but not forgotten."

He heard the soft, sultry laugh in her voice. For an irritating woman, she had the sexiest laugh he had ever heard. "Did you call to reminisce, or was there something specific you wanted to talk about?"

"Oh Alex, you do go on." She let out a sigh. "I called about this rift between our fathers."

Absently, he picked up a paperweight and balanced it in his hand. "What about it?"

"I think we should meet to talk about getting them back together."

The idea of getting his father back with Wally had crossed his mind more than once, but there was no point in admitting it to Paula too quickly. She'd call it a game point in her favor. The woman was far too self-assured as it was. "That's meddling."

Didn't he have any feelings at all, anymore? "No, that's surviving. My father is so upset, he's driving me crazy."

You are already half crazy, he thought. Surprisingly the thought made him smile. "Then have him apologize."

She might have known Alex would take that attitude. "He'd rather die."

Alex examined the paperweight. "That, too, would be a way out for you."

Paula shut her eyes for a moment, wondering how someone so handsome could be so impossibly stuffy and difficult to communicate with. "Alex, much as it pains me to say this, please?"

The phone buzzed again. "Hold it a minute, there's a call coming in." Putting her on hold, he switched to the intercom. "Yes?"

"Your father is on line one."

A headache materialized from nowhere. It was time to take action, and in handling the team of Wally and Paul, albeit separately, he was going to need all the help he could get—even Paula's. "Tell him to hold." He switched over to Paula. "Paula?"

She detected defeat in his voice and wondered what the silent fifteen seconds had yielded. "Yes?"

"When can we meet?"

"This afternoon at one too soon?" She tried to keep the smile out of her voice.

She didn't succeed. He heard it. "Not soon enough. Are you familiar with Anton's?"

She wondered if he meant to be condescending or if he thought that she was only familiar with fast-food places. "I think I read about it in *People* magazine."

"It's on fifty-first and—"

"It was a joke, Alex."

"They pay you for this?"

She didn't rise to the bait. "Usually I have more inspiring material to work with."

He looked down at the blinking red light on his phone. His father hadn't hung up. He had no choice but to meet her. "See you at one, Paula."

"I can't wait."

He had heard that teasing tone before, and knew he was in for an afternoon that he would rather avoid. "I can."

"You do know how to turn a woman's head, Alex."

This time, he laughed. "I usually wind up wanting to wring your neck."

"I remember." The words were fondly uttered, and she suddenly remembered the Alex of the past, the one she used to have so much fun with. "See you."

She hung up.

Alex sat and stared at the receiver for a moment, wondering if he had done something unpardonably stupid by agreeing to meet with her. Something told him that he very well might have.

Well, time would tell. Resigning himself, he pushed down the first button on his phone. "Hello, Dad, what can I do for you now?"

Chapter Two

Alex arrived at the restaurant before Paula. He knew he would. He was of the opinion that Paula regarded time as something decorative to be worn around a wrist. Although she worked regular hours at the studio, he had always thought of her as a free spirit, not bound by common things such as responsibilities and timetables, the way the rest of the world was. It both irritated and fascinated him, although he kept the latter to himself.

There had been a time, he mused, when his and Paula's spirits had been more kindred, but he had been very young then, and reality hadn't intruded yet. As time went on and he became more and more aware of their fathers' life-styles, he knew that he wanted the exact opposite. He and his mother had traveled with the comedy team in the early years, until he turned eight, at which point his mother had decided that he needed to attend a regular school. Paula and her mother had always remained at home. He had envied Paula that. She would have undoubtedly enjoyed tramping from city to city. Though he was quite young at the time, living out of a suitcase, never know-

ing where his bed would be that night, was nothing short of
pure chaos to him. He had needed stability, structure. He
needed to know what the future held. If there was something
within him that cleaved to the more flamboyant, he ignored it.

Paula had called him stodgy, but what did her opinion matter? He thought of her as hopelessly whimsical and irrespon-
sible.

He knew the exact moment she entered the restaurant. There
was no need for him to see her. The sound of her laughter
floated through the air. Low and throaty. It was unmistakable. He had heard it directed at him more than once.

Alex turned and watched her breezily take possession of the
maître d's arm, the light green dress she wore accenting her
every move as she walked. The tall, dignified man was reduced
to a grinning, benevolent giant who escorted her to her table.
She had a way of doing that, Alex thought, to everyone but
him. Men all seemed to brighten around her. He found himself sitting a little straighter, being a little more alert. All his
senses came to life, waiting, anticipating disaster. It was not
unlike, he thought, preparing for an earthquake.

Paula gave the maître d' a flash of a smile, bright, overwhelming and guilelessly genuine, as he helped her with her
chair.

"Thanks, Jon." She turned to Alex as she opened up her
menu. "Sorry, we ran over."

He wondered how anyone could have hair that looked like a
tumultuous storm and still be so attractive. "Was it anyone I
know?"

Using her finger to skim the list, she saw nothing that
tempted her. Her appetite seemed to have vanished in the last
few minutes. "Hmm?" Maybe just a salad.

"That you ran over," he clarified.

Paula closed the menu and fixed her green eyes on Alex. "I
see why you went into law."

There had always been something about her look that made
him defensive. He could never shake the feeling that she could
see right through him. Silly feeling, he would have thought he

would have outgrown it by now. "I went into law because I like order, stability, rules."

"Please," she shuddered, holding up her hands to ward off his words, "you're giving me goose bumps just talking about it."

For the moment, he was amused instead of annoyed. "Everything still a joke to you?"

She ran her fingertips along the edge of the menu, her eyes on his face. "It helps balance the world. You see everything as deadly serious. Mix us together, and you get an average person."

It was an effort to draw his eyes away from her hands. Their motion was almost hypnotic. "Not if you're one of the ingredients."

Paula batted her lashes at him. "Flatterer—"

This was going to be a long lunch, Alex thought, resigning himself.

The waitress appeared to take their orders. "Would you care for a cocktail?"

Paula saw the long look of appreciation the young woman gave Alex. He did look as if he had stepped out of *GQ*. His profile was just rugged enough. He had thick black hair, a nose plastic surgeons would call their crowning achievement if they had had a hand in it and eyes the color of the sky at dusk. She had to admit that there was a lot to admire there. Too bad it didn't go any further.

"I don't know about you, Alex, but I could certainly use one." She turned toward the waitress. "Singapore Sling, please."

"I'll have a Black Russian," Alex added.

The waitress gave him a heartfelt smile and moved away on crepe soles.

"Comedy writing not going well today?" Alex guessed at the source of need for liquid reinforcement.

"It's going fine." She moved her menu to the side. "What isn't is *Life with Father*." She sighed. "If he slams one more thing in the house, I think the whole place is going to fall apart."

Alex offered Paula a roll from the basket the busboy had discreetly placed on their table. "I didn't know you still lived at home."

Paula broke off a piece of bread and took a bite. "I don't— at least, not normally." It needed butter, she decided. "May I?" She indicated the butter dish at his elbow. He nodded as he passed it to her. "I'm having work done on the plumbing in my place—after two pipes broke one wonderful Sunday morning." The next bite of bread was more satisfactory. She grinned at Alex. "But that's another story."

And he knew she could tell them. She was, like her father, a natural storyteller who reeled in her audience. He didn't want to encourage her.

She read as much in his eyes. "The main point," she continued, "is our fathers. I'm assuming that Uncle Paul is as upset about all this as my father is."

Alex buttered his roll slowly, wondering how much to divulge and how much he should leave unsaid. "I don't know about upset, but well..." Alex paused, then went ahead. "He sputters."

A dab of butter smeared on her finger and she licked it off. Alex watched her, and a strange feeling spread through him. He recognized it for what it was, and thought that he hadn't been getting out as often as he should. There could be no other reason for the sudden, unbidden sexual pull.

"Sputters?" Paula repeated. Why was he watching her every move? Did he expect her to do something outlandish right here in the restaurant? Alex was so conservative it made her want to scream at times.

Alex nodded, running a hand over razor-cut jet black hair. "Like an outboard motor. Never finishing his sentences."

She understood, even if she could see that he didn't. "That's a holdover."

The waitress reappeared with the drinks and her pad. "Paula?"

Paula surrendered her menu. "Seafood salad, please." She accepted her drink.

"Two." Alex added his menu to the one the young woman was holding, and gratefully took his drink. He wondered if one was going to be enough. He leveled his perplexed gaze at Paula. "What's a holdover?"

"Uncle Paul never finishing a sentence." She took out the pink-and-yellow umbrella and nibbled on the orange slice that had been skewered on it. "Dad never let him finish a sentence. He always knew what Uncle Paul was going to say."

Alex frowned. Frustration began to gnaw at the edges of his mind, as he remembered several of the evenings he had spent with his father. "Well, your father's more blessed than I am." He wrapped his hands around the stocky glass and moved it back and forth slowly. "Half the time I don't know what my father's talking about these days."

Paula allowed herself a long, studious look at the man opposite her. So good-looking and so devoid of warm, intuitive feelings. What a waste. "You would if you listened."

He recognized the tone. It usually preceded one of their differences of opinion. "Are we here to try to get them back together or to catalogue my faults?"

"The former." She took a long sip of her drink. It was all fruit and no punch. "The latter would take me too long. About Uncle Paul—" She was all ready to launch into her idea, but got no further. To her surprise, Alex put a hand on her wrist.

It was the only way he knew how to stop her. "Paula, you're—how old?"

His hand felt oddly warm, protective on hers. She wondered if he was either of those things. He had been, once, or had she just imagined it? "Old enough to vote." She frowned. "You know perfectly well how old I am. What's that got to do with anything?" She wished he'd take his hand back. It was making her feel . . . odd. Maybe the drink wasn't as weak as she thought.

Alex saw the way she looked down at his hand, and he withdrew it, aptly hiding a wave of self-consciousness that came over him. It always seemed to, in her presence. Only in her presence.

"Don't you think you're a little too old to keep referring to my father as Uncle Paul?"

She could have been annoyed at his pickiness, but she held herself in check. She didn't want to reduce the discussion to a war of wits, at least not yet. "Age has nothing to do with it. It's a sign of affection." She leaned forward and whispered, "You can look it up in the dictionary under *A*, counselor."

Alex raised a brow. "I know what the word means, Paula."

Paula shrugged. She kept her eyes on her drink as she attempted to spear a cherry. "I thought lawyers didn't listen to hearsay."

She got to him. She always did. "Are you trying to tell me that I'm a cold stuffed shirt who doesn't have any firsthand experience with affection?"

A bit of red was visible from beneath the ice chips. Paula pulled the cherry out. "If the laundry mark fits, wear it."

"Look, just because I don't babble like, like—"

The smile she gave him could have melted butter at fifty paces. "Alex."

"What?" Exasperation laced his tone. He realized that he had raised his voice. "What?" he repeated, lowering it. The waitress placed their plates before them and left quickly.

Paula's eyes never left his face. "You're babbling." There was satisfaction in her voice.

He could feel his jaw tightening.

"Alex Hamilton does not babble." He saw her give him a questioning look, and he relented with a pronounced sigh. "Except around you. Why do you think that is?"

She sampled her salad before she allowed herself to answer. "I'd like to think that I bring out the best in you."

He laughed shortly. "Be serious."

Paula opened her eyes wide in innocent surprise. "I am being serious."

It was when she opened her eyes wide like that that Alex was reminded of exquisite emeralds shining in the light of a setting sun. No, the rising sun. Beginnings, not endings. Paula didn't believe in endings. She always said they were too sad. Funny how he knew so many things about Paula without wanting to

Like the scent she always wore. Something subtle and musky. Basic. It made him think of a great many things that weren't connected with the Paula he knew.

That Paula was flip and always had to have the last word. While he secretly admired her wit, he would have suffered a great deal before admitting it to her.

His salad really didn't interest him, but he made an attempt to eat. "You know you always bring out the worst in me, Paula."

She shook her head vehemently. "No, you do that without my help, I'm afraid. And besides, I didn't make you become a lawyer."

For the moment, he forgot the original purpose behind their meeting. "What's wrong with being a lawyer?"

"Nothing," she shrugged innocently.

Just when he thought she had dropped the subject, she went on, "I should have specified an *estate* lawyer."

Alex put down his knife and fork. "All right, what's wrong with being an *estate* lawyer?"

How could she phrase this so that he'd understand? And why did she even want him to understand? What he did with his life was no concern of hers. "Why didn't you go into something more flamboyant? Like criminal law?"

It was the perennial clash of their life-styles again, he thought, caught up in it, nonetheless. "Why stop there? Why don't you ask me why I didn't become something really colorful—like a cat burglar?"

He always looked cute when his feathers were ruffled, she thought, suppressing a smile. A show of emotion, even annoyance, was better than nothing. "You're much too muscular to be a successful cat burglar."

For some reason, he was surprised she actually noticed him in physical terms. Surprised and oddly...pleased. He clamped down the response that rose to his lips, simultaneously wondering what was coming over him. "I'm afraid of heights, too," he added sarcastically. It was true, but it wasn't what he had meant to say.

"That would get in the way," she agreed. She raised her eyes to his face, while keeping her head slightly lowered. It had a devastating effect, which she was unaware of and he refused to consciously acknowledge. "But I think there's something more serious at play here."

Now what was she driving at? "Oh?"

"You're afraid of risks."

"If I were, I wouldn't be here with you."

It was her turn to be caught unaware. He saw it in her face, and he relished the momentary victory.

"Meaning?"

"Meaning meeting with you is like attending my own roast— except that I know I won't be greeted by affectionate applause at the conclusion of the barb slinging." He was a lawyer, used to picking his words very carefully. *Affection* and *Paula* didn't belong in the same sentence. He would have bet his life on it. So why had he used the term? He was getting sloppy.

"I'm as bad as all that, huh?" she asked, suddenly serious.

He was surprised. He didn't think anything would get to her, but to backtrack now would mean surrendering the momentary triumph. "I thought I was being rather charitable." He was paying her back for all the slings she had carelessly thrown at him.

She raised her chin proudly. It was a gesture meant to redefine the lines between them. It didn't quite make it. "The only kind of charity you give is from the pocket."

"Now what are you talking about?"

"Heart, Alex, heart." She waved her hand impatiently, wishing she didn't feel suddenly so unable to express herself, so uncustomarily unsure of herself. There was always that little bit of uncertainty somewhere in the back of her mind, whenever she was around him. "Something you don't have. You don't give of yourself. You don't cross over that very careful line you've drawn for yourself."

He shook his head as exasperation began to mount within him. He could never quite control it around her, the way he normally could in every other situation. If it weren't for Paula, he would have sworn that he was a fairly easygoing man, without a trace of temper. Paula always managed to bring it out, along with a host of other emotions he would have preferred to have left undisturbed. "You use more words to say nothing than anyone I've ever known."

"If that's an insult, it wasn't a very clever one."

"I wasn't trying to be clever."

"Congratulations," she raised her salad fork in a salute, "you've succeeded."

He let out a perturbed sigh and looked at his watch. "Paula, I have to meet a client in an hour. Is there a point to our meeting?"

"There was. There is." She shook her head in self-mockery. "You make me forget myself."

"I only wish *I* could," he muttered.

His regretful tone made her smile again. "Truce?" She cocked her head to peer up into his face as she put out her hand.

He took the slender hand into his somewhat gingerly, as if he expected her to pull it away.

"You're holding it like it's a snake." Her tone was teasing again.

"Not quite a snake. Snakes can be turned into pets." The smile he offered changed his face to that of an endearing boy. It made her remember her crush.

Paula withdrew her hand and proceeded crisply, slightly shaken by the memories that crowded back. "About our fathers—"

"Okay," he leaned back in his chair expansively, "you're the scenario writer, what about our fathers?"

He sounded too willing. It made her suspicious. "They're miserable apart."

"No argument."

"Finally." She laughed, and it sent an intense wave of something deep and basic through him. He took another drink of his Black Russian.

"And we're miserable with them apart."

He nodded. "Agreed."

"Two for two. I'm afraid of going on."

That'll be the day. "But you will."

"I always do," she retorted wryly. "We need to get them closer than just the same town."

"Fine." It was like voluntarily sitting on a powder keg, waiting for it to go off. Just what did she have in mind?

"Like sitting next to one another."

They both knew how stubborn their fathers could be. What did she have up her sleeve? That she had a plan was something he never doubted. Paula was never at a loss for ideas, however unorthodox. "Short of using a gun, how do you propose to do that?"

Paula began rummaging through her purse.

Alex watched in fascination as Paula pulled things out of her purse that had no business being there. He stopped playing with his salad and leaned over toward her. "I lost a pair of gold cuff links in 1986. Could you see if they're in there?" Raising one eyebrow, she awarded him a withering look. "Well, it looks as if everything else in the world is in there," he explained with a shrug. "Just what are you looking for?"

"These!" She held a small envelope aloft and pulled out four tickets. "Tickets to *Laughter and Love* at the Dorothy Chandler Pavilion. You bring your sire, and I'll bring mine—without telling them that the other will be there."

She handed him two of the tickets and then put the others away again. "Once they see each other, they'll have to talk."

"Doubtful." Alex pocketed his two tickets. "Paula."

She knew that patient tone. It bespoke of annoyance just behind it. "Yes?" she asked innocently.

"Why did you bother asking me to meet with you? You've obviously already made up your mind as to what to do." She had this irritating habit of taking charge without thinking things through. She had had it for as long as he could remember.

If she was too flip, Paula knew he might decide not to help. And she needed him to convince his father to attend the performance. She gave Alex a warm smile. "Let's just say I'd feel reassured if you agreed with me."

"That'll be the day." He thought about her plan and shook his head. "I don't know, Paula, this sounds too simple."

Paula shook her head. Alex watched the waves of auburn hair bounce against her slim shoulders. "Lawyers are always making everything complicated. Uncle Paul and Pop are simple men, they just need a little encouragement to get them to iron out whatever it is that's wrong." She patted her purse confidently. "Running into each other at the play will make them do it. They won't act like squabbling children in front of us."

Alex was willing to concede to part of her reasoning. "Well, my father wouldn't."

Oh no, he didn't. "Meaning mine would?"

"Paula," he said helplessly, "I'm not looking for an argument."

"You're certainly doing a bad job of convincing me."

"Finished?"

"With my meal, yes. With you, no."

That's what you think, lady. "Sorry, I just remembered another appointment." He put his napkin on the table. "And don't you have work to do, or do you just mail in those scripts?"

She knew what he thought of television. Mindless entertainment. He probably never took the time to just sit back and enjoy himself anymore. As she began to rise, he came around to her side of the table and pulled out her chair for her. The gallant gesture pleased her, even though she knew it was automatic with him.

"No, I don't mail in the scripts. We work a lot of hours on those little scripts." She realized she had made a mistake as soon as she uttered the word *little*.

"Your word, not mine." She opened her mouth to retort, but he wouldn't let her. He was more taken with the fact that she had let him pull out the chair for her. "I thought you'd be too much of a feminist to let me help you with the chair."

They walked out of the restaurant. A valet stood by the entrance, and Paula handed him her ticket.

"I have nothing against male slaves." Out of the corner of her eye she saw the valet give her a strange look, as he ran off to fetch her car from its parking space.

Her answer didn't have an iota of truth in it, but she couldn't resist saying it. She loved trying to get one up on Alex. He was, without his probably knowing it, a challenge to her each time they met. Stuffy though he might now be, he did possess an excellent mind, and she loved sharpening her wits on it. Besides, he was adorable when he was flustered.

"I bet you don't," he muttered.

She laughed, pleased with herself and feeling oddly light-headed. She decided it was because the end of her father's slamming fit was at hand.

The valet got out of her car and handed her the keys. She handed him a tip in return. "So I guess I'll see you tomorrow night."

She caught Alex off guard. "What?"

"The tickets." She tapped his breast pocket where he had put them. "They're for tomorrow night."

"Oh."

His hand covered hers for a moment before he reached inside for the tickets. He thought he saw something soft flitter through her eyes, then dismissed it. Paula wasn't soft. She was a tongue with legs. Pulling out the tickets, he looked at them. "Right."

"Better get on your toes, counselor." She patted his shoulder. "You'll lose the next case, if you're not careful."

He watched her disappear into her Porsche and drive away as he waited for the valet to bring around his Mercedes. Why did he feel as if her words were some sort of a prophecy?

Chapter Three

Paula came sailing into the kitchen the next morning, wearing a simple light gray jacket, rose blouse and white crisply pleated trousers. In addition to the outfit she was wearing, she was carrying a dress on a hanger. She caught the quizzical look her father gave her as she kissed his cheek. "I'm taking my dress in to work."

Her nose was assaulted with the aroma of French toast. Actually she was being kind. It was assaulted with the odor of burned French toast. It was a credit to her father that he never gave up trying. A credit to him, a trial to her.

She draped the dress over the back of a stool and seated herself at the counter, resigned to another culinary experience.

Wally placed a serving of French toast in front of her. It was, she saw, still recognizable. It could have been worse.

"Why?" Her father nodded at the dress. "Does it feel neglected?"

Paula drowned the burned offering in maple syrup. "No, Pop," she answered tolerantly. "I'm taking it with me so that I can change for the theater tonight, remember?"

The better part of last night had been spent trying to convince him to go with her. She had gone to bed, she thought, victorious. Apparently there had been some troop movement during the night.

Paula sampled her breakfast and decided that there wasn't enough maple syrup available in Southern California to help kill the taste. She desperately cast about for a gracious way to walk away from breakfast without offending her father, who seemed to get hurt easily these days.

"I'll probably have to work late tonight. There won't be enough time for me to come home and change. I'll meet you there." She picked up her glass of orange juice and brought it to her lips, but didn't drink. Her father was frowning. "What's the matter?"

Wally kept his eyes lowered as he mumbled, disgruntled, "I just looked in the *TV Guide*. There's a John Wayne movie on tonight."

She wasn't going to be taken in by his tone. This was for his own good, even though he didn't know it yet. "We'll tape it."

Wally gave an impatient snort. "You know I can't work that damn thing. It's got more buttons than an elevator." He dropped a batter-encrusted pan into the sink and waved his hand in the general direction of the living room.

Grateful for a reason to abandon her breakfast, Paula slid off her stool and marched back into the living room. "Not to worry, I'll take care of it for you."

She thumbed through the *TV Guide* and found the movie listing. Three presses of as many buttons and the machine was set. With less spring in her step, Paula returned to the kitchen. "Done." Subtly she picked up her plate and dumped the contents into the garbage, keeping her back to her father.

Wally had seated himself on a stool and was poking at his own breakfast, but not for the same reason. "I don't really feel like going out, baby."

Oh please don't get stubborn on me. You've *got* to come. "We've been through all this already, Pop." She rinsed off her plate and left it on the rack to dry. "You *need* to get out, if only to give the furniture a rest." She crossed the kitchen and stood next to his stool. "C'mon," she coaxed, tucking both her arms through her father's. "It'll be fun. Just you and me," she lied, hoping he'd forgive her for this eventually. "We haven't gone out together since I can't remember when."

Wally leaned back on his stool and pretended to give her a once-over. "Well," he drawled, "I usually go out with younger women."

She grinned and wound her finger through the wispy hair on top of his head. "Make an exception, just for tonight." She withdrew her hand and became serious. "Please, Pop. I really want to see this play, and I don't want to go alone."

He was still reticent. "Why didn't you just invite a friend?"

"I did." She smiled. The look in her eyes softened affectionately. "You."

Wally sighed. "You really make it tough to turn you down."

The look she gave him was both smug and impish. "I'm trying to make it downright impossible."

Spreading his hands wide, he gave in. "Okay."

Paula picked up her dress and slung it over her shoulder, her fingers wound around the top of the hanger. "You won't be sorry."

Wally stared at the dark piece of toast on his plate. "I will be if that blamed VCR doesn't work. I really like *Rio Bravo*."

"The machine'll work perfectly." She crossed her heart with her free hand. "I promise."

He kissed her cheek as she turned to go. "You, I can believe in. Not like some people."

She knew he was talking about Paul.

Soon, Pop, she silently promised, soon you can believe in Uncle Paul again.

Heartened, Paula left for work.

Nine hours and one complete rewrite later, she still hadn't lost her good humor, although she wasn't all that sure about her mind and body. She felt as if she had been passed through a wringer. In slow motion. This week's episode of *Hayley's House* was exactly one day away from the final taping session. That was the time when the director and at least one of the stars of the show usually began toying with the script and demanding changes. It was the time of the week that Paula hated most. Today had been pure hell with a capital *H*.

Of course, she thought, if things went awry, tonight would be no better.

"Some people go through trial by fire once," she muttered into the mirror in the ladies' room. She brushed her hair away from her face. Stubbornly the swirling auburn mass refused to obey. "I go through it every week. I must be crazy." She stopped and looked around. There was no one to hear. She continued her monologue uninhibited. "I probably am, if I'm getting ready to voluntarily sit next to Alex."

No, it wasn't Alex, it was Paul who would probably sit next to her. No, she amended again, pushing a shell comb in just above her ear, Paul would be next to her father, and she'd be on her father's other side. Alex would get the aisle seat. *Those* were the arrangements she had mentally mapped out yesterday. Slightly frazzled around the edges, she was getting confused. Paula blew out a long breath. She could hardly wait until the evening was finally underway.

As a test, she shook her head. To her satisfaction, the combs held. At least one thing had gone right today. Let's hope for two, she added silently, checking her purse one last time for the tickets.

With one final survey of herself, she decided she was ready. Even if she wasn't, it was time to go. Traffic at this hour, she knew, was going to be murder, and she had a little less than an hour to get to the Dorothy Chandler Pavilion.

Later she was to realize that getting her combs to stay in her hair had been the *only* thing that had gone right that evening. But early in the evening she had no way of knowing that. She thought it was a good omen when she managed to arrive at the theater twenty minutes before the curtain was scheduled to go up.

She was wrong.

Congratulating herself on having time to spare, and mentally preparing herself for the scene that was to come once the two feuding partners saw one another, she made her way down one of the aisles. The four seats reserved for her party were empty.

Okay, she thought, where was everyone?

"Excuse me, Miss Stewart?"

Startled that someone should know her name here, she whirled around to find an usher standing next to her in the aisle.

Having just spent nine hours locked into a continuous argument about the quality of this week's script, the first thing Paula thought of was work. Hayley Halliday's tentacles extended far and wide.

Oh God, Paula groaned inwardly, don't tell me they want me back at the office. Hayley couldn't want *another* change. Even she couldn't be that cruel.

Distressed, Paula still managed to keep her composure as she tried to smile nonchalantly. "Yes?"

"There's a telephone call for you. You may take it in the manager's office."

It *was* Hayley. Why had she mentioned where she'd be tonight? "For me?"

"Yes. If you'll just walk this way." The slender young man turned on his heel and walked back up the aisle.

Reluctantly Paula followed the usher.

The manager's office was wood-paneled and plush, but she hardly took any notice of it and only vaguely acknowledged the manager, who rose when she entered.

"Ms. Stewart?" She nodded. "I'm a great fan of your father's."

Her father? Something clicked in Paula's brain. Of course. Her father had the seat number right in front of him and had undoubtedly charmed the manager into sending someone for her. Now the question was why. The way the manager beamed, she knew that her father wasn't calling from the hospital. That meant that nothing had happened to him.

Still, she hoped his medical insurance was paid up. He was going to need it when she got through with him.

The manager handed Paula the telephone and pushed the third button down for her. Graciously he stepped away. Paula waited until he was several feet away.

"Hello?" A whole range of emotions, led by anger and frustration, were registered in her voice.

"Hi, baby."

"Don't 'hi, baby' me." She turned away from the manager and lowered her voice. "Why are you calling me?" she asked urgently. "Where *are* you? And why aren't you here?"

There was a dramatic pause. "I'm sick, baby."

Well, she conceded grudgingly, maybe he was on the level. This was the cold and flu season. "All right, I'll be there as soon as I can."

"No, no," he interjected quickly. "I said sick, not dying. Just a little fever, that's all. But at my age, you can't be too careful."

"At your age," she scoffed. "This morning you were a young Casanova, who said women *my* age were too old for you. Tonight, you're Methuselah. Make up your mind, Pop. You can't have it both ways."

"No, but I want to live to be Methuselah, so I've got to take care of myself. Stay and watch the play. I'll feel twice as bad, if I make you miss it. I know how much you want to see it. I'll just tuck myself into bed and turn on old John for company."

She couldn't very well admit that she had no interest in the play without giving away the whole scheme. She was stuck here for the evening. "Say hi to John for me," she muttered. "I'll see you when I get in."

"I'm really sorry, baby."

He sounded so genuine, she relented. She was just angry because her first attempt had failed. "Yeah, me, too." More than you know, she added silently, then replaced the receiver. "Thank you," she told the manager.

"Not bad news, I hope," the man said.

"No, my father was supposed to come to the performance with me, but he couldn't make it. I'm sorry about the inconvenience." She nodded toward the telephone on his desk.

The mustached man beamed at her. "It's never an inconvenience to talk to Wally Stewart. He's a great man."

"Yes, I know." And a great con artist when he wants to be, she thought, taking her leave. Oh well, she consoled herself. It could be worse.

It got worse.

Muttering under her breath, she made her way down the aisle back to her seat. She walked directly into Alex, who was on his way to the exit. Alone.

Paula looked around his tall frame to make sure that Paul wasn't behind him. She turned her eyes to Alex. "Where's Uncle Paul?"

"Home." Alex bit off the word tersely.

"What?"

People kept bumping into them. There was nowhere to move in the aisle, where they weren't blocking someone's way. Muttering an oath, Alex nodded in the direction of their seats. He let Paula lead the way. "He just called me on my car phone as I pulled into the parking lot."

She was afraid to ask. "And?"

"It seems his car won't start."

If she didn't know better, she would have sworn this was shaping up like one of her father's old comedy routines. "Do you believe him?"

Annoyed, Alex shrugged. "Do I have a choice? I just came to tell you the 'good news' and couldn't find you here." He looked around. "Where is *your* father?"

She hated admitting failure, but there was no way around it. "Home. Sick. Or so he says." She frowned as she sat down.

Alex sat down next to her. The forest green dress she wore made her eyes seem even more vivid, he thought. As if she needed that. She was already too vivid for her own good. Or his. With her hair pushed away from her face, it made her neck seem more slender, her face more heart-shaped. Damn attractive woman—to some men's way of thinking, he amended. He forced himself to look at the program, wondering what was wrong with him tonight. He had seen her dressed up before. But each time it had been at a function where there were a lot of other people he knew. Somehow this was more intimate.

He laughed at himself. No one in the world would consider sitting in the front rows of the Dorothy Chandler Pavilion intimate. It sat over six hundred people at maximum capacity. Tonight it seemed to be practically bursting at the seams.

"You know, it seems like an awful strange coincidence for both of them not to show." Her eyes narrowed. "You didn't mention to Uncle Paul that I would be here, did you?" There was an accusation in her voice.

"You'd make a wonderful cross-examiner," he quipped, knowing that his comment would annoy her. "No, why?"

She shrugged. It had been a shot in the dark. "Well, if he knew I was coming, he might think Pop was coming, too."

Alex nodded. "A logical, well-thought-out idea. You surprise me." Before she could retort, he continued calmly. "I said nothing, except that I thought we needed an evening out together—as opposed to an evening *in* together."

She caught the inflection and grinned. "Been dropping by a lot?"

Alex pursed his lips together. Paula had never realized how full and sensuous they looked before. "Try every night. He's beginning to drive me out of my mind."

"He's just lonely."

"Then he should try dating."

"No, he should try getting back with his partner," she corrected stubbornly.

"It certainly doesn't look like that'll be tonight, does it?" Below, the orchestra was tuning up, but he hardly noticed. All he seemed to be aware of was the woman next to him. And that bothered him more than he liked to admit. He just couldn't quite fathom why. Alex sought refuge in sarcasm. It was something they both understood. "Well, here we are, just the *two* of us." He looked at her significantly. "Any more ideas, Dear Abby?"

Paula's eyebrows rose mockingly beneath the fringed bangs. "Name-calling. Very good. Is that how you win your cases, counselor? Calling the jury names?"

"I never had to go out with the jury."

"Lucky jury. Well, you're not going out with me, either. We just happen to be at the same place at the same time, sitting together." Calm down, Paula, you're beginning to ramble.

The houselights were starting to dim. "Look, we're here, we're dressed for it, and I bought the tickets. We might as well enjoy the evening and watch the play."

He leaned back in his seat. "Let's just watch the play and not stretch credibility here."

She faced forward. "Fine with me," she answered tersely. This was going to go down as one of the most miserable evenings of her life, she prophesied.

It was a very funny, absorbing play. Paula had to admit that despite the circumstances and plans gone astray, she truly was having a good time. It was a comedy, and Paula loved to laugh. The only thing that put a damper on the evening was knowing that Alex was sitting next to her in the darkened theater. There was something vaguely unsettling about his presence, more so tonight than usual. Probably, she told herself, because she had never had to sit next to him for such a long period of time before.

Alex watched her almost as much as he watched the characters on the stage. Even though he tried to shut it out, her laughter kept drawing his attention back to her. If there was anything that made her stand out in his mind, aside from her barbed tongue, he thought cynically, it was her laugh. It was the kind of laugh that belonged to a woman who could be soft even while she was strong, a woman who knew how to please and exactly what pleased her. A woman of spirit. Something stirred within him, something timeless, primal. It refused to be shut away.

He realized that his hands had closed in his lap and were clenched for some reason. He opened them and tried to relax. Relaxing next to Paula was like trying to relax in a lion's den without knowing if the lion was in or not. Tonight there was something more going on, but he'd be damned if he knew what. Before he realized it, the performance was over.

"Well, the evening wasn't a total loss," Paula said as they moved with the rest of the crowd out into the sumptuous lobby

Without thinking, he placed his hand on the small of her back to guide her out. It was a routine gesture. Strange how delicate she felt beneath his palm. Again, the term seemed a odds with the woman. Paula was *anything* but delicate.

"How so?"

"It *was* a good play." She was relieved when they walked into the lobby and he dropped his hand. For some reason it was far too intimate a gesture.

She stopped for a moment as he helped her on with her wrap His strong hands passed over her bare shoulders, and just for an instance, there was something akin to a flash of electricity that went through her. She would have told herself that it was just because she was shuffling her feet along the carpet, but she wasn't shuffling, and it wasn't a dry night. Rain had threatened since early morning.

Their eyes met and held for a moment. Alex dropped his hands away from her shoulders. "Yes," he took a deep breath inhaling that fragrance that was hers alone, "it was good wasn't it?"

Uncustomarily ill-at-ease, Paula dropped her eyes first "We'd better be going."

But just as they walked out of the building, the sky broke open and it began to rain. People were running for their cars al around them, and it was nothing short of a madhouse.

"Now what?" Paula muttered.

In response, Alex pulled her over toward a place where they could stand away from the crowd but still under the pavilion' roof and safely out of the rain. For a few minutes, they stood watching it come down. The noise of the crowd was in the background, and it might have been nonexistent for all the difference it made to them.

"The weatherman predicted rain," Alex commented watching as it came down in sheets.

Paula sighed. "Wouldn't you know he had to pick tonight to start being right?" She watched in silence for a moment. "I've always thought of rain as romantic," she said unexpectedly having no idea what possessed her to share the thought with him.

He felt like putting his arm around her, but didn't. Here, more than ever, he caught her scent, mixed with the musty smell of rain. "I don't see the connection."

Paula shook her head sadly. "You have no soul, Alex."

"Let's see," he reviewed, amused. "No emotions, no sense of humor, no soul. There's not much of me left, is there? What is it I do have, if anything—according to you?"

She turned to look at him instead of the rain. The answer was simple. "Integrity."

"I'm sure the firm will be happy to hear that."

"Are you?"

"Am I what?" As usual, she had lost him. He wondered if lightning worked as fast as Paula's mind did.

"Happy."

He didn't want to consider her question seriously, afraid that there was more to it than he cared to know. "I was before you started hatching plans."

"No one twisted your arm to come," she pointed out.

"No, no one did."

"Why *did* you come?"

"Because I thought the old man was lonely," he told her honestly. "I don't know what's come between them, but it shouldn't have."

She stared at him in wonder. "Alex, I do believe you can be positively human at times."

His eyes slowly took in the contours of her face. The light played on it, making it seem almost exotic. A gypsy, that's what she was; an exciting, irritating gypsy. "At times, Paula, I think I can be too human."

She felt her breath catch in her throat, and she forced it out. "Where's your car?"

A nice, safe topic. "Parked in Arizona."

She knew what he meant. The parking lot was huge. "Mine's closer. We'll get mine first. I'll give you a ride to yours."

It started to really pour, and the wind was picking up. "I don't know, maybe we should wait."

But Paula shook her head. "There's a man in the lobby collecting two of everything. I don't think the rain's going to get any better."

He shrugged, and then, to his surprise, she grabbed his hand and dragged him off into the rain. They ran, dodging cars that were pulling out sporadically. Suddenly, as she reached her car, her foot slipped out from under her and she began to fall. Alex pulled back hard on her hand to try to steady her. Instead he caused her to fall against him, and they both went down with her sitting on his lap while he unceremoniously found his posterior making contact with a huge puddle. Expecting to hear some sort of an apology or at least a word of sympathy, Alex was surprised to hear Paula burst out laughing.

Her arms went around his neck. "I knew you had your uses." Impulsively, still laughing, with rain cascading down her back, Paula leaned over and kissed him quickly. That was all it was supposed to be, just a quick, meaningless kiss.

It wasn't what it turned out to be.

Caught off guard, Alex went with instincts he didn't know concerned her. His hands gripped her shoulders, and he kissed her, really kissed her, with far more passion than he realized was there, hovering on the brink. The kiss was hot, passionate, wanting.

He expected her to pull away and rap him one. He didn't expect her to kiss back. And he certainly didn't expect passion, not in either one of them, not to this extent. When it came down to it, he hadn't known *what* he had expected, but it wasn't this. When was the last time a kiss had left him reeling? He couldn't remember. He suspected never. She felt wonderful, even though there was nothing more touching than their lips and his hands on her shoulders. His mouth slanted over hers, over and over, taking, giving, creating havoc.

Once she had wondered what it would be like to kiss him. Now she knew. It outmatched any of her childhood fantasies and blew them all apart. His mouth was firm, strong, demanding. Challenged, she met the dare and paid back in kind. And in paying back, she was ensnared, hopelessly, totally, enmeshed.

But she couldn't be. Not with Alex! This was all wrong.

Paula pulled back, breathless, her eyes wide. "We'd better get in, if you want that ride to your car."

Alex went around to the passenger side and waited until she got in and threw the switch to unlock his door. He eyed her as he slid silently into his seat. Why wasn't she saying anything? It wasn't like her.

He felt nerve endings tingle. It wasn't like *him*. He turned his face forward and stared straight ahead.

She had trouble locating his car. Hell, she thought, she was having trouble driving. Her arms were shaky. *She* was shaky. She didn't like the implication.

When Alex finally spied his car, Paula stopped and let him out. Alex turned to say something, but she gunned the motor and sped off, chewing a hole in her lower lip.

Alex got in behind the wheel and just sat there in the dark for a long moment.

It was just a harmless, little kiss.

No, damn it, it was a passion-laced kiss. There was no getting around it. He had felt its impact like a hard punch to his gut. Alex ran his hand through his hair. Paula? No, it was impossible. It was just too ridiculous. Yet there it was. He was attracted to Paula.

Now what gods had he crossed, he asked himself, to earn this sort of a punishment?

Chapter Four

Paula didn't remember getting home, not clearly at any rate. There was a vague image in the back of her mind of swerving headlights as she had veered the car to the right through a large puddle, but on the whole, the trip from the Dorothy Chandler Pavilion to her father's door was just a hazy experience that hadn't completely made it into her memory bank.

She noted with a mixture of annoyance and fascination that her heart was still beating somewhat erratically. It wasn't because of the kiss, she told herself. It was from the realization that there had *been* a kiss, that had been initiated on her part and that, dear Lord, it had felt good. More than good. Wonderful. It had felt, she squeezed her eyes shut now that she was within the confines of the garage, like a kiss was supposed to feel. Like an *important* kiss was supposed to feel.

Not with him, by God!

Paula clenched her teeth as she got out of her car. Thrusting her hand into her purse, she began to hunt for her house keys. She stood, dripping and rummaging, before the door that led to the house in the darkened garage. Her mind was working at a furious pace, trying desperately to assimilate what had just happened and turn it into something *other* than what it felt like had just happened.

The trouble with you, Paula Stewart, is that you haven't taken time out to smell the roses in I-don't-know-when. You accused Alex of being a workaholic, yet you're just like him.

"Heaven forbid," she interjected out loud.

I can't even remember when you had an honest-to-goodness boyfriend. *That's* why you reacted the way you did. You haven't been out there, responding enough.

She had certainly responded tonight.

Searching through her purse more frantically and with growing frustration, she told herself that she also hadn't had dinner. People deprived of nourishment tended to hallucinate after a time.

The time, she knew in her heart, was a bit longer than six hours, but who was counting?

The door connecting the house to the garage suddenly opened, and her father stood there, looking at her quizzically. In deference to her drenched state, he stepped back. "Out for a midnight swim?"

"I couldn't find my keys," Paula muttered as she walked through the doorway.

Wally shut the door behind her. Paula crossed into the family room. In the background the credits to *Rio Bravo* were just winding up, and the theme song filled the room. Wally eyed her purse. "I couldn't find Pittsburgh in your purse."

"That's because Pittsburgh isn't *in* my purse."

Wally cocked his head as he rested his arms on a very ample stomach draped in a frayed pink sweater. The sweater was older than Paula. He squinted at her, and his eyes nearly disappeared. "You seem upset."

"I'm not upset." She dropped her purse on the coffee table and realized that she had answered too quickly and too harshly. She flashed him an apologetic smile. "I'm just tired."

He made a show of looking her up and down. "And wet."

"And wet," she repeated mechanically. "How are you feeling?"

He pulled out his handkerchief and blew his nose, then grinned. "Better."

At least one of us is, she thought. "That's good." She tried to sound cheerful. It rang hollow. She knew she had to retreat. Her father was very good at reading her mind, and she didn't want it read tonight. Paula ran her hand through her damp hair. "I think I'll just slip into something warm and Alex." Her expression froze as she darted a look toward her father to see his reaction. Miraculously he didn't seem to hear her. "I mean, dry."

Make an exit now, Paula, before the other foot goes into your mouth.

With larger strides than normal, she made her way out of the living room and to the stairs. Tiny drops of water marked her path.

A loud commercial for the evening news came on. Wally switched off the set and glanced at Paula. "Are you feeling okay, baby?"

"I feel a little under the weather," she lied. The truth was, she wasn't exactly sure *what* she was feeling, other than surprised.

"You look like you've *absorbed* the weather." He took three steps after her, then stopped. "You know," his voice followed her up the stairs. "Maybe you shouldn't have gone to the theater, either."

Paula stopped on the landing, sighed and shook her head. "Maybe I shouldn't have."

When she walked into her bedroom, she flipped on the light and went straight to the wardrobe mirror. She stood looking at herself for several minutes.

"You don't look like you've been struck by lightning." The image stared back at her, unconvinced. "But you have, haven't you?"

Paula sank down on the bed, her hands wound around the left post of the four-poster bed. "So what are you going to do about it?"

She was amazed, utterly amazed by the obvious physical explosion that had taken place only a short hour ago. It was a reaction she would have expected of two lovers who had been parted for years, not two people who were so opposite that if they had been magnets they would have repelled one another to the ends of the city. For the first time that she could ever remember, she felt something akin to fear quaking in the pit of her stomach. In another setting, at another time, things might have ended quite differently tonight.

She was playing with dynamite.

"I'm going to ignore it, that's what," she said a bit too breezily to fool even herself. She dragged her hand through her wet hair. "Wouldn't Alex have a good laugh if he knew what I felt," she muttered aloud.

No, Alex wasn't nasty. He wouldn't laugh. At least, she amended, not out loud. He'd probably grin. A lot. Well, he didn't know, and he *wouldn't* know. It was as simple as that.

But it wasn't simple, not at all. She had come up with an alternate plan this afternoon in the event that things hadn't gone right at the theater. And they sure as heck hadn't, she mused. But now, in light of what had just transpired, could she risk going through with it? Could she voluntarily pick up matches and play with them of her own free will?

She shook her head. She was making a mountain out of the proverbial molehill. So she had kissed Alex. So he had kissed back. What did that really mean? Nothing, right?

Right.

She looked back at her reflection. The face in the mirror didn't look altogether convinced.

"You look like hell, Paula," Ted told her the next morning when she walked into the office.

"Thanks, I think you look lovely, too." She shrugged out of her cardigan and draped it on the back of her chair. Shifting her coffee mug closer, she sat down before the word processor. She saw Ted looking at her over the top of his coffee mug. "You'd look this good, too, if you only got two hours' sleep."

"Hot date, Paula?" Ted's face was wreathed in an open, friendly leer.

Paula switched on her word processor. "Just thinking about the script."

"What a novel change. Let's get to it, shall we?" Marty proposed.

"That's why I bucked traffic this morning," Paula replied with false cheerfulness.

They worked for two hours, and her mind kept wandering. It was an effort to concentrate. Usually bits and pieces of thoughts and dialogue kept crowding her mind. Today her mind could have been declared a vacant parking lot for all the productive activity that was going on there. It was because of last night. She knew she had to shake this feeling of disbelief mixed with she-had-no-idea-what. She had to talk to Alex to set things straight.

Every opportunity she had, she called Alex's office. And every time a cool, reserved British-accented voice informed her that he wasn't in. Paula kept trying until six-thirty, at which time she was put in touch with his answering service. Her natural good temper was in danger of evaporating.

Well, if Mohammed wasn't going to come to the mountain, the mountain was just going to have to pay him a visit, she decided. She wasn't going to get any rest tonight, if this wasn't laid to rest. Besides, she had to tell him of her new plan.

It had been a long day for Alex, one that seemed to stretch out endlessly. First his senior partner, a man he admired, had almost literally dumped a client on him. With good reason. The woman was incredibly enamored with the sound of her own voice. She needed help drafting her will. After Alex had finally managed to partially satisfy her, he was then stuck in a meeting that had resolved nothing. And when he was through with that, he was forced to spend the better part of the afternoon in court involving the contesting of a will. Ugly names had been hurled back and forth, and the judge had adjourned the court until Monday morning when hopefully tempers would have cooled.

To make matters worse, laughing green eyes had plagued him throughout the day, taunting him when he least expected it. He had spent a great deal of time thinking about last night's kiss in the rain. Or actually, he had spent a great deal of time trying *not* to think about the kiss, which was tantamount to the same thing in the long run. The impression it had imprinted on him had been on his mind all night and then all day, materializing at the oddest times in court. Once he had caught the other lawyer looking at him with a quizzical expression and had realized that he was smiling somewhat foolishly.

She managed to create havoc in his life even when she wasn't around. Somehow, it seemed par for the course.

In an act that now struck him as bordering on desperation, he had allowed Olivia, the senior partner's secretary, to set him up on a blind date. It seemed her friend was visiting from out of town for several days. He had never been on a blind date, had never seen the sense in it. But after his reaction to Paula, he began to think that he needed to get out more. There was no other explanation to cover the magnitude of his reaction to what had literally exploded between them.

Going out with another woman would banish Paula's very real, very unsettling presence from his mind.

He glanced at his watch. He had an hour before he had to get ready. He needed, he decided, a drink. A strong one. Never much of a drinker, he felt that tonight was definitely an exception. He was halfway to the bar in his living room when the doorbell rang.

"Now what?" he muttered. He wasn't expecting anyone. But then he hadn't been expecting his father all the other times the older man had showed up. With a sigh, Alex pulled open the door and then stared. For a moment he thought he was imagining her. After all, her face had flashed through his mind all day.

But she was real, and standing out in the hallway.

Why?

"How did you know where I live?" His own voice sounded foreign to his ear.

"You're in the book. Under Prince Charming." She peered over his shoulder and caught a glimpse of the decor. Not bad. "May I come in, or did I come at an inappropriate time?"

He stepped back, holding the door open wide. "For you, there is no appropriate time. You might as well come in now."

"Always the last word in hospitality," she murmured, breezing in.

See, pulse regular, breathing normal. Last night was a fluke, she told herself.

"I wasn't aware that anyone was allowed a last word in your presence." He took her jacket and purse and put it on an antique table that stood against the wall next to the door.

"Only if they're quick-witted."

She looked around his living room slowly. It looked, she thought, just as she would have imagined. Masculine, tasteful, neat. Everything in its place and waiting to be photographed by *Good Housekeeping*. The man didn't have a messy bone in his body. At least in that respect his future wife, whoever she might be, was lucky.

And in other respects? a tiny, annoying voice whispered. Would she be lucky there, too?

Paula refused to entertain any further answers.

Alex saw her looking around his living room, as if she were about to criticize his taste. Seeking to forestall such a digression, he asked, "What can I do for you?"

Paula turned to face him, her eyes level with his mouth. She quickly raised her eyes to his. The view was obstructed by auburn fringes. With a short huff, she blew away the bangs that were hanging in her eyes. "Well, first of all, we have to talk."

"'We?'" he repeated with mock alacrity. "As in a dialogue? You mean I get a chance to answer?"

She ignored his sarcasm and began to move about the room restlessly. "About last night..." she began.

He watched her pace. Bothered you as much as it did me, did it? he thought. Interesting. And damn complicating. His face remained blank as he moved to the bar. "Care for a drink?"

"Absolutely," she said too quickly. "White wine if you have it." Whiskey, straight, if you don't, she added silently. She was going to need it, she decided.

She watched his hands as he poured the wine. They were strong hands. Hands that were extremely capable. Were they gentle hands, as well?

Careful, Paula, the only thing you want this man handling gently is your father's ego.

"Yes?"

She blinked. "Yes, what?"

"You were saying about last night?" A glass of whiskey, neat, followed.

She had been blanking out all day. This *had* to stop. She whirled on her heel suddenly, as if she were attacking. What, she wasn't certain. Probably just the absurdity of the idea that was haunting her.

"It never happened."

His dark brows moved together until they practically touched. "*What* never happened?" He offered her the glass of wine.

She smiled with satisfaction as she accepted the glass. "So, we understand each other." He wanted to erase that moment, too. If the thought bothered her, she didn't let on, even to herself.

Paula raised her glass to take a sip, but never completed the movement. Alex stopped her.

His drink still on the bar, Alex put his hands on either side of her shoulders, as if capturing her in the parentheses of his hands would help him assimilate what she was saying. It didn't. "Paula, I *never* understand you."

She looked up at his face. Pieces of last night floated through her mind as light through a prism. The warmth, the yearning, the— She stopped. If it had been anyone other than Alex . . .

But Alex was Alex, and she wasn't in the business of changing people. "Yes," she said softly, "I know. That's just the problem."

"What's just the problem?" The woman was a walking enigma. He dropped his hands and picked up his drink.

She shook her head. "Never mind."

It was best not to harbor dreams, however small, of what might have been *if only*. Best to get on with the real world. Freed of his hands, she moved over to the sofa and sat down, still holding her glass. She twirled the stem around in her fingertips. Light from a nearby lamp caught in the light yellow liquid, gleaming and sending out shafts of beams.

Alex looked down at her and realized that he wanted to touch her, wanted to kiss her again. Maybe the whiskey was doing him less good than he thought. Or maybe, he thought with a touch of foreboding, it was something else entirely goading him on.

Paula raised her eyes to him. "About our fathers."

He held on to his glass with both hands, afraid he might do something very, very stupid if his hands weren't otherwise occupied. Looking ahead rather than at her, he sat down next to her. "Second verse, same as the first."

How could she have *ever* harbored romantic thoughts about him, even for one instant? "Don't quote silly lyrics to me. That's my department." There, annoyance was good. Just keep it in place, she coached. "Do you realize that their act is in danger of breaking up?"

Alex smiled as he turned to her. Now the light from the lamp was playing on her hair instead of the wine. It made her hair look like flame, adding to the gypsylike, seductive quality about her. He took a long sip of his drink. It felt hot going down. It didn't do a thing to dull his reaction.

"Well, I'd say that's a logical assumption, when two people refuse to speak to each other for the rest of their lives."

She was annoyed at the cavalier way he was treating the whole situation. Didn't he care about his own father? In her attempt to raise her anger, she momentarily forgot that he had gone along with her scheme last night. "Their act can't break up. It'd be a crime!"

Alex took a deep breath, as a buffer against the storm he felt was coming. "Embezzlement is a crime," he corrected calmly, almost feeling her indignation grow. "This," he gestured in the air, indicating their fathers' argument, "would be a shame, I suppose."

Paula stared at him. His heart was as chiseled as his profile, she thought in frustration. "You suppose?"

He placed a free hand on hers, then withdrew it. Touching was out, he warned himself. "Paula, it's not as if they're a national monument. All the great comedy teams break up, eventually."

Her wineglass met the coffee table abruptly, creating a tidal wave of white wine that leaped over the side and onto her fingers. She didn't seem to notice. "Laurel and Hardy didn't."

He suddenly had a great yearning to sample just a drop of white wine, served on long, slender fingers.

You've got a date in an hour and a half, he reminded himself.

But it didn't alter his feelings. It would have been like summoning a flyswatter as defense against a falcon. He cleaved to sarcasm. It was what they both understood. "Does contradicting me come naturally to you, or do you work at it?" He raised his glass and took another fortifying sip. A long one.

She relented slightly. "A little of both." She smiled. "But it's worth it." The dry tone fell away as she launched into the crux of her idea, a very thin, shaky idea, but the only one she had, at the moment. *He* wasn't coming up with anything, and half the fault lay with his father. "You know, if we're going to be lovers, we're going to have to stop this sort of thing, at least in front of our fathers."

The whiskey halted in mid-descent down his throat, and he began to choke. Eyes made watery focused in on the woman next to him in disbelief. This was crazy, even for Paula. "Lovers?" he coughed out.

She took the glass away from him calmly. It seemed to her that she was always calmest whenever Alex was not. Except for the kiss . . .

She refocused her mind to the present. "Not really, Alex. That's just what we want our fathers to believe. If they think we're romantically involved, they'll try to resolve their differences for our sake. So what do you think?"

He gave her a long look. She *was* crazy. "Do you really want an answer to that?"

"No," she said honestly, knowing what he probably thought of the idea. "What I want is cooperation."

"What you need is to be committed. Ever hear of the Hatfields and the McCoys?" he asked. "A romance there did nothing to quell the family feud."

"That was a blood feud. This is just a simple misunderstanding. I'm sure of it. I'd stake my life on it," she added a bit more urgently.

He raised an interested eyebrow at her words. "Can I hold you to that if you're wrong?"

She wasn't afraid of backing up her opinions. She stuck out her hand. "Okay."

He looked at it, but didn't take it. "Tempting, Paula, very tempting."

Paula let her hand drop. "Alex, will you help me? I can't do it without you."

"No, not even you could pull that off."

"So what do you say?"

Lovers. What if—? No, it was ridiculous to even entertain the notion. Alex shook his head. "Paula, it'll never fly."

She was always at her best when facing opposition. Sometimes, she thought, she seemed to live for adversity. "I don't want it to fly, I want it to play. Oh listen, Alex, they're both probably dying for the other to make the first move. This'll give them the excuse they want. After they get together, we'll admit to the hoax. They'll be too happy to care."

She saw the look of doubt on his face, and her voice speeded up. "A few days—a week, maybe. You can spare a week out of your life for your own father, can't you?"

She could see that he was wavering.

She frowned, thinking of what lay ahead. It was going to be nothing short of a test, as far as she was concerned. A test, if she were honest, to see if she could keep from making a fool of herself over a silly thing such as physical attraction. She plotted a course for herself of cold showers and a lot of exercise. "Listen, Alex, it's not going to be any more pleasant for me than it is for you."

She had never been logical, he thought. Not since they were children. No, not even then, but then he hadn't noticed. He had been struck with her colossal energy and zest for life, then. Alex shook his head. "They'll see right through it."

He *was* wavering. She could feel it. She wasn't sure whether to celebrate or panic, then upbraided herself for being silly. She was a mature, adult woman. Nothing was going to happen that she didn't want to happen. Which was what bothered her.

"Not if you're convincing."

"I don't like deception—"

She clutched at his arm and tugged. "I'm not asking you to become a spy, I'm asking you to do a good deed."

He laughed. She was incredible. If only she didn't smell so good. "Only you could see things in that light."

"We'll talk about my clairvoyance later." Her eyes searched his face eagerly. For the moment, she shut away thoughts of potential complications. "Will you help me, Alex?"

Slowly, a grin spread over his face, and the chiseled features softened. Definitely a good-looking face, she conceded. He leaned back on the sofa and took a long look at her. "I never thought I'd see the day when you said you needed me."

She laughed. "Don't let it go to your head. This is only temporary."

This time he leaned forward, until his face was inches away from hers. "As long as it isn't fatal."

She felt his breath on her face and stifled a shiver. He saw something, she thought in a moment of unconscious panic. Something inside of her, something that he had stirred last night. She forced herself to look confident and in control.

"Not a chance." Her voice was almost formal. "Now are you going to help me?"

God help him, he was entertaining the idea. "Just what did you have in mind?"

"I haven't thought that out yet." She saw the knowing smile touch his lips. "I didn't know if I could talk you into it."

"What, the mighty whirlwind had a moment of doubt?"

She patted his cheek, her fingers lingering just a moment too long. "Only about you, never about me." She rose suddenly, finding the sofa too confining. "All I know is that we can't invite them separately to some event again. This time they'll grow suspicious."

He laughed, incredulous at how her mind worked. "And they won't if we tell them that after years of one-upmanship, we've realized the error of our ways and have fallen madly in love?"

She raised her eyebrow at his tone. "I think I'll do the talking, when I explain this."

He shrugged. "It's what you're good at."

She ignored the barb. "They'll appreciate all the trouble we've gone through, once they're back together." She put out her hand. "Shake on it?"

He raised one eyebrow as a slight smile began to bud at the corners of his mouth. "If that's all we do, we're not going to convince anyone."

It was only through sheer willpower that she didn't edge away from him. She felt heat suddenly flaring through her. "Dress rehearsal was last night, okay?"

"Last night?" His lips curved in a smile. "I thought last night never happened."

"You're infuriating, you know that?" But she couldn't keep from returning his smile.

"So you keep telling me. Still want to go through with this ruse?"

"I have no choice."

"You always have a choice, Paula."

It was time to leave. Something warned her that staying here with him under these circumstances wasn't wise. She just might call another "dress rehearsal" herself. "Not in this matter."

She wondered, only for a moment, if she was only talking about the ruse.

Chapter Five

She saw Alex look impatiently at his watch. "Timing me, Alex?"

"In a manner of speaking." He hadn't meant to be so obvious, but he absolutely hated being late. "Well, I can't say that this hasn't been interesting, Paula, but if that's all you wanted to discuss—" Alex's tone indicated that it was time to reacquaint herself with the door.

Paula shifted slightly as she watched him. She wondered what was up. "If I didn't know any better, Alex, I'd say you were in a hurry to get rid of me."

He placed his hand on the doorknob, turned and looked at her. "And I'd say you were right."

In order to avoid any further discussion, Alex knew that he'd have to get her out quickly. Strike before she caught her breath. He began to place his hand on the small of her back to help move her along. But then he dropped his hand abruptly. There was to be no touching, he reminded himself.

Paula noticed. He saw humor rise in her eyes. It was incredible how much he could see there when he looked, he thought.

"Now, Alex, is this any way to treat a lover?" She pretended to pout seductively.

She did that well, he thought. He knew she was putting him on, but that didn't change the latent air of sexuality humming between them. He found it more than a little difficult to ignore.

"It is," he told her tersely, "if you're trying to get rid of your lover, to get ready for a date."

Paula's eyes opened wide and looked nothing short of spectacular. Alex wondered if they looked like that when she made love.

"A date?"

Why did he feel like throttling her and embracing her at the same time? It was because, he told himself, any prolonged time spent in her company seemed to make him totally irrational. "A date," he repeated, knowing she wouldn't drop it there. This time he opened the door wide, a blatant hint.

"You?"

He didn't like what her intonation implied. "Why do you say that as if you were reading this under Ripley's 'Believe It or Not'? I do date, Paula."

She thought of last night's kiss. And then she thought of someone else being in the receiving end, instead of her. The smile she offered Alex was forced. She wasn't altogether sure why.

"I'm sure you do, Alex." She elaborately brushed imaginary lint from his lapel. "It's not that you're not attractive." She looked up at him to emphasize the point, and hesitated. Their eyes held for a moment, and something flipped over and then tightened in Paula's stomach.

Very, very attractive, unfortunately. Why hadn't I really noticed that before? And why did I have to notice now, of all times?

"It's just that I don't think of you in that light."

The hell I don't. Maybe that's what's so wrong with this picture, suddenly. I'm thinking of Alex as someone of the opposite sex, instead of being just Alex.

"Oh? I know I'm going to hate myself for asking," and he knew he would, but he couldn't resist knowing, "but why not?"

"Because, my friend, dating is fun. I didn't know that you knew how to have fun. Anymore." She smoothed down his collar.

He gathered her fingers together, removed them from his shirt and held them with both hands. When she touched him, it made him want more. And he told himself that he didn't want more. Not from Paula. "Maybe you'd be surprised."

"Would I, Alex?" Her eyes challenged him to show her, even as her mind told her she was asking for trouble. "Would I really?"

She was doing it to him again, tripping up his mind and jumbling his well-ordered thoughts. She was absolutely dangerous to the well-being of any intelligent life-form. "I think you know the answer to that. Now, if you don't mind... The door." He inclined his head in that direction.

Paula picked up her jacket and folded it over her arm. She took her time, as she tried to steady something that seemed to quiver with an unnamed anticipation that was almost overwhelming. "This date of yours, is it someone... steady?"

He braced himself. "Just what do you mean by 'steady?'"

Paula laughed. He was being cautious, just as if he was standing before a judge in a courtroom. "You know, someone you care about, someone you share your innermost secrets with."

There was never the chance of a simple yes or no with her. Everything became involved, confused. There was never the natural evolution of ideas. Conversation with Paula was a challenge at best. One he wasn't up to, at the moment. He shook his head in exasperation.

She saw his frown and went on, delighted that she had riled him. "I was just wondering if you'd shared your nickname with her, *Smarty-pants*?"

His eyebrows narrowed, as he took hold of her arms for emphasis—or perhaps subconsciously he hoped if he held her still for just a second, she would *be* still and listen. His no-touching edict was momentarily forgotten. He stared at her, annoyed, ready to give her a piece of his mind. She smiled. Her lips parted slightly, invitingly.

Paula didn't know quite what to expect. Unconsciously she ran her tongue over her lips. The action wasn't meant to be sensual.

But as he stood there, all the things he was about to say disappeared. All he wanted to do was kiss her. This was crazy, he thought. Where had his anger gone? Where had his *mind* gone?

"No one ever called me that but you, *Sugar lips*." Realizing that he was holding her, Alex let her go.

She smiled as she purposely sauntered past him out into the hallway. When she turned back around, her skirt swirled slightly about her knees. It was enough to lead his thoughts astray again and make him swear at himself for it.

"Better not tell her about that one, Alex. She might not buy the story about my being only six years old at the time, with my mouth outlined in white from a powdered doughnut."

"She would if she met you."

Paula cocked her head to one side as she playfully regarded him. "Meaning?"

It was a gesture he had seen her father use, time and again. On him it looked comical. On her, it was appealing. Very, very appealing. "That you still act like a six-year-old."

"Always young at heart, Alex." She winked. "Take care, Alex. And don't forget to be in early tonight. I like my lovers fresh."

He leaned against the doorjamb, his interest aroused, despite himself. Did she have lovers? *A* lover? Someone special? Did she share herself with someone, laughing that deep, throaty laugh of hers that always seemed to manage to get under his skin? It was no business of his if she did, he reminded himself tersely. The question was purely academic, nothing more. "You sound like you go through them like tissues."

She gave him a sly smile. "Tissues aren't very durable."

"I see your point." Anyone who would get himself mixed up with Paula would have to be a man of iron in more ways than one. He began to wonder if he was up to this agreement he had let himself be talked into.

"Goodbye, lover." With a laugh, she quickly kissed his lips, taking care to do so while in motion. That way there would be no temptation to discover if last night's reaction was a fluke.

But even a fleeting kiss left an indescribable tingle dancing through her body and down her spine. It seemed ridiculous to react this way to Alex, of all people, she told herself. Yet there it was, and she couldn't readily deny it.

But she was going to give it one hell of a try.

Alex closed the door slowly. Her lips had barely brushed against his, yet something heated and warm had risen up, then faded away at a slower pace. It disturbed him. Maybe he shouldn't have let himself be talked into this scheme of hers. Their fathers were basically reasonable men. They would eventually resolve this dilemma on their own. There was no need for any covert machinations on his part or hers.

If he knew all that, why had he allowed himself to get roped in by Paula?

He knew the answer to that, too. He hadn't. Alex never did anything he didn't want to. But that opened up a larger mystery to him. *Why* had he wanted to?

He told himself he had no time to thrash that out. He had a lady to escort, and less than an hour to get ready now that Hurricane Paula had zipped in and out of his living room. He crossed the room and went into his bedroom to change.

Lovers.

Alex shook his head as he pushed open the closet door. Maybe he should have his head examined. If he knew anything at all about Paula, he knew that chaos lay ahead for all of them. He didn't want chaos. He had a well-ordered life and liked it that way.

Then why had he agreed to do it? Maybe it was boredom. Maybe not. Or maybe... He didn't let his mind drift to that end.

What was he worried about? No one was going to believe this. They had spent too much time whittling each other down to size to convince anyone that they had suddenly seen the er-

ror of their ways and fallen head over heels for each other. Even
with lines like "The lady doth protest too much," having made
their way into the vernacular, this charade tested the bounds of
credibility.

Lovers, ha.

It wasn't going to work.

Alex got ready methodically. He was a systematic person, by
nature, given to following strict schedules he made up in his
head. Everything in his closet was neatly laid out, and he never
spent any time looking for things because they were always
where they were supposed to be. He could just guess at what her
closet looked like. Like the aftermath of an earthquake. An
eight-point-seven tumbler.

Why the hell did he keep thinking about her? he demanded,
as he slid on a fresh pair of trousers.

Maybe it was because next to her, everything else always
seemed to dull in comparison, he thought. He jammed his
shirttails into his trousers in annoyance at the realization.

But it was true.

Because he was a precise person who could exercise extreme
control whenever necessary, he forced himself to calm down
and look at the situation the way he examined everything else.
With little to no emotion, objectively.

He closed his narrow belt and swore softly under his breath.
It was hard to be objective, when matters involved Paula.

Now that he had agreed to this charade, just how was he expected to play his role? How attentive was he going to have to
be? Could he do it? And would it work? Or would it be a disaster, just like last night's scheme had been?

Perhaps, he thought, remembering the previous evening,
disaster was a little too harsh a word to use.

He was just knotting his gray silk tie when the doorbell rang.
Alex automatically glanced at his watch. Who would be calling on him at this hour? Paula. She had probably hatched the
rest of her plan and wanted to spring it on him while it was still
fresh in that riotous cavern she called a mind.

Alex crossed from his bedroom to the living room, dropping his jacket on the back of the sofa. He didn't have time to

go over anything with her now. If he spent any more time with Paula, he was going to be late picking up Gayle, no, Gwen, that was her name, he remembered.

Alex pulled open the door. "Look, Paula, I told you that I can't—"

The tall silver-haired man in the doorway appeared a little puzzled. He ran a hand over his thick hair apprehensively, then peered into the room. "Is Paula here, Alex?"

"No, Dad," Alex sighed, "but she just was, and I thought that she forgot something." Alex had no choice but to step away from the doorway and let his father come in. He'd seen that look on his face before—for the last several days.

Paul Hamilton shoved his hands into the pockets of his charcoal-gray slacks. "I didn't know you were seeing Paula socially."

"I'm not." Alex suddenly remembered the charade. Taking a deep breath, he amended his denial. "That is, I wasn't until recently."

Lies didn't come easily to him, not even for a good cause, and he found this one particularly heavy and out-of-character for him. Were his father not in such a deep emotional fog, he would have seen through it immediately, Alex thought.

The elder Hamilton walked into the living room. He moved fluidly. It was easy to see that as a young man he had been exceptionally handsome. He had retained his looks, which had mellowed from utterly heart-stopping to gallantly distinguished. He still did not lack for female companionship whenever he wanted it. Seeing him, Alex knew exactly what he would look like in another thirty years. Except that he hoped he wouldn't look nearly so forlorn and lost.

If there was no traffic, almost an impossibility for this time of the evening, he'd still be able to make it. "Dad, I have a date tonight."

Paul beamed. "With Paula?" Then he looked puzzled. "But you said she just left."

This was not getting any easier. "No, not with Paula. Someone else."

"Someone else?" The expression on Paul's gaunt face showed that he didn't approve. He loved Paula as if she were his own. In a way, he thought, she could have been, had the timing been right. "Does Paula know about this 'someone else'?"

"Yes," Alex said impatiently, "she—"

Paul shook his head in disbelief. His sigh seemed to say that the world was a strange place and he didn't fit in so well anymore anywhere. He sat down heavily, his long, lanky frame almost spilling out over the edges of the sofa. "She's an outstanding, rare girl, Paula. Not many women would stand for that."

Alex reached for his jacket. "For what?"

"For not being the only woman in a man's life. Two-timing can only lead you into trouble, son." He looked away, and his mind drifted to another time, another place. "I ought to know," he said softly, more to himself than to Alex.

Alex saw that it was fruitless to try to clear up the misunderstanding. He was caught up in Paula's lie already, and it was less than a half hour old. He was afraid to anticipate what lay ahead now that the scene had been set.

But what captured his attention was his father's last reference. His father was as moral as they came, even though he was exceptionally handsome and women had always thrown themselves at him. As far as Alex knew, his father had always been faithful to his late mother. That was one of the most admirable things about him.

"When did you ever two-time anyone?" Alex laughed at the thought.

"I didn't, but that doesn't seem to matter."

Alex looked at his father, totally confused. Was the man getting senile? Was the situation between his father and Paula's father affecting him so much that he was no longer rational?

Paul riffled through the television guide, trying to find the listings for that evening. "What's on television tonight?"

"I don't know." Alex slipped on his jacket, still carefully watching his father. He looked so alone sitting there. The thought gnawed at him. "Do you want to stay here tonight?"

Paul looked over his shoulder at his only child, his thumb marking his place in the guide. "Unless you plan to bring the young lady back. Then I'll make myself scarce." Paul turned back around. "I'm getting kind of good at that."

Alex knew that he shouldn't be taken in by this. He had spent a great deal of time alone with his father in the last eight days. There wasn't a thing for him to feel guilty about. Yet the act of leaving the man alone, looking so forlorn, seemed somehow tantamount to leaving a puppy chained out in the rain. He didn't much care for the image.

Alex stopped buttoning his jacket and weighed his options. On one hand was a totally unknown woman whom he had agreed to go out with in a moment of weakness. He meant to test out his theory that his reaction to Paula was the result of keeping away from the fairer sex for too long. There was no prospect for a relationship, lasting or otherwise. He wasn't interested in one, at the moment, and besides, the woman was only in town for a week. It was awkward at best, he thought.

On the other hand was his father, who wasn't asking anything of him but who obviously needed a friend or at least a living, breathing person in his vicinity.

Maybe he could call Paula and have her come over to stay with his father. She was the bleeding heart in this scenario. No, that was out of the question. He wasn't about to ask Paula for a favor. She'd hold it over his head for the rest of his life. Possibly longer if she could swing it.

He made his decision.

Alex took out his wallet and sorted through the various slips of paper arranged in the back compartment until he found what he was looking for. He pulled out a blue note with a phone number scribbled on it.

He pointed toward the television set. "Flip the switch on the VCR, Dad. There's a movie in it I think you might enjoy."

He had already seen it himself, but he could stand to watch it again. He heard the machine click into position as he crossed over to the telephone on the other side of the room.

Turning his back to his father, Alex tapped out the number on the slip of paper, then took a deep breath. He had never done anything like this before, not shown up when he was expected. It went against his basic instincts. He believed in responsibilities, in regulations. Stability was very important to him. It was the cornerstone of what he was. It had been what was missing in his life when he was growing up.

"Hello, Gwen?" A nasal voice replied in the affirmative. "This is Alex Hamilton."

"Yes?" There was no sign of recognition in the woman's voice.

Suddenly he felt relieved. The whole idea of a blind date was foolish, as far as he was concerned. He didn't know what had come over him. Yes, he did. Paula. She was to blame for this. Now that he thought of it, she was to blame for a lot of things.

"I'm afraid that I won't be able to make it tonight." He glanced over his shoulder at his father. The man sat, straight as a rail, on the sofa. He didn't think his father knew how to slouch. "There's been a family emergency."

"Oh, *that* Alex Hamilton." The response this time was none-too-bright. "Olivia's friend."

He had never seen himself in the role of Olivia's friend. Olivia was in her late fifties and had been born at a keyboard. She was James Corbett's secretary. He respected her capabilities, but friendship had never entered into it. Given the situation, though, he saw no reason to correct Gwen's impression. "Yes. I'm sorry about the short notice."

"Ah, that's okay. I was feeling a little tired. Can't seem to get over jet lag like I used to. I'll be in town for a week. Some other time, maybe."

"Some other time," he echoed, knowing that there wouldn't be. "Thank you for being so understanding."

"Sure thing. Bye, sweetie."

Alex hung up. Maybe his father had done him a favor, after all.

Alex turned back to his father and crossed over to the sofa. When he sat down next to him, Paul looked at him in surprise. "Lady friend coming over, instead? I could go—" He began to rise.

Alex placed his hand on his father's shoulder to urge him back down. "I canceled out."

Paul nodded, thoughtfully digesting the information. "Better that way. You wouldn't want to take a chance on hurting Paula's feelings."

Right about now, Alex was intently contemplating hurting Paula's long, slender neck. He laughed shortly, dismissing the notion. "Dad, Paula has the hide of a rhino."

Paul peered at his son through sad gray-blue eyes. "For a lawyer, you don't notice much do you?"

Alex shifted slightly in his seat, draping his arm over the sofa's arm. "I notice that you're upset."

Paul gave a short, dry laugh. "My partner, worse, my best friend of twenty-seven years said he's never going to speak to me again. I think that goes beyond the definition of upset."

"Dad," Alex began patiently, "what's this feud all about?"

"It's something Wally wouldn't want me to talk about," Paul said stoically.

A lot of patience was going to be needed here. Alex didn't honestly know if he was up to it. "But Dad, he's not talking to you—"

Paul shook his head slowly. "Honor is honor, son. It doesn't matter that one of the parties involved is a pigheaded son of a—well, it doesn't matter, that's all. I can't change the way I am just because Wally is so stubborn."

"He's always been stubborn," Alex pointed out.

"You noticed that, too, did you?" Paul chuckled dryly, thinking back over the years.

Definitely a lot of patience. "Dad, what I'm saying is that nothing's changed and—"

"Oh, something's changed all right."

"What?" He was surprised he didn't shout the word. He felt like it.

"I can't talk about it."

Alex gave up and turned his attention to the action on the screen. Credits were finally fading, and a street scene was coming into focus. He resigned himself to the fact that it was going to be another one of those evenings.

"Thanks for staying, son." Paul barely whispered the words his eyes on the screen. "I appreciate it."

Any tender communication between the two of them was rare. Alex felt strangely warmed, yet uncomfortable. He thought about the situation. His father had to miss Wally's companionship an awful lot. The two men did everything together. Tonight was their usual night for poker. Alex had no such inclination. "Have you eaten?"

"Yes," Paul answered vaguely, leaning forward as he watched the screen.

"Recently?"

He looked at Alex. The expression on his face was a mixture of confusion and thoughtfulness, as he tried to remember. "I'm not sure."

Par for the course. "I'll fix dinner." Alex rose with the intention of heading for the kitchen.

His father's voice stopped him. "Would you mind if we sent out?"

Heartburn served on a kaiser roll. Oh, what the hell, why not? "The Stage Door Deli?" Alex guessed.

Paul smiled broadly. "You read my mind."

"No, just remembered your tastes. The Stage Door, it is."

He knew the phone number by heart now. Delicatessen food was an acquired taste from his father's starving comic days on the road. Even though now both he and Wally could well afford to eat at the most expensive restaurant that either coast could boast of, a pastrami on rye could still make Paul's mouth water.

Alex called in the order and then sat down on the sofa next to his father.

"You know, Alex," Paul murmured, never taking his eye off the television set, "not many sons would put their love life on hold and sit around with their old dad in front of the TV."

"Not many sons have fathers like you," Alex muttered under his breath.

"Thank you," Paul beamed.

And then he sighed, and his countenance became sad again.

Okay, Paula, Alex thought grudgingly, this plan of yours had better work. I'm not sure how much more of this I can take.

Chapter Six

She couldn't shake the restlessness. Try as she might, Paula's thoughts would not stay on her work. She was too concerned about her father and about the plan she had jumped into, as always, feet first.

Being unsure of herself was something that she was not accustomed to. All of her life she had proceeded confidently ahead with no wavering, no hesitation cluttering her mind. And she would have gone on in like manner in this particular instance, except that this particular instance concerned Alex, and for some reason that made a world of difference.

"It shouldn't. It shouldn't make a bit of difference," she murmured to herself.

But it did.

She sat on her bed, tailor-fashion, with the intention of jotting down notes for next week's script of *Hayley's House*. That was why there was a clipboard and pad plopped on her jean-clad knees. But nothing was happening on the pad. The script didn't keep her attention for more than a few seconds at a time.

The scenario she was scripting in real life kept overshadowing it.

Paula stared at the page before her and realized that for perhaps the first time in her life, she wasn't sure. She needed an encouraging word, something or someone to tell her that she hadn't totally lost her mind with this idea, that what she was doing made sense, even if she was doing it with Alex.

Where was her self-confidence? Since when had she needed someone's encouragement, to tell her that she was right?

Since now.

Reaching over to the nightstand, Paula pulled the princess phone to her and mechanically pressed the buttons that connected her to Erica's Restaurant. Erica was her cousin. More importantly, she was related on her father's side of the family. That gave Erica the ability to give support where angels feared to tread.

"Good evening," a smooth falsetto voice announced, as if it was a foregone conclusion not to be debated. "Erica's Restaurant. How may we help you?"

Paula cradled the phone against her neck and was rewarded with a series of musical notes. She had forgotten that the buttons were in the receiver. The phone in her own bedroom in the condo was different.

"Hello?" the high voice inquired with just a touch of impatience. "Anyone there?"

Paula recognized the unmistakable squeak at the end of the question. It was Hugo, Erica's temperamental head waiter. He spoke five different languages, and knew how to be petulant in each one. "Yes. I'd like to speak to Erica Stewart, please."

There was an impatient expulsion of air. "If it's about a reservation—"

Paula could just picture Hugo, his long, aristocratic nose pointed upward, lips pressed tightly. "Don't get huffy, Hugo. I'm not trying to go over your head. It's about her Uncle Wally."

"Paula?"

Paula grinned. Uttering only the single word, he sounded a lot friendlier. She could always tell. His native New York accent surfaced when he felt at ease.

"The same." Paula pushed the clipboard off her lap. No use in even pretending she was going to get any work done tonight. "Is Erica around?"

"She's in the banquet room, fussing over a wedding party that's up to their eyeballs in schnapps. I'll fetch her for you."

"Thanks, Hugo."

Music intended to soothe filled the receiver as Paula waited. She glanced down at the clipboard. The page facing her actually did have some writing on it. Exactly three words: Episode Number Fifteen. She began to sketch a chrysanthemum in the center of the page. It made the page look a lot better.

"Paula?" A high, breathless voice asked. "Hi, what's up?"

Paula snapped to life. "I wanted to bounce something off you."

"Shoot."

The chrysanthemum gained leaves as Paula talked. "You know about that feud between Pop and Uncle Paul?"

"Know about it?" Erica laughed. "Honey, I was caught in the cross fire."

Paula stopped doodling. "What do you mean?"

"Well, it erupted in my restaurant."

The pen dropped from Paula's hand. She hadn't thought of calling Erica to shed light on the situation. It never occurred to her that someone in the family would know more than she did about her own father. "Then you know what it's about?"

"Nope."

"But you just said—"

"What I would have said, if you'd ever let me finish a thought," Erica explained affectionately, "is that one minute they were talking and laughing, and then the next minute I looked over and Uncle Wally was shouting at Paul who looked very, very pale."

Paula sighed. Back to square one. "Pop didn't say anything to you?"

"Yes, he said something."

"What?" Paula cried impatiently.

"He pointed to Paul and said 'he pays the check' and then stormed out. I've never seen him act like that before, Paula."

"You're not the only one." Paula dragged her hand through her thick mane, loosening it from the clip that was ineffectually holding it in place. She tossed the clip on the bed. It bounced and fell to the floor. "Pop won't talk to me about it, and he's absolutely miserable without Uncle Paul and too pigheaded to admit it or do anything about it." A crescendo of music swelled and threatened to overpower their conversation. "Erica, what's that awful noise in the background?"

"That's Everly and Brighton. Second marriage for her, third for him. I think everyone wants to party frantically now because they figure that there may not be a get-together for the silver anniversary."

"Cheery." But Paula had other things on her mind beside the ultimate outcome of the Everly-Brighton union. "Anyway, I think I've come up with a way to get Pop and Uncle Paul back together."

"That's my cousin, the quintessential schemer. So what did you have in mind?"

Paula took a deep breath before she answered. "Alex and I are going to pretend to be lovers." There was a long pause. "Erica, did you hear me?"

"It might work," Erica conceded slowly. "Uncle Wally and Paul might laugh themselves to death over that one, and then there won't be a feud."

"That's not quite what I had in mind."

"Paula, that just might qualify for the dumbest idea I've ever heard."

Paula drew an *X* through her sketch. "Thank you for that vote of confidence."

"Confidence?" Erica echoed. "Honey, does *Romeo and Juliet* mean anything to you?"

Paula thought of her pre-writing days when she had fancied herself an actress and had found out that she wasn't. "Yes. Four weeks in out-of-town tryouts and closing on opening night. I was the nurse. The padding they put on me was atrocious.''

"I mean the story."

"It's fiction, Erica," Paula insisted stubbornly. She knew what Erica was driving at. Too late she remembered that Erica was the stable cousin in the bunch. Maybe *Erica* should be the one matched up with Alex for this charade. They certainly had more things in common than she and Alex did.

"Ever stop to think that maybe Shakespeare was onto something?"

"Yes, that violence sells. Television found that out a long time ago."

"Paula—"

She hadn't called Erica in order to defend her point of view, but now that she was doing it, she found that it was strengthening her own convictions about the plan. It would work. She'd *make* it work.

"Besides," Paula went on doggedly, "as I pointed out to the very stubborn Mr. Alexander Hamilton when he cited the Hatfields and the McCoys, that was a blood feud. This is a tiff."

"Smart man, that Alex."

"Fine. When we're through, I'll make you a present of him."

"If I know you, by the time you're through, there won't be anything left of the man. Besides," Erica stood up, "if this is a tiff, as you call it, then why not just wait for it to blow over?"

"Because Pop's miserable. Besides," Paula grinned, "when have you ever known me to just stand by and do nothing?"

"Forgive me. I don't know what came over me. You really talked Alex into this, huh?"

"It really wasn't too difficult, actually." Paula liked to think that he wasn't a match for her when it came to persuasion.

"Uh-huh."

Paula heard the broad smile in her cousin's voice. "What's that supposed to mean?"

"Shall I be reserving the banquet room for you two? Provided I have one left," Erica amended, and Paula heard the noise level rise even higher.

"Only if you want to leave it empty. That was the most off-the-wall remark you've ever made, Erica. There's absolutely nothing between Alex and me except years of animosity and a desire," for some reason, she paused over the word, "a desire," she went on hurriedly, "to get our fathers back together before we both lose our minds."

"Right, whatever you say, cuz. I've got to go and try to save some of the crystalware before there's nothing left. Keep me posted."

Paula hung up and replaced the phone on the nightstand. Erica was working much too hard. There would be no other reason for her cousin to even contemplate suggesting something so absurd as Alex and she getting together in real life....

Paula shoved her clipboard next to the phone, silently declaring her workday at an end. There was no point in belaboring her mind. It just wasn't coming. She knew when it was fruitless to keep pushing.

She sat for a moment, staring at the wall, her mind wandering. Suggesting that she and Alex were a real duo was absurd. She wasn't his type.

Just what was Alex's type of woman? The thought came out of nowhere, surprising her. She linked it up to the fact that he had told her he had a date tonight.

What was the woman he was going out with tonight like? He had been, she thought, rather evasive when it came to talking about her. Did that mean it was something serious, or that he was just being his usual closemouthed self? Paula plopped down on her stomach and hugged her pillow. She wished he'd let loose a little. He never ran off at the mouth, but he had talked to her more when they were younger. Not nearly as much as she did, of course, but he had talked. Back then he had made her think of the strong, silent type.

Unfortunately she thought, as she continued hugging the pillow, you couldn't get into a person's feelings and thoughts if he was always quiet, always holding back. Alex had made restraint, she mused, into an art form, one not to her liking. What frustrated her the most about him, she decided, was that he wouldn't let her in. She always felt cut off. Other people didn't do that to her. In fact, she couldn't cite a single person who didn't open up to her. Besides Alex.

What type *was* he attracted to? Probably someone with sensible shoes, a sensible way of dressing and a sensible hairdo that was *not* sexy even when all the pins were pulled out. Paula's mouth curved in a smile. She rather liked her creation of the perfect woman for Alex. Work-oriented, stable, meat-and-potatoes without a dash of imagination to her. That was what he probably liked. The total antithesis of what she was like.

She rolled onto her back. His loss, she thought.

A thought struck her, and her smile grew broader. Maybe it would be fun to rattle his cage a little. She had felt a reaction from him in that kiss they shared. Very efficiently she disregarded the fact that she had been totally affected, as well. Maybe he wasn't as restrained and controlled as he'd like to think. It might be fun to find out.

And then again, something warned her, it might be dangerous.

A loud crash in the other room brought her musings to an abrupt halt. On her feet quickly, she hurried to her father's room.

"Pop? You okay?"

When there was no answer, she pulled open the door quickly. Her father was in his robe, apparently ready for bed. He was standing in a puddle of black-and-white and colored photographs scattered in a jagged semicircle around him. An upended shoebox was off to the side.

"Yeah. I'm all right," he grumbled, looking at the photographs on the rug. "Even his pictures are trying to get me."

"Pop, what are you talking about?"

He scooped up the box which was now empty. "I was just getting down some old photos out of the closet, and they fell on me."

Paula bent down and picked up the photograph closest to her. It was one of a much younger, much slimmer Wally and an incredibly dashing Paul. He looked a lot, she suddenly realized, like Alex. The two men were standing, arm in arm, before a sign that proclaimed the area to be "Redlands, the Hottest Little Town in the West."

Paula rose to her feet and looked at her father. It wasn't going to be so hard to arrange this reconciliation once she got the ball rolling, she thought. Not if he was secretly traveling down memory lane. "You know, it's high time you put all these into an album." She held up a few to emphasize her point.

He grabbed a handful and tossed them into the box. "It's high time I put these in a fire."

"What?" she cried.

"They're pictures of Paul," he accused.

"And you."

"That can't be held against me. They were taken before I knew the kind of man he is."

"What kind of man is he?" she prodded, hoping to trip her father up and finally hear the whole story instead of just muttered accusations.

"The kind you wouldn't want to know. I sure don't." Wally squatted down, his wide robe pooling around his short, stubby pajama-clad legs. He grabbed another fistful of photographs and threw them into the box. "Now help me get these together so that I can throw them out."

Paula joined him on the floor, taking care not to wrinkle any photographs. To her they were precious memories marking her father's career, and more importantly, his life. "I'll get them together, but you're throwing them out over my dead body."

Wally shook his head philosophically. "If that's the way you want it, but the trash collector's not going to like the added weight on Tuesday."

Paula rocked back on her heels and stared at him. "Pop!"

He shrugged. "Your suggestion."

She pried his fingers off the pictures he was holding, and gently deposited them in the shoebox. "The first one you've taken. How about my other suggestion?"

The rusty eyebrows drew together. "You mean about getting together with him?"

"Yes, that one."

"I liked the dead-body suggestion better." He reached for another scattered group of photographs.

Paula beat him to it. "I'm not going on with this routine."

"Neither am I." He reached for the refilled shoebox, but Paula pulled it back.

"These are my memories, too, Pop."

"You need a new set."

She thought of telling him about Alex now, but something held her back. "I'm working on it. Until then, I want yours." She put her hand on the box, and for a moment they eyed one another.

Wally pulled his hand back and raised it in an act of temporary surrender. Paula took the opportunity to pull the box to her. Her father lumbered up to his feet and shrugged mightily. "I'm too tired tonight to argue."

"That's a first," she murmured as she began leaving the room, box in hand.

"I heard that."

"You were supposed to," was her parting shot.

Back inside her own bedroom, Paula put the box down on the bed. He wasn't fooling her. She knew him inside and out. She could tell how much he ached to get this thing between him and Paul resolved. Tomorrow, when he was up to his theatrics, she'd tell him about Alex and her. Maybe she'd even get Alex to come over and add strength to the lie—no. The first time she told Wally, she should be alone. Alex might ruin it all by laughing.

She turned the box upside down and let the photographs fall out haphazardly. They landed on the gray-and-blue comforter like so many disjointed snowflakes heralding the past. When she was a child, she used to do this. She'd picked up pictures at random, making up stories about her father and Paul and their adventures. It made her feel a part of their lives beyond the time that they spent at home.

She sifted through the jumble of photos now with a clearer eye, or so she thought. Here on her comforter was an entire chronicle of her father and Paul's upward climb to fame. Mixed in here and there were photographs of their families. She pulled

ut one, and a sliver of a memory flashed through her mind.
Alex, aged eleven, looking very skinny in a bathing suit. She
was standing next to him. She looked like a rail in her two-piece
suit. The color was rather faded, but she thought she remem-
ered that her suit was strawberry. She liked it because it
rought out her hair. She grinned, remembering. Vain even
hen.

Paula settled back against her headboard, pillows nestled on
ther side of her. Both she and Alex were clutching a pail in the
hotograph. It was filled to overflowing. There were sea ur-
hins in it. She remembered she cried when she discovered that
hey died on their trip back home from the beach. It was Alex
ho had comforted her.

Paula turned the photograph over in her hand, then let it fall
ack to join the others. The memory tasted bittersweet. He was
entler, sweeter then.

"Oh Alex," she whispered to the boy in the photograph,
when did you change? When did you become so upright, so
motionless?"

She began to put the photographs back into the box, unwill-
g to continue the game.

Chapter Seven

The annoying buzz of the alarm clock cajoled Paula into restless state of consciousness.

Daylight.

Shutting her eyes again, refusing to come face-to-face wi the small rectangular instrument of torture, Paula groped abo and searched for the answer to her prayers, the off switch. H fingers came in contact with the right button, and she jamme it down so hard the little clock fell over.

The incessant buzzing ceased. But it was too late. She w awake. And tired.

Morning.

Alex.

Paula's eyes flew open as she bolted upright.

Alex! Had she really gone to his apartment last night a proposed that they pose as lovers? What had seemed like su a brilliant stroke of genius last night now seemed much less in the light of a brand-new day.

She dragged her hand through her hair. A sigh escaped h lips. Yes, she had. She had really gone to Alex's apartment a done that. Last night came back to her, frame for frame, word for word, in living color.

Funny how she always seemed to remember her conversations with Alex so completely. For a man she often labeled as a stuffed shirt, he provided her with a great deal of wit-sharpening entertainment. If only he wasn't so different from her, then maybe...

She kicked off the covers and stumbled over to her closet. There was no "maybe." The simple fact was that they *were* different, and nothing was going to change that. Nothing.

Pulling out one outfit and then discarding it for another, she stared at her reflection in the mirrored wardrobe door, not seeing it, nor the outfit she held up before her. Her mind was too full of other things. A smile began to grow on her lips.

She had to remember to look at the situation in the right light. In addition to accomplishing her goal of reuniting her father with his partner, this whole venture might even prove to be fun. She'd get a chance to tease Alex, to ruffle his neat feathers. She had always enjoyed doing that before, right? She enjoyed the way his rejoinders always kept her on her toes, right?

Okay, so if she was going to be enjoying herself so much, why did her stomach feel so queasy?

Opening-night jitters, she pronounced as she headed toward the shower. Nothing more, just opening-night jitters. She was no stranger to that in her profession. Neither her father nor Paul was going to be easily fooled. This was going to take some concentrated effort on her part *and* on Alex's, if he was up to it. It was going to take some very convincing playacting.

Her stomach fluttered again as she thought of having to pretend to be Alex's lover and just what that might entail. A fearful excitement was beginning to grow within her. She had a dangerous habit of leaping before she looked, and running with a feeling instead of worrying about the consequences. But *that*, she reminded herself, would have made her more like Alex.

"God, what a ghastly thought," she muttered. With that, she turned up the shower-head spray and let it hit her in the face.

* * *

By the time Paula came down the stairs, she had her immediate plans mapped out. She was going to spring the news of her romantic involvement with Alex on her father at breakfast. But when she entered the kitchen, he was nowhere to be seen. Neither were there any preparations lying around for the disasters he liked to refer to as breakfast.

Her father was an early riser when he wasn't performing. It wasn't like him to oversleep. Concerned, Paula went upstairs to his room.

She rapped softly on the door. "Pop?"

When there was no response, she opened the door a crack. Her father was in bed, but he wasn't asleep. His blanket and sheet were rumpled and tangled around his round body. He was lying on his back, staring at the ceiling.

"Pop, didn't you hear me?" She pushed open the door and crossed to his bed. "What are you doing in bed?"

Just as she reached his bed, Wally turned his face toward her. "I'm laying in it."

Well, at least that was more like him. She felt his forehead. Cool. Just what *was* the matter with him? She sat down on the edge of the bed next to him. "Are you feeling all right?"

He moved his shoulders up and down vaguely. "I suppose."

She tried to find a clue to the situation in his eyes, and failed. "Then what's wrong?"

"I couldn't seem to fall asleep last night, and now I can't seem to get up. There's just nothing much to get up for." He sighed loudly.

She eyed him for a moment, not knowing what to think or say. Her father had always been the embodiment of perpetual motion for as long as she could remember. The situation was getting serious. Depression was setting in. She would have never believed it of him. Yet what else could it be? Without his act, without his partner, it appeared that her father didn't feel he had much of a purpose. He had always loved to make people laugh. It had always been his driving goal. But now, because of this ridiculous, mysterious feud, it had been taken away from him.

She'd let him rest this morning, then corner Alex and force him over tonight. She decided that it would be better that way. They'd tell her father together, and that should light a fire under him.

"There's plenty to get up for, Pop."

"Easy for you to say."

She bent over and kissed him on the cheek. "Okay, stay in bed for as long as you like." I'll get you up and running with my news tonight, she vowed silently. Paula rose. "I'll call you later."

"I'm not going anywhere," he answered mournfully, turning his eyes back up to the ceiling.

Oh God, she couldn't stand seeing him like this any more, she thought. It just wasn't like him. She hesitated at the door, debating telling him right here and now. But something held her back. It was, she thought, as if she was waiting for the cavalry to come riding in at the last minute and come up with an alternate solution. It was, she realized, almost as if she was *afraid* to set her plan in motion.

Silly notion. She just wanted him to get some rest, that's all. If she knew her father, he was going to need all his energy for the dramatics that would follow the announcement of her affair with Alex.

An affair with Alex. Now *that* she told herself as she slipped out, was a damn silly notion indeed.

For once, the trip in to work wasn't plagued with mile-long, bumper-to-bumper traffic, and she drove into her parking space less than forty-five minutes after she left the house. Excitement tingled through her as she mentally expanded her plan. She'd call Alex during a break and tell him that tonight was the night. Provided, that was, she could reach him. He was always so darn busy.

Just part of his charm, she told herself, then laughed. The words *charm* and *Alex* were not usually put together.

Whistling, Paula entered the small office where she worked. "Hi, gang."

Her cheeriness subsided as soon as she took a good look at the other two occupants in the room. It was a given that at this time of the morning their faces were portraits of grumpiness. This morning, however, the word that came to her mind was *morose*. Marty wasn't even touching his doughnuts, and Ted just leaned against the wall, staring out the window.

"What's the matter, somebody die?" She deposited her purse in the lower right-hand drawer of her desk and then closed it with the toe of her shoe.

"Yeah," Ted answered moodily.

Paula sank into her chair, horrified that she had been so flippant about the matter when it was actually true. "Oh, I'm sorry." She looked from one man to the other. "Who?"

"We did," Marty told her.

Paula looked at Ted, and he nodded. They were making less sense than usual. "Run that by me again?"

Marty shoved his hands into the pockets of his baggy trousers as he glared at the poster of Hawaii on the wall next to her. Maybe he'd get a chance to take that vacation, after all. The thought didn't buoy him. "We've been put on temporary 'hiatus.'"

She knew that was a euphemistic term for "as good as canceled."

"Yes," she said numbly, "That is death. Ratings?" she asked in surprise. Overall their ratings had been good. She knew because she had been following the figures religiously. And the show's time slot was excellent. Pulling the show didn't make any sense. But then, things rarely made sense anymore. Look at her reaction to Alex. Quickly she shut the last thought out of her mind.

"Temperament," Marty corrected. He shuffled the papers on his desk from one side to another.

Paula watched him. She knew how he felt. If he didn't actually start packing anything, he didn't have to admit to himself that it was really true, that the show was dead. *Hayley's House* was Marty's first job as head writer.

"Hayley?" Paula guessed.

"None other." Ted picked up his coffee mug and drained the last of the dregs before continuing. "Ms. Halliday and the production company have come to a parting of the ways over 'contractual problems.'"

"She wants more money," Paula filled in.

Marty whirled around and pointed a finger at Paula. "The lady gets a cigar." The expression on his boyish face became somber. "And they won't give it to her."

"Smart people," Paula muttered.

"Meanwhile," Ted said, rising, "we're out of a job." He began to put the things on his desk into an open cardboard box. He glanced over his shoulder at Paula. "Just when I was going to have you eating out of the palm of my hand, too." The grin on Ted's face seemed a little halfhearted.

At least his spirit was still there, Paula thought fondly. She made a face, then said sweetly, "Maybe biting it off, Hammerstein, but never eating out of it."

She leaned back in her chair. Things moved quickly in this business, she thought. Working one day, out selling pencils on the street corner the next. Well, this would give her more time to devote to her "performance." Wouldn't Alex be pleased?

"You look like a Cheshire cat," Ted observed, peering at her face. "You know something about all this that we don't?"

She hadn't realized that she was smiling. Paula shook her head, wishing that she did. Finding work as a comedy writer wasn't easy. "Just thinking about relaxing a little."

"Relaxing can get old when you've got bills to pay," Marty said with a trace of bitterness.

Paula rose and crossed to him. She placed her hand on his shoulder. He was even more hunched-over than usual. He had taken the blow personally, and for the moment it was defeating him. She had seen it happen before. "You'll find something."

He looked at her, appreciating the warm vote of confidence. "Sure." False bravado filled his voice. "I'm the best in the business."

"Next to me," Ted interjected.

She was really going to miss them, she thought. They had only been together a little over a year and a half, but a strong bond of respect and affection had formed in that time. "If you two comedy giants will excuse me, I've got to find a box to clear out my desk."

Ted held his box up in front of Paula. "You can throw your stuff in with mine," he offered. "And then you can move in with me and sort it all out."

"If I moved in, it'd be my head I'd have to sort out." She patted his face. "Nice try, Hammerstein."

He hefted his box under one arm and opened the door with his free hand. "Always leave them laughing, that's my motto." His expression grew serious as he looked at them. "Well, see you around."

The other two nodded, knowing that it might be a long time before they were called back, if ever.

Paula had just finished packing her things when the phone on her desk rang. She put down the carton and picked up the receiver. "Paula Stewart."

"Paula, Maury."

In all the years that she had been with Maury Anderson, she had never heard her agent say hello when he called. "You heard?" she asked in surprise. News traveled fast, especially bad news. She sat down, making herself comfortable at her desk for the last time.

"Heard? I'm calling you to tell you. When did you hear?" Maury sounded annoyed at having lost his edge of surprise.

Paula laughed. If Alex had trouble understanding her, what would he do with someone like Maury? Suddenly she frowned. Why was Alex invading her thoughts so often? This charade of hers didn't require her bringing him into her thoughts, only physically into her life for a week or two. Or three. She had to stop getting so carried away.

"Okay, Maury, from the top," she urged. "What are you calling about?"

"The special."

"The special," she repeated patiently. When he said nothing, she asked, "What special?"

"It's the deal of a lifetime—for me. Not bad for you or your old man, either." He chuckled, sounding very pleased with himself.

"English, Maury, speak English. Now, what special?" she enunciated carefully.

There was another long, self-satisfied chuckle on the other end. "I just put together a deal for you to be the head writer on Wally and Paul's special."

She sat up straight, stunned. The first thing that came to her was that this meant she and Alex wouldn't have to go through with their charade. Their very own television special would pull their parents' faltering partnership together far more quickly.

That's what you wanted, isn't it? So where's the excitement? She hadn't the faintest idea why she felt so leaden all of a sudden.

"You still there, Paula?"

"Yes," she said, forcing herself to sound chipper, "I'm still here. Just a little speechless, that's all." Feeling oddly hollow, she ran her hand along the naked desk. "You know they're feuding, don't you?"

"Who?"

"Pop and Uncle Paul."

"News to me."

Odd. She would have thought that Maury would be the second, if not the first to know. He'd been with her father for over twenty-six years and was part den mother, part agent to the two men. But then, the man had a whole stable of clients to see to. "It happened about seven or eight days ago. They've had some sort of a fight—"

"Fight, shmight, this'll make them kiss and make up. It's what they've always wanted. Nice credit for you, too, kiddo. See if we can arrange for a leave of absence from that show you're wasting your talent on."

She looked around the empty room. Even the posters were gone. Marty had taken custody of them. "Not necessary. We just went on hiatus."

She could hear the broad grin in Maury's voice. "Couldn't've arranged it better myself. This'll be a real feather in your cap."

"Yes, I know. Thanks, Maury," she said without feeling. She couldn't understand why this left her so cold. She should be jumping up and down. Maybe her father's malaise was contagious.

"That's what I'm here for. You start next Wednesday. Call you back with details later today, after I meet with the producers."

"Maury?"

"Yeah?"

"Do me two favors."

"Yeah?"

She could hear the note of caution in his voice. He was always cautious when asked to promise something, even with someone he had known since she was in diapers. "Have you told Pop yet?"

"No. I just finished putting the deal together a couple of minutes ago. Yours was the first number that came to mind."

"Let me tell Pop."

"Stealin' my thunder, eh? Guess you're entitled this one time. So long as I get my ten percent."

"Always."

"And two?" he prodded, still a little suspicious. "You said two."

"When you see the producers, see if you can get them to agree to Marty Sorensen and Ted Hammerstein as two of the writers."

"Sorensen and Hammerstein." He rolled the names over on his tongue. "Aren't they the ones on your—?"

"Yes, they're the ones. I work well with them, Maury. They've got real talent."

"I'll see what I can do."

"You're a prince."

"I know."

Paula hung up with Maury's triumphant chuckle still ringing in her ears. She didn't move. Toying with a pencil she had forgotten to pack, she sat there, rethinking the conversation. She should be elated. So why wasn't she? What was the matter with her? Was she just shell-shocked? Or disappointed?

Disappointed about what? About being deprived of being in Alex's arms while safely hiding behind a charade? She *had* been working too hard.

Just what was her problem? This morning she had been restless because she'd be in close contact with him. Now she was restless because she no longer had to be.

You can't have it both ways. Which way *do* you want it?

This way, she decided firmly. She reached for the phone to tell Alex that his services were no longer necessary, and then stopped. His office was on her way home. She'd stop by and tell him in person.

Picking up the box containing her belongings, she took one last look around, then walked out, heading toward the parking lot. That it would be simpler just to call him on the telephone didn't complicate her thoughts for more than a moment. She preferred face-to-face contact, she told herself. That this came from a woman who could spend hours on the phone talking, didn't seem to be any sort of a contradiction to her.

My God, it wasn't bad enough that she infiltrated his thoughts, now he was hearing her voice, Alex thought looking up from the file on his desk. He could have sworn that he heard Paula's voice coming from the outer office. But how could he? She had no business being here.

"You can't go in there."

"Why? Is he seducing a client?"

It *was* Paula.

Alex began to brace himself for this newest invasion, when Paula burst into his office with Bianca on her heels. It was hurricane season again, he thought.

"I'm sorry, Mr. Hamilton—" Bianca gave Paula a look that could kill at twenty paces. Paula remained unharmed and unfazed.

"That's all right, Bianca, I'll handle it from here." He had his sincere doubts about the truth of his statement, but he ushered his secretary out the door, anyway. Closing it, he gathered his strength together and turned around to face Paula.

Paula seated herself, not on a chair, but on his desk. "Why does that woman feel she has to guard you like the lost national treasure?"

He tried not to notice the way her skirt hiked up around her thighs. "It's her job to screen my calls and my visitors. She's supposed to weed out the undesirables."

Paula couldn't resist smiling up into his face one last time and playing the game. "Right now, I thought I was supposed to be desirable."

As a matter of fact, you are, he thought. Too damn much for either one of our goods. "I didn't see a reason to inform her of our suddenly ignited passion."

Paula toyed with the strap on her shoulder bag, feeling suddenly as listless as her father had appeared this morning. "You don't have to bother informing anyone."

"Well, if we're supposed to play this thing right—" Why was he explaining this to *her*? It was her idea. She should be the one up on details. Then he remembered that details were never her strong point. That was his department. It always had been.

She let her purse fall to the gray-carpeted floor with a thud. "We're *not* playing this thing."

Paula shifted slightly, and he realized what she was sitting on. Leaning over, Alex tugged gently on a neatly typed letter that was partially under her very trim posterior.

"Why, Alex, watch your hands," she murmured, fluttering her eyelashes. She always felt better when she could take refuge behind humor.

He sighed patiently. "You happen to be sitting on Mrs. Grimaldi's will."

"Sorry, Mrs. Grimaldi," she addressed the paper, then moved to the side so that he could retrieve it.

He let the paper drop on top of a stack behind her. "Why aren't we playing this 'thing'?" He wondered why he was even bothering to ask. "Cold feet?"

She looked down at her shoes. "My feet have nothing to do with it. Pop's agent just called. Pop and Uncle Paul are finally oing to get a shot at that special they always wanted to do, o-o-o," she drew a breath, "there'll be no reason for us to retend anything. This is guaranteed to smooth over any prob-ms they have."

He ran his finger over his desk calendar, then pulled back his and. He had gotten a paper cut. It figured. With Paula round, things never went his way. "Well, that's a relief," he aid in a toneless voice. It was a relief. Why he didn't feel that ay was beyond him. He pulled out his handkerchief and abbed it against his finger.

She watched, curious. "Paper cut?"

Self-consciously he dropped his hand. "I'll live."

"Let me see." When she reached out, Alex took a step back. he slid off the desk.

"Why, do you want to see me bleed?" That seemed to be her peed. "Then you could tell people you actually drew blood."

She tugged at his hand and he reluctantly let her look at it, eeling foolish. "I'm just trying to be nice, Alex."

"If you were really trying to be nice—" His voice trailed off.

She raised her eyes to his. "What?"

"You wouldn't have walked into my life to begin with."

"As I remember it, I was carried in, bundled in a pink blan-et. I didn't have much choice. But I'm walking out of it now." he gave him back his handkerchief. "You're right, you'll live."

"Yes, I know."

She noted his tone and wondered about it. They both knew hey weren't talking about a paper cut. "You don't sound very elieved."

For some reason beyond me, I'm not, he thought. "You al-ays said I couldn't express emotion."

"Except anger," she reminded him.

He smiled, tucking away the handkerchief. "You do have a ay of bringing that out."

"I do, don't I?"

Was it that, that he couldn't express feelings? Or was he ex-eriencing the same sort of odd disappointment that was nawing at her? No, she was reading too much into it. He just ouldn't express his emotions. He would probably be clicking his heels up for joy if he knew how. Time to wind this up Paula, before he realizes that you don't sound overjoyed your self.

"Well, thanks for your help, such as it was."

"Feel free to call on me again any time, not to be your lover.'

"My number-one candidate," she muttered.

Why wouldn't that damn sinking feeling leave? she won dered. Why didn't *she* leave?

"What did your father say when he found out—about the special?"

"He doesn't know yet. I asked Maury, our agent, to let me tell him first. I was going to call him." She sighed.

"What's the matter?"

"I should have called him by now." She had meant to call Wally from her office. But deciding to see Alex had made her forget all about it. Well, that would no longer be a problem, she told herself. She'd only have to see him at the next family get together. If he came.

"Would you like to call him from here?" Alex heard him self offering.

She glanced at his phone, then back at Alex. "You're being unusually nice, Alex."

"Everyone else I know thinks I am nice."

She shrugged. "Maybe they're right," she said softly. Then her smile grew broader. "And then again, maybe there's jus something in the water they're drinking."

The door opened, and a man in black-rimmed glasses peered in. "Oh, sorry, didn't know that you were busy." He began to close the door again.

"No, that's all right, Owen." Alex crossed to the door "What's on your mind?"

The man eyed Paula appreciatively for a moment. "Mind i I see you a minute, Alex?"

"I'll be back in a few minutes," he told Paula, wondering why he was bothering. If she was gone when he came back what of it?

"I'll be waiting with bated breath," she called after him.

"Who's the lovely lady?" she heard Owen ask Alex.

"No one you'd want to know." Alex's voice faded down the corridor.

Good old Alex. Maybe this was for the best. Alex could have never pulled off the charade.

Maybe? What did she mean, "maybe?" Of course this was for the best. This was exactly what she wanted. A simple, quick way of getting her father together with Paul. She jabbed impatiently at the buttons that connected her with her father.

Her father answered with less than his customary cheeriness. This would bring it back, she assured herself. "Hi, Pop. It's me. Maury just called. You know that television special you always wanted?"

"Yeah?" Wally responded guardedly.

"It's yours!"

"Damn."

This wasn't the response she was expecting. "What do you mean, 'damn'?"

"Well, it couldn't have come at a worse time."

"Why?" she asked, exasperated. If he were in front of her, she'd swear she'd be shaking the man by his shoulders, trying to get some sense into his head.

"Because I don't want to do it with him."

She closed her eyes. Maybe her father was going through his second childhood. No, it wasn't that. He had never come out of his first one. That was part of his appeal. But not today. "Pop, don't you think you're carrying this just a little too far?"

"Not far enough. Think they'll take me by myself?"

"No, I don't think they'll take you by yourself." Screaming at him wasn't going to do it, she told herself. But the urge was strong. "You and Uncle Paul are a team, remember?"

"We *were* a team."

She couldn't take it any more. "Well, you're going to have to be a team again. You can't let this opportunity go by." She could even hear him being stubborn. There was a certain way he drew a breath when he was standing firm. "You and Uncle Paul can't go on feuding this way."

"Give me one good reason."

"The special."

"Not good enough."

She wasn't sure how it had happened. In her frustration, the words just tumbled out. "Because Alex and I are involved, and we can't stand seeing you act this way. Now you and Uncle Paul had better resolve whatever the hell it is that's going on between you."

"What do you mean 'involved'?"

"Lovers, Pop, lovers," she cried in frustration. Nothing but silence met her words. "Pop? Pop, did you hear me?"

"I heard you."

"Don't you have anything to say?" This was her ace card. If he stayed stubborn after this, she didn't know what to do.

"I'm going to have to think about this."

She let out a sigh. "You do that. But think fast."

"Full of surprises, aren't you?"

She wasn't quite sure how to take that. He wasn't being glib, and he wasn't angry, either. Probably in shock. Well, at least that was better than listless. "You don't know the half of it. We'll talk when I get home."

"Count on it."

Paula hung up, then stared at the phone for a long moment. Oh God, she was going to have to go through with it, after all.

She was surprised to find that she was smiling as she contemplated her fate.

Chapter Eight

"What?"

Alex looked at Paula in surprise. His conference with Owen had only lasted ten minutes. In that time, it seemed that the world had turned around one-hundred-and-eighty degrees.

Paula pushed herself away from his desk, but remained sitting in his chair. She gripped the armrests unconsciously for support. "I said that the special doesn't seem to make any difference to my father. He still refused to talk to Uncle Paul."

Alex moved over to the small reading table next to a wall of leather-bound law books. The coffee maker that Bianca oversaw so protectively was still half full. He poured a cup. Black. The extra caffeine suddenly seemed vitally necessary. "Clearheadedness doesn't stand much of a chance in your family, does it?"

Paula watched him, thought of asking for a cup herself, then decided against it. She was tense enough already, as if she was waiting for something to happen, a bomb to go off somewhere. "If that's the best snappy patter you can come up with, it's no wonder law became your calling."

He turned and leaned against the table, nursing his cup. "Cutting to the chase—does this mean that we're an item again?"

She shrugged innocently, as a wide grin suddenly began to flourish. Suddenly she felt good, alive, almost giddy. She liked feeling this way and refused to analyze the basic reason behind it. She wanted no complications. She just wanted to continue feeling this way. "Unless you have a better idea."

"Not at the moment."

There was a tinge of superiority in his voice. It didn't go unnoticed. But right now, Paula felt magnanimous enough to forgive him his bit of chauvinism—just this once. "But you will if you think about it."

Alex took another sip, let it slide down, then acknowledged her statement. "Probably."

"Well until that time," she rose to her feet, "we'll do it my way."

He laughed and shook his head in disbelief. She was one of a kind, probably by popular demand. "Was there ever any doubt?" one of a kind, probably by popular demand. "Was there ever any doubt?"

"Not in my mind." Paula circled the desk and crossed over to where he was standing, deliberately swaying her hips in a somewhat exaggerated fashion.

Alex watched every movement. Coffee finished, he placed the cup down on the table. "I take it you use the term loosely."

She saw humor in his eyes, liked it and let her own tone match it. "Not as loosely as when I use the term *human being* when applying it to you." She batted her eyes at him playfully.

He never could quite get that edge on her. "Want to put down the gloves?"

She pretended to lift her chin pugnaciously, inches away from his face. "What's in it for me?"

Why did he have this sudden urge to run his hands along that throat, to run his lips along that throat? Instead, he crossed his arms before his chest and leaned back. "Cooperation, for one."

"Consider them down."

Deciding maybe she *could* use coffee, she reached around him and poured half a cup. She felt his eyes on her every move. Used to attention, it still made her self-conscious. She hadn't a clue why.

His pose was relaxed, yet she could feel the tension in his body. That, too, matched her own. There was tension in the air, even though they were bantering. She could smell it, feel it, taste it. It wasn't just his, it was hers. Theirs. As if something inevitable was going to happen but neither knew when and the waiting was making them edgy.

Deliberately playing for time to steady her nerves, Paula took a long sip of coffee. Then she cocked her head to the side and looked at him. "What's 'two'?"

He watched her hands. They weren't steady. It pleased him that she was as unnerved as he was. "I think we'll find that out together, don't you?"

"Maybe."

Dangerous ground. The words flashed through her mind, and although it wasn't like her, she retreated. Taking another long sip, she placed the cup down. As she pulled back her hand, it brushed against his thigh. Such a tiny contact, such an intense reaction. She shouldn't have had the coffee, she told herself.

"You make a good cup of coffee, Alex," she said a bit too brightly, stubbornly refusing to step back. "You might not be a total loss as a husband, after all."

"Bianca made the coffee."

"Oh." She pretended to examine the cup distastefully this time.

"But to concede to your point, to the right kind of woman, I'd be the perfect husband."

"And she'll undoubtedly know by the *P* on your pajamas."

"I don't wear pajamas."

She looked at him, oddly startled by the piece of information. "You don't?" That didn't sound like Alex at all.

"No."

Her pulse quickened as she thought of him, lying in bed, with nothing but sheets around him. Her body tingled in response.

"Why, Alex," she put her hand to her throat, a shocked woman, "that sounds positively decadent. I wouldn't have believed it of you."

He knew she was trying to cover the fact that he had ruffled her. He liked the way her eyes widened and the wide, open curiosity that was there. It made her look guileless, vulnerable. And highly desirable. Everything seemed to make her more desirable these days. He felt he was engaged in a losing game, but he was bound to play out the hand. "There are a lot of things about me you don't know."

"Apparently." She looked down at her hands, not knowing why she kept feeling self-conscious. "Look, the thing is, Pop wasn't going to do the special until I told him about us."

The absurdity of the coupling struck her, and she laughed that throaty laugh that was his undoing. He noted that she sounded a good deal cheerier than she had when she had first walked into his office. He wondered if it was because she saw this as another chance to make him jump through hoops. Or if, perhaps, it was something else.

"You sound like Don Quixote, suddenly given a breath of life on his deathbed and crying, 'Sancho, my horse!'" he observed.

She knew she should be going. There were errands to run and an overwrought father to talk to. Yet she stayed and wanted to stay. Maybe she needed a long vacation. Maybe there was something in the coffee. Maybe if she kept dragging out absurd reasons, she wouldn't have to face the truth.

"Is that how you see us, as Don Quixote and Sancho Panza?" She smiled prettily. "Who gets top billing?"

"That would be you. I'm not about to fight you on that."

"Thank you. But you're not short and fat, either. Or loyal, like Sancho."

"Try me." He let himself trail his fingers along her hair, barely touching it. It was enough. "Part sorceress, part hurricane," he murmured, more to himself than to Paula.

Air became scarce as it lodged in her lungs and didn't move. She realized that she was holding her breath. "Interesting combination."

He looked into her eyes, those laughing, mischievous green eyes that always looked as if they held some sort of a secret joke. And always about him. But she didn't look as if she had one now. Her eyes were wide, questioning. "Yes, isn't it?"

Somehow she had known it was coming. Paula had felt it in her bones, sensed it in the air. Alex was going to kiss her. It was only a matter of time. And the time was now.

She might have known, but he was taken completely by surprise. Just as he was by her. He hadn't a clue that it was going to happen until it did. He would have put money on it *not* happening again, or would have earlier that day. It didn't make any sense.

It didn't have to.

Oh God, here it came again, that feeling like a flash flood, drenching him, leaving no part of him untouched. It was even worse this time than the last. And the more he struggled, the farther down the waters pulled him, snatching him away from the shores of good sense and lifting him to a land ruled by passions.

He was no stranger to desire. It was a common enough feeling. He had desired women before. But need? He had never needed a woman before, never needed to hold her close, to kiss her, to feel her breath on his face. He needed Paula. And the more he fought it, the greater the need grew.

He held her against him, molding her to his body, letting her know of his needs, his wants. He wanted her. Wanted her next to him, in his bed, with her hair spread out beneath her like a flaming halo.

He *had* to be crazy. Paula and halos. Pitchforks was more like it.

Madness was more like it. He had never experienced anything so gripping before. Her mouth was sweet and giving, yet as it gave the passion grew, feeding on the sweetness until his mind spun and he didn't know who or what he was. Only that he needed this, needed her.

The rush in her ears wouldn't stop. Even as she dug her fingertips into his shoulders, clinging for all she was worth, it wouldn't stop. It rocked her. The kiss rocked her. He made sky rockets and colors and everything she always thought was just a myth appear in her head when she closed her eyes.

She pulled back, afraid she was falling and would never reach the ground.

Paula blinked several times as she tried to focus on Alex's face, trying to regain her own ground, wherever that was.

Maybe it was a sugar imbalance of some sort.

"Alex," she took a step back and bumped against his desk. She sidestepped it, still backing away, "I think we have that part down pat. There's really no need to practice any more." She ran out of breath, and hoped that he didn't notice.

He noticed. "No," he said softly, knowing they were both lying, "no need, at all." There was a need, a very great need, not to practice, but to explore, to find out just what this was all about.

Slowly, as if drifting, yet knowing she had to get away fast, Paula crossed to the door. She felt like a child at a horror movie, wanting desperately to open her eyes and see, yet at the same time terrified of what she might see. As she opened the door, she turned around. Her pulse was still beating hard. She looked down at her wrist, wondering if it showed and if he could see.

"Alex?"

"Yes?"

"Thanks." He lifted a brow. "For going along with this," she added quickly. He nodded. "I'll call you later with our next move."

"I can hardly wait."

"I know." She tried to grin, found that she could, then grinned wider and closed the door behind her.

Alex stared at the closed door. He had a problem. He definitely had a problem. And he didn't know what the hell he was going to do about it.

The door opened again, and he tensed. She was returning for some reason.

But it wasn't her.

"Ah, there you are." James Corbett, the senior partner of the law firm, walked into Alex's office.

The disappointment Alex felt unnerved him. He covered it well. "What can I do for you, Mr. Corbett?"

James Corbett was a big, booming man with a zest for living and for the finer things in life, to make that living even more worthwhile. He loved his work, his golf game and his family in varying degrees of order, depending on the date in question. Corbett had apparently seen something he liked in Alex and had taken him under his wing almost from the first day. As time passed, Alex had worked hard to prove Corbett's basic instincts correct.

"Coffee's almost gone," he commented, pouring the last of it into his cup.

He savored the brew while Alex waited patiently to hear why the man was in his office. Social calls were rare. There wasn't time for them during the day. And though he and Corbett had gotten together after-hours, always at a dinner party held at Corbett's estate, those were few and far between, as well.

Corbett passed a hand over his thinning iron hair, which was meticulously combed back to cover as much as was physically possible without being ludicrous. "Sorry about Mrs. Joyner the other day. I'm afraid that couldn't be helped."

"She was rather interesting."

"The woman is a bore, Alex. No need to shy away from that." Corbett eased himself into the chair in front of Alex's desk and stretched out his legs as he studied his junior partner over the rim of his cup. "But I didn't give her to you because she was boring. I gave her to you because I knew that you'd be the one to do the best job and be able to weed through her words."

Alex acknowledged the compliment with a smile that said he understood. The question of capability had never been raised. There was no need. He gave the way Corbett expected people to give. One hundred percent. Anything less was not acceptable to Corbett. Or to Alex.

"And," Corbett leaned back in the chair, "I had an errand to run."

Alex smiled again as he tried to picture the hulking man running anywhere. Things came to Corbett, not the other way around.

"My daughter, Diana, needed to be picked up at the airport." Corbett closed his right eye slightly as he looked at Alex. The thought occurred to Alex that he was being sized up rather carefully. "You remember my mentioning Diana, don't you?"

It was the look Corbett wore when he was in the midst of a negotiation. Alex wondered what was up. "She was in Europe for three years. Wasn't she going to marry that count?"

"'Was' is right. The romance, or whatever you want to call it, fell through. She's come back here to nurse a broken heart and spend a little more of my money to raise her spirits." He chuckled dryly. "I'll probably find out the size of her hurt by the size of the diamond tennis bracelet she picks out today. I asked her to meet me here at four." He watched Alex carefully as he let his words sink in. "Thought we might have an early dinner together at Anton's."

It sounded like a harmless conversation, but Alex knew better, knew Corbett better. "We?" he repeated. "Am I invited?"

Corbett leaned forward and placed the coffee cup on Alex's desk. "I've always liked the way you pick up on things. I think Diana might like you."

It seemed to be his week for being chosen as an escort, Alex thought. "Well, I am free tonight, but from what you've mentioned about Diana, I think that your daughter might prefer the freedom of selecting her own male companions."

"Of course, of course." Corbett rose, his perfectly cut imported suit moving with him like a second skin. "Still, there's no harm in bringing out the best for her to meet, is there?" He smiled expansively. "You'll forgive me my flight of fancy, but I never liked her intended. No sense. Head in the clouds, hand in a pocket, never his own. Not a thing like you. You've got your feet planted firmly on the ground."

He made him sound like an oak tree, Alex thought, then wondered where the comparison had come from. He was spending too much time with Paula.

Corbett gave him a confidential, approving look. "You know exactly where you're going."

To hell in a toboggan, so it seems, Alex answered silently.

"She needs a man like that. I need a man like that."

It was only by exercising the strictest of control that Alex managed to keep his mouth from falling open. "I beg your pardon?"

"In the family, my boy. I'm talking about in the family. Now don't misunderstand me." He held up his large hands. "Diana's a beauty, not an old horse I'm trying to palm off. Doesn't look a thing like me, fortunately. Got her mother's genes and delicate bone structure. But you'll see all that for yourself." He turned on his heel and went to the door. "Well, see you at four."

Corbett closed the door behind him. The phone on Alex's desk began to ring, but he ignored it until it stopped. His secretary would undoubtedly take a message. He didn't feel like talking to anyone, at the moment.

For the life of him, he couldn't shake the feeling that he had walked on stage smack into one of his father's routines. Any minute now, the lights would turn up and the audience would applaud. There could be no other explanation for the bizarre situation he found himself in.

He pulled his desk calendar over and penciled in neatly "Dinner with Diana," by the empty space next to four o'clock. Letting the pencil drop, he wondered how this newest development in his life was going to mesh with Paula and her plans.

His secretary peeked in after a sharp knock on the door. "Mr. Hamilton, you didn't answer your phone. Are you ill, sir?" she asked. There was no concern on her long, gaunt face. Only curiosity.

"I'm thinking about it, Bianca," he answered still staring at the words he had written on his calendar. "I'm sincerely thinking about it."

Bianca walked away, shaking her head. "Let me know what you decide, sir," she said, shutting the door quietly in her wake.

"You'll be the first to know," Alex said to the door. "With any luck," he said to himself, "I'll be the second. Maybe."

This was all Paula's fault, all of it. He just hadn't quite figured out how to pin this on her yet. But given time, he would. He never doubted it.

Chapter Nine

Wally heard someone struggling with the front-door lock. A burglar wouldn't be that inept, he reasoned. It had to be Paula. He was agitated and fairly leaped over to the door. As he yanked it open forcefully, he pulled Paula along with it. Her key was still stuck in the lock. She nearly tripped over the threshold.

"Are you sure about this?" he demanded.

Paula glanced at him, then back at the lock as she turned the imprisoned key back and forth. "Your lock sticks, Pop."

"Hang the lock," he said impatiently.

"That might not be the only thing I'd like to hang by the end of today." With a mighty yank, she pulled the key free. Sighing, she looked at her father. He looked as vital as he ever had. Good—the news of her "involvement" with Alex had his blood moving. "Well, I see that you're off the critical list."

Wally pushed the door closed dramatically. "No thanks to this new turn in your life. Have you lost your mind, Paula?"

She dropped the key into her purse and let that fall on the hall table. "In this case, isn't it a little like the pot calling the kettle black? I'm not the one charging around like a raging wounded bull."

"No, but you're involved with the son of one."

She put her arms around his neck and smiled broadly. "Don't say that. Grandpa was a very nice man."

"I'm not talking about me. I'm talking about Alex, Paul, them."

"Oh." She withdrew her arms and gave him an innocent look that she knew would goad him on. She was milking this for all she was worth. She wanted him to stay revved up and running.

"Yes, 'oh.'"

"Pop," she linked her arm through his and gently drew him toward the family room, "wouldn't you rather talk about the special?"

He didn't budge. At the mention of the special, his eyebrows rose up high on his forehead. He looked, she thought, for all the world like a mischievous greeting-card jack-o'-lantern.

"No I wouldn't. C'mere."

He gestured toward the sofa. They never sat in the living room unless there was a formal talk coming. He reserved the living room for his business associates, the ones who hadn't gotten to know the inner man. The ones who had, he herded into the family room.

Puzzled, Paula followed her father to the sofa and sat down.

"Am I being evicted?" she asked lightly. Paula had a feeling she knew what was coming. With elaborate movements, she smoothed down her skirt and returned his penetrating gaze, waiting.

Wally took his daughter's hand into his. It looked even smaller as it rested on his wide paw. "Baby, I know you've been independent since the day you were born, and nobody's ever been able to tell you anything, but . . ." He hesitated, groping for words.

Seriousness did not fit him very well, she thought. He was much more at home striking a comedic attitude. But she kept her silence, letting him struggle.

Wally took a deep breath and tried again. "Don't get me wrong. I like Alex, but seeing the family you're getting into—"

Since Alex was an only child and his mother had died five years ago, that left only Paul to hide beneath the umbrella her father labeled "family." Enough was enough. Paula was now annoyed. It showed plainly on her face. One look and Wally knew he had overstepped his bounds. "A 'family' we've been mingling with since I was in diapers. Before that, even."

Wally dropped her hand and rose abruptly. He stuffed his fists into his pockets and roamed around the room in silence. She'd never, ever seen him like this. Why wouldn't he talk about it? Why wouldn't he tell her what was wrong? What could be so horrible that he kept it bottled up inside, instead of letting it come gushing out the way he always did with things that annoyed him?

"Pop?"

He turned. For a moment, he looked every one of his fifty-seven years. Whatever was between them, she thought, it wasn't a small thing. It wasn't a tiff he had overdramatized the way she had surmised. What was she going to do about it? She couldn't just stand by and watch this happen. She had never been one of those people who looked on from the sidelines as life played itself out. She had to jump into the center, even if the center threatened to drag her down.

Wally began to pace behind the sofa. "I'm not sure I can be civil to Paul after what's happened."

She twisted around to watch him. "What *has* happened, Pop? Can't you tell me? You've always told me everything."

Wally laughed softly to himself. "No, not everything, kid." He looked as if he was about to say something more, but then his expression grew somber. He shook his head. "No, it's my problem, not yours. I don't want to burden you."

"Pop, you're not 'burdening' me. I'm your daughter. If something's bothering you, and it sure as hell is, I have a right to know."

The cherubic smile she was so familiar with suddenly resurrected itself on his face, as he took hold of both her hands once more. "Forget about me. This is supposed to be the best time of your life. You're young, you're in love, and you don't have to pick up after him yet. Enjoy. Forget what I said, too. I always did like Alex, and there was a time I had hoped you'd both see past your bickering and get together. So now it's true." He kissed her cheek. "Be happy, baby."

She couldn't stand it. He looked so happy. Happy over a lie. She had *never* lied to her father before. There had never been a need to before, nor any inclination, either. While she had grown up living with her mother, it was her father who was her friend, her father to whom she could always turn, no matter what the problem. He was always there for her. No matter where he was, he always had time to stop and talk to her on the phone. Once, when she was sixteen, going through her first serious romantic breakup and feeling as though she would just die from it, he had flown home after the last show just to hold her hand and talk. He had to fly back the next morning. But he had been there for her. He had always been there for her. She couldn't deceive him now.

Paula bit her lower lip. "Pop—" she hesitated, wavering between telling him the truth and going on with the charade. How to step lightly in the mine field between truth and lies and still do some good? She hadn't a single clue.

But she never got a chance to form her confession.

"Listen, baby," Wally interrupted, his shoe-button eyes dancing, "if you're going to do this, we're going to do it right."

Something in his expression should have warned her. But she was too worried about his state of mind to realize where this was all leading and what kind of an impact it was going to have on her immediate life.

"Just what do you mean, 'right'?" Half-formed thoughts flashed through her mind. Her father was not one to do things in half measures. His enthusiasm usually got the best of him, and he tended to overdo everything.

He circled around the sofa, sitting down next to her again, completely transformed from the morose man she had seen lying in bed this morning. Words came at her fast and furious. "We'll get the family and some of our closest friends together, have an informal dinner.'' He clapped his hands together, savoring the idea. "And make the announcement then.''

Paula had a sinking feeling in the pit of her stomach. Too far. She was letting this go too far. "What announcement?''

Sometimes, Wally thought his only daughter's mind wandered around too much. "Why, that you two are getting married.''

Paula cleared her throat, and she stared at the Monet lithograph on the far wall. "Well, we hadn't—''

"You're not getting married?'' Wally's voice went up, and so did his body as he jumped to his feet. He hovered over her, an indignant, protective bulldog.

"Pop, I—'' She reached out to him in an effort to calm him down.

He should have known. This was Paul's son they were talking about. Hadn't Paul fooled him? Why should Alex be any different? "You mean he's just stringing you along, having his way with you?''

The angered look on her father's face surprised her. She could almost see him grabbing a shotgun and comically demanding that Alex "do the decent thing.'' "It's not called that anymore.''

"I don't care what the popular term for it is. Is he trifling with your emotions or not?''

"Not.''

"Then he'll marry you.''

"I suppose,'' she said slowly. It was either lie or see Alex's hide nailed over the mantelpiece. That was all she needed. Guilt.

"Then he'll marry you,'' Wally repeated firmly.

"Then he'll marry me.''

So they'd have a little more to pretend about, she told herself, trying to assuage her conscience. They would call off "the engagement'' after their fathers resolved their differences. No harm done. The scenario was just getting a little fleshed out, that was all.

She could just hear Alex's reaction now.

"So we'll have the formal announcement—''

Paula licked her lips. Well, at least he wasn't talking about renting billboards to advertise the wedding date. But if she didn't stop him, he soon would be. "Pop, it's not like we're merging two kingdoms here—" she began. God, Alex was going to have a fit with this newest development.

Why did she care what his reaction was? She was being embroiled here, too.

The round head bobbed up and down in agreement with her pronouncement. "No, more like a kingdom and an inconsequential principality—"

Paula suddenly saw herself going down for the third time. "Pop—"

"—but who's quibbling?"

"You are," she cried. "With Uncle Paul. And you know we can't have this formal announcement without his being there."

"I can do anything I please."

"Pop—"

Wally pondered this for a moment, really wrestling with the situation. And then he gave her the wide, guileless grin he was famous for. "I'm a big man. For you, I'll bury the hatchet."

"Hopefully not in Uncle Paul."

"Don't tempt me."

"Pop, don't do it just for me. Not just for me," she pleaded. Although she was doing this for all the right reasons, she didn't ultimately want her father patching up his argument solely because of her. She just wanted it to be the catalyst that set him in motion. He had to be made to see that he was being unreasonable about the situation. Whatever the situation was, it wasn't worth giving up a lifelong friend. They had been through so much together over the years.

Wally looked at her squarely, a stubborn look forming on his face and in his eyes. There was hurt there, too. "*Only* for you. If it was for anyone else, I couldn't be dragged to the same city as that man."

"How are you going to do the special?"

"Very simply. I'm not."

He couldn't do this. She had to make him see that. "Pop—"

"No," he waved a chunky hand over his head, slicing the air. "I don't need the special."

"Maybe you don't, but I do. *Hayley's House* got canceled." She was stretching the truth a little, but only a little, she told herself. A hiatus notice was almost as good as a cancellation. "I need this special, Pop. I need you to do it for me. And I need you to do it with Uncle Paul."

Wally closed his eyes. The temptation to tell her his reasons was great, but it would only hurt her, as well. Above all else, he didn't want to see her hurt. He opened his eyes and looked at his daughter's face. So young, so pretty. No, she didn't need to know his reason. "Okay. But I don't want to talk about that now. I want to make plans for your party."

She threw her arms around him. "Thanks, Pop. You're the best."

"Yeah, I know." He looked at the Monet over the fireplace. He had bought that for Cecilia on their first anniversary because she liked it so much. He felt a pang and let himself nurse it for a moment. "Your mother should have known, too."

Paula backed up and looked at him quizzically. "What?"

"Nothing." His whole countenance changed. He was infinitely more buoyed. "Listen, I've got phone calls to make."

She nodded her head numbly, her mind whirling. If she knew her father, what he meant by close, intimate friends would probably turn into a gathering containing only a handful of people under the maximum amount allowed at Madison Square Garden. She turned toward the stairs, needing to get away so that she could sort things out.

He called after her. "We can hold it on Saturday night, before we get all caught up in that special thing, and—where are you going?"

"To call Alex." *He's going to want to kill me,* she added silently.

Wally laughed softly, but loud enough for her to hear. "I remember what it was like."

"No, you don't, Pop. No, you really don't," she said under her breath.

* * *

"Mr. Hamilton's office."

"Bianca, this is Paula Stewart."

"He's not available—"

Oh no, you don't. She was now onto the secretary's method of operation. "Bianca, I need to talk to him, and I need to talk to him now, so put me through or I'll tell immigration that you're here illegally."

"Well, I never—"

"I'm sure you haven't, but they won't know that, will they?"

Paula was rewarded with total silence, as Bianca put her on hold. Paula counted to ten and then heard Alex's voice. He was not pleased.

"What did you just say to my secretary?"

"That there's a Kelly Girl just itching to take her place, and if she didn't let me talk to you, I'd send the temp over. Listen, never mind Miss London of 1955, we have a problem."

Yes, and I'm talking to it, he thought. He exercised patience. It was getting to be a habit around Paula. "Whatever it is, it'll have to wait. I'm going out to dinner in a few minutes."

Paula thought of the woman that he had said he was seeing last night. "Is this a regular habit, then?"

"Eating dinner? Yes. I do it every night." He listened to his own answer. He *was* hanging around Paula too much.

"You're improving." His answer tickled her. The writer in her always admired a good quip, even if it was at her own expense. "With company, I mean."

"Are we officially lovers, yet?"

She curled up on the bed. Somehow the word made her stomach tighten. She worked hard at ignoring the feeling. "Yes." She kept her voice light.

"Then I wouldn't want to jeopardize our relationship by answering that. I'll meet you for lunch tomorrow and we'll discuss your problem."

"Our problem," she corrected.

"That's what I like about you, Paula. Share and share alike." She heard someone knock on his door and then someone ask,

"Ready?" "I have to go, Paula. I'll see you at one at Anton's."

She answered "Fine," but she said it to the dial tone. He had hung up. Probably couldn't wait to get going, she thought, annoyed.

Paula replaced the receiver and then rolled onto her back and stared up at the ceiling, thinking. Who was this person he was having dinner with? Did he like her, or was it just a business meeting? He sounded too evasive for it to be business. No, this was pleasure. A tinge of jealousy rose up, and she banked it down, refusing to recognize it for what it was.

She had never thought about Alex seeing someone seriously. Was he going out with that woman he had seen the other night? The one he had hustled her out of the apartment for? Again? Maybe there was more to him than met the eye. Restless, Paula got up and paced about her room, picking up odds and ends and replacing them.

Well, as long as he helped her with this charade and got their fathers together again, she didn't care how many women Alex Hamilton saw and what he did with them, she told herself.

She was honest enough to admit that she couldn't quite make the statement ring true.

Chapter Ten

Diana Corbett was sophisticated, well-bred, well connected and very easy on the eye. In Alex's judgment she was beautiful. He strongly suspected that they were in agreement with that assessment. There was nothing lacking with Diana's self-confidence, either. He saw that immediately, as well. In fact, he couldn't have asked for a more perfect example of the kind of woman he had, until a short while ago, envisioned would be at his side through the middle and later years of his life. She met all the requirements of the ideal wife for a young lawyer on the rise.

But she wasn't Paula.

And that was a point in her favor. At least, that would have been his immediate answer, if anyone would have asked. In his right mind, he would never have wanted one Paula, much less two. But, he thought as he faced his senior partner across the table at the restaurant and kept an attentive eye on the charming woman at his left, he apparently wasn't in his right mind. Not for several days, now.

All through cocktails and the main course, Alex involuntarily compared the two women. When Diana laughed, he thought of Paula's deep, throaty laugh, which moved through him like languid wine. If a witticism left Diana's lips, he thought of the kind of barb that Paula would utter in the same instance. Even Diana's lips made him think of Paula's. Diana's were thin, perfectly shaped and given to small, gracious smiles. Paula's were full, quick to pull back in a grin, and tempting. So damn tempting.

No doubt about it. He was losing his mind.

Alex raised his water glass and took a long drink.

Corbett eyed his junior partner with a measure of curiosity. "Are you feeling all right, Alex?"

Alex placed the empty glass on the table. "Fine. The fish was a little salty, that's all."

Corbett smiled and nodded, then made a show of looking at his watch. "Then you wouldn't mind taking Diana home for me, would you? I have a late appointment to see to, I'm afraid. Can I count on you, Alex?"

Alex knew it wasn't a question. It was a politely worded command. It was also a setup, but knowing that didn't alter his obligatory answer. "It'd be a pleasure, sir."

Diana's smile grew warmer. It didn't reach her eyes, though, where Paula's smiles always started.

What made him think of that? His boss, the man who held his immediate future in his hands, was practically making him a gift of his daughter, giving him keys to the family estate and saying, "Welcome home, son," and he was comparing smile patterns. What *was* the matter with him?

He had a strong, nagging suspicion that he knew.

Corbett rose, carelessly throwing down a large bill. "There, that should cover the damages and whatever else you two might order," he laughed. Then he placed a hand on Alex's shoulder and said warmly, "And I think that you've been with the firm long enough to call me Jim."

The older man bent over and brushed his lips against his daughter's prettily positioned cheek. "I'll see you tomorrow,

Diana. Don't keep him out too late. I need him alert in the morning.'' He laughed at his own remark as he walked away.

Alex found himself growing restless through dessert, now that there was just the two of them. Diana seemed not to notice. Probably, he thought, because she was amusing herself with reciting her adventures in Europe.

''Would you like to leave now?'' Alex asked after the waiter had cleared away their dishes.

Diana ran her cocktail napkin delicately through her fingertips. Her eyes never left his face. Things were going on behind those eyes, Alex thought. He wondered if she was sizing him up as a potential consort. There could be no other label for the role he had been so blatantly selected for.

''Yes,'' she said in a soft, melodious voice. ''I think I'd like that.''

He couldn't help wondering what else she'd like.

The ride back to Diana's apartment was not uneventful. Diana, Alex decided, did not fit under the heading of shy and retiring. What she wanted, she went after. This time, it seemed to be him. Knowing that it made no logical business sense, whatsoever, he felt himself wanting to put distance between them. Quickly.

Diana had other ideas. ''Father's having a party this Saturday for Judge Wilkins,'' she informed him as they pulled up in front of her apartment building. ''I like to call him Willy.''

Alex had trouble envisioning the gruff-looking older man responding to anyone who called him Willy. The judge had a fearsome reputation on the bench. ''Have you known Judge Wilkins for a long time?'' Alex found that he had to search for things to say. That was never the case when he was with Paula. Then it was a matter of searching for patience, he reminded himself.

''Absolutely forever.'' Diana waited until Alex came around to her side of the car and opened the passenger door for her. She stepped out lightly, making certain that her long legs were fully admired before she rose. ''Would you like to attend the party, Alex?''

How to skirt around this one tactfully? "To the best of my knowledge, I wasn't invited."

"You are now." She lifted a perfectly shaped dark brow and waited for his answer. It never occurred to her that it might be a negative one.

Alex noticed that she didn't acknowledge the security guard as they passed him upon entering the building. Paula never would have done that. More than likely, she would have stopped to talk to the man. Paula never encountered strangers without making them into friends. It was one of the qualities about her that he had always envied.

Alex returned the guard's nod. The elevator was standing open, and he breathed a silent sigh of relief as they entered. Almost over.

"I'll have to check my—"

Diana pressed five. She tried to suppress her annoyance. She wasn't used to having to convince someone to comply with her wishes. "There'll be a lot of important people there," she interrupted. "People who might be influential in helping a rising young lawyer's career."

"I'm perfectly happy the way I am." Until that moment, he hadn't really thought about the matter. Was he happy? No, he didn't believe he was. He wasn't certain why, but he knew now that he wasn't. But at the moment, he felt the lie was necessary.

Diana stepped out into the lushly carpeted hallway, then looked at Alex with mounting curiosity. "You don't always plan to be an estate lawyer, do you?" She laughed, as if the idea was absurd and they both knew it.

Ambitious, too. But for whom? "What did you have in mind?"

She looked content that he had asked her. Amused, he guessed that gave him points for good sense. He followed her to her door.

"A political career."

Good God, the woman wanted to be in the White House, he suddenly realized. "I hadn't really thought about a career in politics."

The smile on her lips was smug. "It's never too early to start thinking."

No, it wasn't, and he knew that she'd be surprised at what he was thinking. And of whom. He was a little surprised, himself, at the frequency with which Paula kept cropping up in his mind.

"I'll think about it," he promised. "And now, I'm afraid that I have to be going."

She hadn't expected his retreat. Men never retreated from her unless they were told to. "I can't convince you to come in for a nightcap?" Diana looked ever so slightly petulant.

"Not tonight. I'm sorry." He wanted nothing more than to retrace his steps down the thickly carpeted hallway that led back to the elevator. "I have some papers to go over."

She let one long, delicate hand linger on his shirt front. "You'll impress Father, but you're disappointing me."

"One out of two isn't bad." He flashed an apologetic smile. "Sorry, it really can't be helped."

"I like a man with a sense of humor." Drawing closer, she turned up her mouth to his.

He knew what was expected of him. To leave now would be insulting, and to insult Diana Corbett was to incur her father's wrath. He had absolutely no doubts about that. Besides, he told himself, this would be a good way to put his theory about rampant hormones to the test. Taking Diana in his arms, he kissed her.

And waited.

No explosions went off in his head. His blood temperature remained the same, even though her body was pressed provocatively against his. When he opened his eyes, everything was just where he had left it. No spinning head, no disorientation, nothing. He felt the way he had always felt when he kissed a woman. In control of the situation. The only time that wasn't true was when he kissed Paula.

Diana smiled at him as she stepped back into her opened doorway. "I suppose your motto is 'always leave them wanting more.'"

At the moment, it was "go while the going is good," Alex thought. "More like never put off until tomorrow what you can do today."

Diana raised a brow as she stepped into her apartment. The invitation was there. She tossed her head, and her dark hair brushed against her shoulders. "Well, then?"

He could go in and ride out whatever came his way, or he could retreat. "I meant my papers." Casual encounters didn't interest him. Neither did advancement by deception.

"Oh, I see."

For a moment, he thought he saw anger flash across her face, but if it was there, it quickly receded. "Until Saturday, then."

He was crazy. Absolutely, positively crazy. The boss's daughter was throwing herself at him, and he had just neatly lobbed the serve away. She was making eyes at him, and all he could think of was that they weren't the color of Paula's eyes. Diana was a beautiful woman, with wealth and drive, and she had singled him out.

And all he could do was compare her to Paula. And find her lacking.

He *had* to be crazy. Either that, or Paula was a damnable witch who had cast a spell on him. That, too, was a viable possibility. Why else would he have such a strong reaction to her?

He walked to his car, muttering to himself. The security guard eyed him curiously.

Alex jabbed his key into the ignition. They were as incompatible as oil and water. So why couldn't he get her out of his mind? And why now, after all these years? The car came to life, and he pulled away from the curb, driving mechanically. It wasn't as if he had never seen Paula before. She was like an annual cold, a perennial allergy that could always be counted on to return, get under his skin and irritate the hell out of him. So why had she suddenly infiltrated the disciplined sanctuary of his mind with such intensity?

Cars honked behind him, and he realized that he was standing at a green light. He pressed his foot down on the gas.

Because he had kissed her.

So it was all physical, nothing more than physical. He threaded his way down Wilshire Boulevard. And if he believed that, then there were ten people vying for the opportunity to sell him swampland in Florida as a beach resort.

Alex proceeded home in the worst of moods.

He entered the restaurant the next day to meet Paula, in the same frame of mind. He was ready to lynch her for having ruined him.

By some strange twist of fate, he was late and she was early. Like Halley's Comet, he knew it would never again happen in his lifetime.

As he approached the table in the dimly lit, subdued restaurant, he was struck by how alive, how animated Paula appeared, even sitting still. What a contrast to the woman he had been here with last night. Paula was a mysterious box of surprises, while Diana was just an ornate empty container. He found himself wanting to pull the ribbon off the box of surprises.

Maybe this would pass, Alex told himself as he slid into the booth. Paula looked up, startled. She had been, he guessed, deep in thought. Somehow he knew that didn't bode well.

A waiter appeared discreetly to take his order. Alex decided to skip lunch and simply ordered a cocktail.

"You can't get very far on just one drink." Paula closed her own menu.

He lifted a brow. "I can always order a second one."

"I meant for lunch. Since when do you need artificial courage to face me?"

"It's suddenly become a necessity. I'd feel better with an army, but the cocktail will have to do." His drink arrived and he took a sip before asking, "Okay, what's the newest bulletin?"

She toyed with the stem of her glass. When she raised her eyes to his, she discovered that he was looking straight into them. It took her a moment to remember what she was going to say. "We're going to have to go public."

"Someday, you're going to learn not to start sentences in the middle. Public as in what?"

"As in a formal announcement, at a party hosted by my father for us."

"What kind of a formal announcement?" he asked suspiciously.

Paula looked down at the table and moved her napkin to the side. "It's about our engagement."

He took another long sip. "Our engagement?" Paula pressed her lips together and nodded. "I thought I was just supposed to be your lover."

A passing waiter gave them both a knowing look. Alex gave him a stony look. The man moved on quickly.

"You got upgraded," Paula told him.

"That's your word for it," he commented dryly. "Just when did I lose my head and propose?"

"When my father threatened to turn you into a rug for trifling with my emotions."

Maybe he *should* have ordered two drinks to start with. "I always do make smart decisions." There was no reason to be annoyed. After all, this was all still just playacting. Pretending to be her fiancé was no different than pretending to be her lover. Either role would be over in short order. "How many people is he inviting to this little party?"

Paula hesitated only a fraction of a moment, but he noticed.

"My guess would be half the immediate world."

He might have known. "Ah, it's going to be an intimate party, then."

She looked at him, pleased. He surprised her. She expected him to make some kind of angry comment. He still could be a good sport, when he wanted to. "What do you want to do about it?"

He shrugged. "Attend. It'd look a little odd if I didn't, wouldn't it?"

A grateful smile spread on her face. "You're going along with this?"

How could he have not noticed just how radiantly beautiful she was before? Where had his eyes been? "I thought I signed on for the duration of this little drama, when I initially agreed to this."

She left her salad alone. It didn't hold her attention nearly as much as Alex did. "That was when it was just between the four of us."

He laughed. "I can just see the honeymoon arrangements."

Grateful as she was at this display of good-humored patience, Paula still couldn't get over the fact that he hadn't flatly changed his mind when she had told him about the latest development. "I really don't understand you, Alex."

He watched the way the muted light seemed to catch in her hair. Fire, pure fire. It should have been a warning. "The feeling is mutual."

"I mean about all this." She gestured about, feeling suddenly helpless to get her point across. "Why are you being so nice?"

"I called my father this morning and told him that you and I were...involved." It wasn't the only reason he was doing it, he realized, but it was the only one he was giving her.

She leaned forward. "And?"

Alex felt an urge to bring her face even closer, to touch her lips with his. He straightened in his seat. "He's overjoyed. He said he always loved you like the daughter he never had. Maybe he will get together with Wally because of this. I guess I owe it to him and my sanity to give this my best shot."

"Oh Alex!" Her hand covered his and she squeezed it warmly. "You know, you really can be very nice when you want to be." She stopped as he leaned over toward her. There was a warm, smoky look in his eyes. Something turned over in her stomach again. "What—what are you doing?" Warmth flooded through her, prodding at all her pulse points.

His fingers brushed her cheek lightly. "You have an eyelash..." His breath seductively caressed her cheek. Her heart began doing erratic things.

"I have lots of eyelashes," she whispered, her mouth engaged even if her mind wasn't.

Their lips were inches apart. She almost felt him smile rather than see it. A surge of excitement went through her. Was he going to kiss her? It was dark in the restaurant, soothingly so, and they were alone in a booth. The stubby candle on their table flickered, casting romantic lights around the small enclosed area.

Well, *was* he going to kiss her?

Her pulse accelerated. This was just what she didn't want— and yet, she did. With all her heart. It was all she wanted, all she seemed to think about, since that kiss in the rain.

She almost moaned when he drew away.

Alex placed his hands on her shoulders to steady himself. He wanted to kiss her so badly that he could hardly contain himself. He tasted it, felt it, ached for it. His demanding need unnerved him. He'd never felt this out of touch with himself, this reckless. When he was with any other woman, there were always clear-cut lines. When he was with Paula, everything was a breathtaking blur. He didn't know if he liked it, but he did know that it was addictive.

"Well," he said simply, "now you have one less eyelash."

She couldn't help herself. She was never one to be indirect. "Were you going to kiss me?"

He might have known that she could see it in his eyes. She could see everything. "Is that how you usually have people get rid of your loose lashes?"

A quip. She deserved that. She would have done the same to him. Feelings were too important to talk about for Alex. Suddenly the same seemed true for her. At least the feelings she was having about him. Paula withdrew behind a quip of her own. "No, but they don't usually get that close to do it. I was just wondering if you were getting in the mood for Saturday night."

"Saturday night?"

"That's when Pop plans on holding his gala."

Alex shook his head. More complications. "Bad timing. I can't come."

"Why not?"

"Because I promised Diana I'd attend her father's party." And though he found that he really didn't want to, he knew that for the sake of his position in the company, he would have to attend.

"Diana?" She knew her voice sounded a little too innocent to be genuine. By the look on Alex's face, she knew she wasn't fooling him, either. "Is she the one you went out with the other night?"

He was going to explain and then stopped. It was too involved. Besides, it would be admitting that one of the reasons he had gone out to dinner with Diana was because he was trying to get Paula out of his mind. "Yes. She's James Corbett's daughter."

"James Corbett, as in the name in gold lettering on your door?"

"The same."

"The boss's daughter." She grinned suddenly.

"Something funny about that?"

Paula shook her head, then took a last sip of her wine. "No, but that explains it."

"Explains what?"

"For a moment, I was overcome with an image of you lost in a passionate embrace with some wild vixen who had caught your fancy." And I hated it, she added silently. "Now I understand."

"Well, that makes one of us. Understand what?"

His voice was low, but she didn't fool herself into thinking that there was no emotion behind it. Paula felt her own adrenaline rising. She loved getting Alex's temper up, and right now it was taking the edge off the inexplicable hurt she was experiencing. Why should it matter to her who he spent his time with and how?

"And I warn you, Paula, you're on dangerous ground here."

She held up her hands in front of her, pretending to ward off blows. "Don't beat me in front of witnesses, Alex." Paula lowered her hands, but her eyes still teased him. "It's just that marrying the boss's daughter is something I can see you doing. It's really very traditional."

Marrying? Where had she gotten that ridiculous notion? And what right did she have in pigeonholing him like that? "You are, by far, the world's most exasperating, most infuriating female."

"I know." She laughed low, sending a shiver up his spine. "It's on my birth certificate."

He sighed. He was practically shouting at her, and she was tossing back glib retorts. "Do you always have to get in the last word?"

"Yes."

"Why?"

"Why not?"

He took hold of her by the shoulders. "Paula."

"What?" she breathed, her smile still teasing, hiding the fact that her pulse was in her throat again.

"Shut up for just a minute."

"Okay, but only for a minute," she said against his lips.

Her lips met his almost hungrily. There was the taste of wine on them, making them just that much sweeter, that much dearer to her, that much more necessary for her very life's breath.

When, when did this happen? Why did this happen? It wasn't going to lead to anything but problems. Oh, but while the merry-go-round was here, she was going to ride, to pretend that the path did lead somewhere instead of just a circle.

She threaded her fingers through his thick black hair, drawing strength from the fact that she was touching him and she needed strength to survive the wild ride and the madness that beat inside her.

Passion rose up like lava shooting from a volcano, hot and bubbly. Every time he kissed her, he only wanted more. Alex knew he was doomed, but it didn't keep him from fighting it. Yet, still he was kissing her.

"Will there be anything else?"

The question, followed by a light cough, drove them apart.

"Not here," Paula murmured glibly to the amused-looking waiter who hovered over them.

Alex marveled at the quip. Wasn't she as dazed as he was by all this? Didn't she feel what he did? "Never forget your training, do you?"

"Never." Just my bearings, she thought. Paula smoothed down her skirt. Everything was in place, and yet she felt as if she had been whisked away by a hurricane.

"When God created your mind, He said 'let there only be one.' And there was a good reason for that," Alex told her. He pulled several bills from his wallet. "I have to run. This should cover the bill."

Paula frowned. "What are you doing? I can pay for my own meal. You didn't have anything."

He looked at her pointedly as he rose. "I had more than I bargained for. Humor me. We're supposed to be a duo." He gave the money to the waiter. "Let the lady have anything she wants."

Paula turned her face up to the waiter and said sweetly, "I'd like a tennis bracelet, please. Four carats."

Alex saw the waiter draw back a step, looking at them both rather uncertainly. Alex drew out another five as an added tip. He had a hunch the man would surely earn it this afternoon. "Maybe he can scrounge up a straitjacket instead."

Paula leaned her head on her upturned palm and looked at Alex. "For whom?"

"At this point, I'm not honestly sure." He paused, ready to leave, yet reluctant. "About the party, have your father switch it to Sunday."

"Sunday it is." She smiled. It felt a little brittle around the ends. And Saturday you'll be with *her*. Not that it matters to me, of course. "Are you sure you can make it? You won't be, uh, sleeping in?"

He patted her shoulder in a patronizing gesture that he knew would infuriate her. "In either case, I'll make the party. See you."

"Only if you're very, very good," she called after him.

Now what had made her mention his date with Diana? Did she want her feelings to be totally transparent to him?

Alex turned, smiled enigmatically at her, then left.

Whoever Diana was, she hated her, then told herself that she was being ridiculous.

"*Will* there be anything else?"

She looked up at the waiter. "You wouldn't have a cup of hemlock, would you?"

"No, madam."

"That'll be all, then."

The waiter slipped away.

She had made her own bed, Paula thought, and now she had to lie in it, spikes and all.

What was the matter with her?

Paula sighed as she pushed aside her plate. Maybe she knew, at that. Maybe she just didn't want to admit it to herself. Not yet. Not ever, if she was lucky. After all, it looked as if Alex had a love interest. A serious one. That left her out of any picture but a make-believe one.

How could he have someone else and still kiss her that way, damn him?

She had always enjoyed the lighter side of life. It was in her genes. And maybe, just maybe, she thought, it kept things from getting too serious, too complex, too involved. It kept words such as *commitment* at bay.

So what was happening here?

He had her running scared, that's what was happening. She both loved and feared what was going on inside of her.

"Like a moth drawn to her death by fire," she muttered.

What if it all turned to ashes on her? What if she committed and he didn't? Wouldn't that be the ultimate laugh?

But it wouldn't be very funny. No, not funny, at all.

She closed her eyes. Something told Paula she was in deep trouble.

Chapter Eleven

The feeling that she was going to wind up with more than she bargained for grew stronger for Paula as Sunday drew closer. She tried to get lost in the thousand details that went into throwing one of her father's so-called intimate parties, which seated five hundred. But Alex kept creeping into her thoughts, always when she least wanted him to. She tried to tell herself that it was only natural. He was, after all, a good-looking man and she was a red-blooded American woman.

But it *wasn't* natural to be having the kind of thoughts she was having. Not about Alex. He wasn't her knight in shining armor; he wasn't going to sweep her off her feet and do wild, wonderful things. He was a straitlaced, stable man who didn't know how to have fun. They had absolutely nothing in common except a few hormones that seemed to be out of whack.

Despite her faultless reasoning, when the evening of the party arrived, though she played the perfect guest of honor, she caught herself watching the door with far more intensity than the occasion called for. There was no use in pretending that it was only a case of party jitters. She didn't *have* party jitters. She was waiting for Alex to appear.

The doorbell rang incessantly from seven until nine. And still no Alex, no Paul. There were guests on the patio and in every room of the house, mingling with waiters while caterers kept scurrying off to the huge truck parked on the side and producing an endless supply of food.

"So where's Prince Charming?" Wally cornered Paula in the hallway.

"He'll be here. He's probably stuck in traffic." She gave him a wide smile. Maintaining a constant smile was beginning to make her face ache.

She was worried. And angry. Had Alex decided at the last moment not to go through with it, after all? How could he *do* this to her? Paula took a glass of wine from a passing waiter.

Easily, the answer returned. It would be the ultimate way of getting back at her for all those quips she had pelted him with over the years. Alex would get in the last laugh.

Or perhaps, she thought with a strong stab of bitterness, the party at Corbett's house had been such an unqualified success that he had decided to sleep over. With Diana. He had probably forgotten about coming here tonight, the rat.

"Do you know you're spilling wine on the rug?" Wally asked her in a stage whisper.

"Just testing its stain-resistant capabilities." Annoyed with herself, Paula took a napkin and bent down to blot the glistening drops from the rug.

"You know, you do look rather natural in that position."

Paula jerked her head up. Alex. This *would* be the time he'd pick to arrive, when she was on her knees like a suppliant servant. She tried to pull her annoyance to her like a protective cloak, but nonetheless, something inside of her hummed, and the smile that came to her lips was far less forced than it had been. Paula held her hand up. Alex took it, helping her to her feet.

"You're late," she murmured sweetly, in case anyone was eavesdropping.

The dark green strapless satin dress she wore seemed to be held up by magic. It took considerable control on his part not to stare or to skim his hands along her soft, bare shoulders. All he trusted himself to do was brush his lips against her cheek. "The pumpkin broke down, and we had to find six more white mice to pull it."

It took her a moment to pull her thoughts together. Her cheek felt hot where he had touched it. Damn, she had to stop this nonsense. "Have you been drinking?"

He inclined his head toward hers and whispered into her ear, warming her bones, melting them. "No, should I have been?"

She stepped back, a response on her tongue, and suddenly looked at him. Really looked at him.

She had seen him all of her life, yet tonight, his presence seemed to fill the entire room the way a crowd of people couldn't. Why? What was so different this time? Maybe, she thought, she was seeing him tonight for the first time. But that was absurd. He wore a navy blue suit that brought out the smokiness of his dark blue eyes. The almost stark white shirt beneath the jacket brought out the exotic hue of his olive complexion. He brought up her pulse.

"What you should have been was here. Two hours ago."

Despite her words, he saw relief in her eyes. She thought I wasn't coming, he realized. So, she wasn't so confident, after all. He liked the trace of vulnerability he detected. It made him feel that he wasn't dealing with superwoman. Just a very, very desirable woman. He had trouble getting past that thought. Perhaps, for tonight, he didn't have to. Just for tonight.

"Missed me, did you?" Alex laughed.

"Something like that."

To Paula's surprise, Alex slipped his hands around her waist and kissed her again. It was a soft, teasing kiss that almost made her stumble. She felt the kiss in every part of her body, and it made her want things that had no place at a public party. Paula backed up and stared at him. She saw a smile curving the corners of his mouth. Was he doing this on purpose? Did he even *know* what he was doing to her? She hoped not. But two could play this game of his. A smile rose to her lips to match his.

Now what's all that about? Alex wondered, sensing that something was up. He could always read her body language, even though her tongue often left him confused as hell.

"Now that's more like it." She recognized her father's voice booming above the rest. "That's the way an engaged couple should kiss—well, in front of people, anyway." Good-natured laughter met his remark.

Paula turned toward Alex. "What's gotten into you?" she whispered as she purposely smiled up into his eyes. The crowd began to close in around them.

He shook hands with several people he vaguely knew. "Just giving everyone their money's worth," he whispered between his teeth. He looked around the packed room. "Who *isn't* here?"

She knew what he meant. Everywhere they looked, there were people. "The janitor at the studio. He has the flu."

Standing together nearby were Wally and Paul. The satisfaction that swelled within Paula was quickly squashed.

"So, you came," Wally said, his voice ten degrees colder than usual.

"Why shouldn't I come?" Paul responded. There was anger as well as hurt in his voice. "He's my son."

"That's his problem."

Distress mounted. "Oh God, they really are at each other's throats." She exchanged looks with Alex.

There was no help from that quarter. "This was your idea."

"Thanks a lot," she retorted through clenched teeth. Paula quickly positioned herself between her father and Paul.

Aware that everyone was watching, she linked one hand through her father's and one through Paul's. "C'mon, you two," she coaxed, "time to start out fresh."

"He's the fresh one," Wally mumbled.

"Pop!" Her voice was stern, even though it was low. The stubborn look didn't leave her father's face. "I can't believe you're acting like this. This is supposed to be one of the happiest nights of my life."

Releasing her hold on both men, Paula moved back and stood beside Alex. He put his arm around her shoulders, and although they were only pretending, she was momentarily grateful for the support.

"I think it's time you made the announcement." She looked to the two men she had loved all her life. Neither moved. They looked like two feuding children, she thought. It was almost too much. She had never known Paul to act this way, either. "Both of you. Uncle Paul. Pop." She nodded at each. "Speak."

"She trains animals on the side," Wally told the person closest to him. Uneasy laughter echoed around them. Then he clapped his hands. "Everybody! Everybody, listen! This is the reason I'm giving all this food away." He beamed as he stepped back, gesturing at the couple behind him. "My daughter, Paula, has agreed to make Alex the happiest man in the world."

"Your father's got a great imagination," Alex whispered against her ear. To everyone else, it looked as if he was kissing it affectionately.

Paula shivered. If she broke out in goose bumps, she'd kill herself—and him—right here and now. What was happening to her? This was just Alex, Alex of the stone expression, Alex of the disapproving frown. Why did he suddenly look like the best thing since sliced bread?

"Hey, honey, they're playing your song," Wally prompted. "Dance."

The band that her father had somehow managed to squeeze into the crowded house was playing "I've Always Loved You."

What kind of a monster had she created? Paula thought in despair.

"I don't have a song," she informed her father between smiling lips.

"You have now. Dance," Paul urged.

She looked around her. There was no space. "Where, on the head of a pin?"

"Give 'em room, everyone. Give 'em room." Wally waved back groups of people.

Miraculously an area around them opened up.

Paula raised her eyes to Alex. He shrugged and took her hand in his. He pressed the small of her back with his other hand until her body was close against his. Almost indecently close.

Deliciously close.

"The man said dance," he told her.

As if in a trance, Paula began to sway slowly to the dreamy music. It was, she thought, as if she always belonged here, curved in against his body like this. It seemed right, natural.

But it wasn't. This wasn't her place, she told herself fiercely. It belonged to Diana or whatever her name was. Someone of Alex's choosing. Someone who could help further Alex's career, be the dutiful little corporate wife. That would never be her. Not in a million years. Not even if she wanted it to be.

Which she didn't. This was all a charade.

Her body was responding to his nearness. Cravings she would never have associated with Alex began to flower and grow.

She was losing her mind.

With determination, Paula looked up at Alex and smiled. He was doing this on purpose. He knew just how close he was to her, just what sensations that was creating. Well, he was going to get as good as he got, starting now.

As Paula moved even closer against him, and a few people around them whistled their appreciation, Alex had a very strange feeling that war had just been declared.

"May the best man win," he whispered in her ear.

"Thanks. I fully intend to," she whispered back.

They understood each other.

"A toast!" Paul announced, snaring a glass of champagne. "A toast to my son and the wonderful taste he's finally shown in women." He raised the slender glass high, and a sea of arms went up all around Paula and Alex, holding goblets of champagne aloft. Waiters rushed back and forth to supply the demand.

"I always liked your father," Paula murmured as she sipped from her glass.

"He does possess insight, at times." Alex slipped his hand around her waist as he drank to the toast. "This, of course," he added with a wry smile, "is not one of those times."

She knew he was goading her, and she rose to the occasion. But before she could manage a response, Paula found herself engulfed in well-wishers. It seemed that everyone had something to say about their finally pairing off. The comments ran along the lines of "It's about time." And "I always said you made a wonderful couple." She saw that Alex seemed to be bearing up to it all far better than she had hoped.

Face it, the man's got many good qualities that you've overlooked.

If she wasn't careful, she'd be pinning a medal on him and losing the edge she had in their dealings.

Paula glanced over toward her father. He was standing by himself. This wasn't going right, at all. Alex was having a field day, making her aware of feelings she didn't want brought to life, she was beginning to feel as if she was ensnared in her own trap, and her father was *not* getting together with his partner.

"Excuse me for a moment, won't you?" she said to the couple that she was talking to. Alex gave her a quizzical look, as she disengaged herself from him.

"I need to have a word with your future father-in-law," she explained.

He nodded, as if giving her permission. He knew it irritated her. She smiled up broadly into his face, and he got the clear impression that he was going to be in for it later. For some strange, illogical reason, he was looking forward to it.

He watched her as she made her way over to her father, the perfect hostess in motion. She seemed not to walk so much as glide through the crowded room. She also had the amazing ability to hear all the conversations aimed at her and could respond to each with just the right words.

She was, he admitted, rather amazing, more like a heady experience than a woman. Something in the realm of a giant, breathless roller-coaster ride like the Cyclone at Coney Island.

A woman with an ample bosom clothed in a vivid purple dress took hold of his arm. He was forced to focus his attention on her, but kept an eye on Paula, finding himself far more fascinated than he liked admitting. For to admit so would be putting everything else in his life in jeopardy.

Paula slipped her arm around her father's shoulder. "Why aren't you over there talking to Paul? You know you want to."

His expression was unusually somber. "What I know is that I wouldn't have invited him if you hadn't insisted."

"Pop."

It was the voice she used when she saw right through him. She did have an amazing ability to do that. Just like her mother had. At the thought of his ex-wife, his pain returned, but he tried to bury it. He shrugged haplessly. "Maybe you're right."

"Of course I'm right." She tucked her arms through his and nestled her head on his shoulder. "C'mon, Pop. Be a man. Make the first move. You'll make everyone happy, especially yourself. Okay," she amended raising her head as he gave her a penetrating look, "especially Paul."

Wally looked over to where Paul was standing. And then he saw Cecilia approach his partner and exchange a few words. Though they had been divorced for over ten years, he and Cecilia had remained friends of sorts because of Paula. And feelings had remained, as well. At least on his part.

Paula felt her father's body grow rigid. What was wrong? "Well?" she prompted, somehow knowing that the moment was gone.

Wally turned around, forcing Paula to drop her hands to her sides. "Well what?"

Paula looked at him, stunned. "Aren't you going to make up with Uncle Paul?"

"Not in this lifetime."

Her frustration flared. "You can be so stubborn. What about the special?" What *was* it? What could have transpired that would have shaken a friendship that had weathered so much and endured so long? She had been so certain that if she could just get them together, talking, that the feud would die. Now she didn't know what to do.

"I'll go through with the special. Just for you. I wouldn't want you to be unemployed because of him," he jerked a thumb in Paul's direction.

Paula saw Paul looking at them. He was alone again. Both of these men would be, until they resolved their differences, she thought sadly. Well, perhaps having to work on the show would eventually bring them back together.

She brushed Wally's cheek with her lips. "Well, thank you for that, anyway."

"Why don't you go back to your fiancé and practice bossing him around?" Wally suggested, gesturing toward Alex.

But it was her mother she singled out when she left her father's side, not Alex. Suddenly she needed answers, not to her father's problem, but her own. It was time to call a spade a spade. She had a problem. And its name was Alex.

As always, Cecilia was perfectly attired, perfectly coiffured. Tall and slim, she looked years younger than she was. In height, looks, breeding, deportment, she was the complete antithesis of her ex-husband. Paula was never more acutely aware of that than she was right at this moment. They had been people from two different worlds when they married. And they hadn't stayed married.

"Mother, why did you marry Pop?"

Cecilia turned toward Paula, obviously surprised by the question. "Isn't that a rather strange question to be asking me after twenty-six years?"

Paula shrugged. "Maybe I never wondered about it before."

"And you're wondering now?" Cecilia looked through the crowd in the direction of Alex.

"Yes."

"He made me laugh."

Paula stared at her mother. It didn't sound like a very intelligent reason to get married, especially not coming from her mother. "That's all?"

"No, he was warm and sweet and kind." Cecilia paused. "When he was there."

"So if he was warm and sweet and kind and made you laugh, why'd you get divorced?" She wanted something concrete. No, she wanted something encouraging. She also knew she wasn't going to get it.

"Because he wasn't there very often." Cecilia looked at Paula carefully. "I needed someone there for me. He wasn't. We had a totally different outlook on life. He always thought everything was supposed to be funny."

Paula felt herself getting defensive. "And you were too serious."

"Perhaps, but that didn't alter the fact that we were different. Too different. He was always out on the road. I wanted to stay home, to raise you in one place. He thought the road would be good for you. I didn't. There was a world of differences between us that laughter couldn't bridge. He's a very good man, your father, but he's not the man for me. Does that answer your question?"

"Yes." And it just reinforces my feelings, she added silently. The momentary sadness she felt was almost unbearable.

Cecilia placed a hand on Paula's shoulder. "You're asking about Alex and you, aren't you?"

"No," she lied, "not at all. Now if you'll excuse me, Mother...." Paula deliberately made her way toward Alex.

He wondered about the strange, sad expression on her face when she rejoined him. "Trouble?"

She didn't want to talk about her conversation with her mother. Instead, Paula looked over her shoulder. Wally and Paul were each working a separate part of the room. "He won't talk to your father. He almost did, but then he saw Uncle Paul talking to Mother and that stopped him."

"Is it too early to say I told you so?"

"Yes."

"Let me know when I can say it."

Paula glared at him. "You should live so long."

"The dynamic duo having their first engaged disagreement?" Erica asked, coming between them and taking hold of each of them by the arm.

"She knows," Paula explained to Alex.

He looked at Paula quizzically. "Is my secret identity showing?"

"I told her, Alex."

He nodded, finally understanding. "With that mouth, it was just a matter of time."

Paula smiled up at him, patting his shirtfront a little too hard. She saw him try not to wince. "See why I love him?" she asked her cousin.

Erica made a show of looking Alex over from head to foot. The smile she wore was not difficult to interpret. "Well, if you don't want him, I get first dibs," Erica announced, and then made her way over to her uncle.

Alex drew Paula over to the buffet table. Picking up a plate, he began to fill it. He put the plate into her hands. "Well, things certainly aren't going the way they're supposed to, are they?"

Paula took the plate without thinking. There was something in his voice that told her he wasn't talking about her plan to get their fathers together. "What do you mean?" she challenged.

Alex created another plate to match hers. "Fork?" he offered. "I think you know."

"Thanks." She took it, her eyes on his face. "If I knew, I wouldn't be asking, would I?"

He raised his eyes from his plate and looked directly, knowingly, into hers. "Not unless you were trying to be defensive."

Damn his smugness. "Defense is your line of work, not mine."

His eyes touched her face, and that strange, hazy feeling danced along her skin. "And fantasy is yours."

She looked down at the plate in her hands, wondering how it had materialized there. Yes, fantasy was her world. And it was pure fantasy to even imagine that she and Alex would stand a chance together. "Two different worlds," she said softly.

"I wonder."

"I don't."

Abruptly she put the plate, untouched, on the table. Still wearing the smile she had put on for the benefit of the party, she turned on her heel and walked away. "I've got guests to see to," she said over her shoulder.

He remained where he was, thinking.

Toward midnight, Alex found himself growing increasingly restless. He hadn't seen Paula for over half an hour and began looking for her.

This is a switch, he told himself. A week ago, he would have counted himself lucky for the breathing space. Now the air felt different, subdued, shallow, without her around. He wondered if he was going through some sort of early mid-life crisis. But the only thing that came under the heading of crisis in his life was Paula. She was the source of it all.

He was drawn to the source.

He found her standing alone in the gazebo, oddly still, staring up at the stars. The party was thinning out. He knew he should be going home, yet here he was, looking for her, missing her. The very realization made him wonder. About himself, about his life. About her.

For a moment, he just stood and watched her. Was he losing his mind? Last night Diana had made it very clear to him that she had selected him as the man of her choice. More importantly and more directly, Corbett had made it clear that he heartily approved of the match. The rest of his life was secured, if he merely went along with things. It was everything that he wanted.

No, not everything. Paula had shown him that. It wasn't what he wanted by a long shot. Now moments of peace were shattered with memories of her laughter, of her teasing smile.

Damn her, damn her wild, swirling hair that made his hands ache, damn those green eyes that stirred things in his soul. Damn that taut, athletic body that kept calling to him. She had unseated his well-ordered world with her harebrained scheme.

And he had let her.

She had shaken up his world from its very foundations. But could she have, if he were satisfied? He knew the answer to that. No. He had striven for so long to reach where he was today, and victory had turned out to be hollow. His life was boring. The people he dealt with daily were artificial. Paula had shattered all that when she whirled into his world with her plan. Compared to her, everything else seemed even more lifeless, more dull, more boring. She had him taking a second look at everything. And his dissatisfaction was growing.

But where would the other road lead? He didn't know, but he was beginning to realize that more and more he wanted to find out.

Standing in the gazebo, outlined in moonlight, she looked every bit the sorceress he had called her, he thought. And he wanted her. God help him, he wanted her in his arms, in his bed. He wanted to know what that teasing, laughing mouth would feel like skimming along his skin, what her long, tapered fingers would feel like, touching him, exploring his needs. She was taking control out of his hands and he needed that. More than that, he needed her.

He came up behind her, and still she didn't hear him. "You were missed."

Startled, Paula swung around. Something raw and confused showed in her eyes before she hid it away. "Oh," she tried vainly to keep her voice emotionless, "it's you." She turned around to look at the moon, pretending that his presence hadn't rattled her.

"Yes, it's me," he acknowledged.

Stepping into the gazebo he fitted his body against hers. Slowly he threaded his hands around her waist. She kept her face forward, but he could feel her reaction. A slight relaxation and then a sudden stiffening as she realized what she was doing. It pleased him, and worried him at the same time. What they had here was a situation. What were they going to do about it? What was *he* going to do about it? He hadn't a clue.

Go away, Alex. You're part of my problem. "I came out here to be alone."

"Obviously." The words were whispered against her hair. She ached to lean into him, and didn't.

"Do you have to hold me like that?"

"Yes."

She pressed her lips together, searching for strength. "I wish you wouldn't."

"No, you don't."

He was right, but that only made things worse. She turned in the circle of his arms and instantly realized that she had made a tactical error. Now she faced him, with moonlight and magic highlighting all his best features—and he had so many of those.

She searched her mind for something to put him off. "So now you're a mind reader."

It's not going to work, Paula. I know what you're doing. I know *you* too well. "Do you think that you can stop being a comedy writer for five minutes?"

"I don't know." She shrugged, her arms moved against his. Neither one of them might have been wearing any clothing for the way the bombs were exploding within her. "What do you have in mind?"

Lots of things . . . holding you, making love to you, finding out what really makes you tick and why I'm suddenly so attracted to you. Or have I always been? "A discussion, a serious discussion."

She tried to look away, and he wouldn't let her. He brought her eyes back to his with a touch of his hand on her cheek. "I'm not sure I'm up to that."

"Try," he coaxed.

He probably made one hell of a lawyer. "All right, what's on your mind?"

He wanted to kiss her, long and hard. Instead he answered, "You."

She tried in vain to hang onto her words. It was her only weapon. Otherwise he'd see what was happening, what he was causing to happen to her. It might amuse him. Above all else, she didn't want to amuse him, not like that. "If that's your idea of a serious discussion, I'd love to see what you think is a short word."

He tried again. He was up against an expert, but he wasn't going to let her win. "Paula, I'm usually good with words. Around you, I become some sort of tongue-tied adolescent. . . ."

His arms felt too good around her. Much too good. She had to make him let go of her without being obvious before she succumbed to the urge to throw her arms around his neck and lose herself in his kiss. "Instead of the wise, aged man that you really are."

"Damn it, Paula, you talk too much."

She opened her lips with a protest and wound up welcoming a kiss instead. And *welcome*, she realized with growing unease, was exactly the right word. Ever since he had kissed her when he came in, she had been waiting for this, eager for his touch, for his mouth on hers.

Damn it, she was falling for him, really falling for him. And it was too late and much too complicated for that to happen now. She loved happy endings, and there wasn't going to be one.

But for now all there was was his mouth, hot, consuming and hers. She rose up on her toes, savoring this precious moment.

One hand low on her back, he pressed her to him. Her hips cradled against his. The hot, hard evidence of his needs spurred her own on. Every pore was alive, thriving, thirsting. Her head swam even as she searched for some cornerstone of reason. She was an adult, sophisticated woman, not some trembling teenager. And this was Alex, someone she had known all her life.

Or had she?

Had she really taken the time to know him? He disapproved of things she did, and she loved goading him. That didn't cover a whole lot of ground. There was a great deal more to the man than she had realized, a depth that had gone undetected until this moment.

Why did she have to uncover it now? He was spoken for. He was going to align his life with the boss's daughter. He was lost to her, and this was all a ruse, destined to melt away very, very soon. If he seemed interested, at all, it was probably because he wanted to test different waters just this once. But he would leave, of that she was certain. He was career-oriented. That was all that mattered to him. She couldn't help him there. She could only love him. And she was sure now that that wouldn't be enough for him. She had started all this. She had tempted fate and told herself it might even be fun. But now it wasn't fun anymore. It was becoming too serious.

His kiss left her aching, wanting. He was draining her of her resilience and making her mind swim with desires that couldn't be fulfilled. Not now, not ever.

Alex drew away, his own breath ragged. He was stunned by the extent of his desire. He would have sought some way to make love to her right here if it was possible. He was thinking as recklessly as he had always accused her of doing. Shaken, he searched her face for a sign that she felt the same. "Now do you understand?"

Paula looked away. "No," she lied, hoping he didn't see how her heart hammered in her throat.

She understood. Only she wouldn't admit it, he thought. He knew her well enough for that. "Something's happening here," he said softly.

She hated when his voice dropped like that. It was seductive. She didn't want seductive. She wanted banter, wits clashing. She wanted her old sparring partner back, not this man who threatened her peace of mind, who threatened regions she had never known existed.

"Yes," she said finally, her voice tight, "we danced, we had a little wine—maybe a lot of wine." She licked her lips, unconsciously savoring the taste of him.

Though she moved back, he wouldn't release her. "It's more than that." His voice was still low, but his tone was insistent.

She looked up at him, daring him to go on, pleading with him not to. "Is it?"

"Yes, and you know it. Despite all your words, you know it. I want you, Paula, and you want me."

Trust him to hit the truth so quickly. Well, he wouldn't get it out of her. "I want you to let me go." Before I do something stupid, like dissolve all over you. It's not supposed to be like this, Alex. I had a crush on you years ago, and it's gone, done with. Don't bring it all back. Nothing can come of it. You know that.

"I want you in my bed, Paula."

She wanted to cry. "Alex, we're just pretending," she insisted vainly.

He thought he saw fear and wondered why. "No." He brushed a hair from her cheek and followed it with his lips. "We're pretending to pretend."

She closed her eyes, drinking in the sweetness, telling herself she was going to be sorry. "Suddenly you've gotten good with words."

His words were breathed against her skin. "Must be the company I keep."

She tried to move her head back but couldn't. In a minute. Just one more minute. "Alex, it won't work between us."

Her body felt warm, pliant against his. It was driving him to the brink of madness. "I thought you were the adventurous one."

"Adventurous, yes, crazy, no."

His lips slipped to her neck. "I beg to differ with that."

She held onto his arms because she suddenly felt that if she didn't, she'd sink to the ground on liquid limbs. "Flatterer," she murmured, trying to keep the conversation going. If he talked, he couldn't kiss.

He opted for kissing.

She was never more glad of anything in her life. And never more frightened. This overwhelming feeling was entirely new to her, and entirely terrifying. As exhilarating as it felt, she wasn't in control anymore. She could only follow it wherever it wanted to take her.

Over and over, his lips met hers, feeding the hunger she felt and yet leaving her insatiable. She thought she'd never get enough of him. She wove her fingers through his hair, wanting to touch him, wanting to have all of him. Wanting desperately to anchor herself before she was swept away beyond reason.

Who are you kidding? You're there already. Alex is right. You want him. You want to go to bed with him. You want to make love with him until you both explode or die.

"Alex? Have you finished saying good night?" Paul stood only a few feet away, hesitating. "Or do you want me to call myself a cab?'' He looked from one to the other and Paula thought that she had never seen him looking more pleased.

Alex cleared his throat, squared his shoulders and seemed to transform back into the conservative man she knew. Paula watched, fascinated. How could he pull back like that? She was still on fire.

"No, I'll take you home, Dad." He looked at Paula meaningfully. "We'll continue this discussion later."

"In my day," Paul chuckled, "we had another name for it. It was called necking." He kissed Paula's cheek fondly. "I can't tell you how happy I am about this."

"Yes," she answered, her voice hollow, "me, too."

She watched the two men cross the lawn and walk back into the house. She felt too numb to move.

Chapter Twelve

Paula sat at the kitchen counter, rearranging a mound of scrambled eggs with her fork. She ate without tasting, which was just as well. Her mind was elsewhere.

Wally noted the faraway look in her eyes and assumed that she was preoccupied with thoughts of Alex. He was right, but for the wrong reason.

Paula was worried about what she had started, worried that if things got any more out of hand she would be hopelessly in love with Alex. The last time she took an honest look, she was more than halfway there already. Paula shivered.

Wally pushed an inky-black cup of coffee toward her. "Cold?"

"Goose bumps," she mumbled. Gratefully she wrapped her hands around the coffee cup.

"Love does that," Wally laughed softly. He lifted his considerable bulk onto the stool next to hers.

Yes, love did that. And love also hurt. That was what she was in for. Hurt. Once the charade was put to rest, Alex would go on with his life and probably to a neat and tidy marriage to this

Diana-boss's-daughter person. And what would she go on to? A lonely feeling in the pit of her stomach.

She should put a stop to this charade. She could end it all with just a few sentences. But so many people were involved. If it were just Alex and her, maybe she could just call a halt to it all. But with all that they had done, it would be extremely difficult. She wondered if she had somehow done this intentionally. Had she purposefully put herself in a situation that she couldn't easily extricate herself from with a few well-chosen words? Perhaps she wanted this forced entanglement with Alex more than she realized. No, that was ridiculous. This was just one of those innocent situations that had somehow gotten out of hand.

And then some.

If she went on with the charade, she'd have to go on seeing Alex, and that made things difficult for her. But ending the charade was difficult, too. Ending it now, before she accomplished what she originally had set out to do, would hurt several people. It would seem as if it were all just a big practical joke.

But going on with it would hurt her.

She saw no way out for her. Except one.

Paula looked toward her father, hoping that perhaps she could prevail upon him to resolve his difference with Paul. Why this plea should work when the others hadn't didn't trouble her. She was too tangled up in her own state of affairs to try to be logical now.

"Pop?"

Wally stopped plopping cubes of sugar into his cup. "I know that tone. There's a favor attached to it, isn't there?"

She grinned. "Yup." With one quick movement, she pushed the sugar bowl out of his reach.

Wally frowned, then stirred his coffee. It wasn't easy. "What kind of a favor?"

Paula watched his spoon do battle with five cubes in various stages of meltdown. It was no wonder the man was *built* like a sugar cube. "The prove-you-love-me kind."

Wally ran his hand through his thinning rust-colored hair. "Who do I have to kill?"

"It's not that easy."

Wally cocked his head to the side and studied her. His tone grew serious. "It's about Paul, isn't it?"

"Yes."

"You want me to talk to him and patch things up."

"When you're hot, you're hot." She looked at him hopefully.

He covered her hand with his own. "Baby, it's not that easy."

"That's what I said." Paula turned the stool to face him squarely. "Pop, you know you can't stand this. And you know that you'd much rather have things the way they were."

"Things," he said so softly that it worried her, "will never be the way they were."

Paula refused to give up. In the balance hung her sanity. And maybe something more. Paula had a great survival instinct. And it was at odds with her situation. "And they never will be, if one of you doesn't make the first step. Let it be you. You're a big man, Pop."

He patted his stomach. "Every soft little pound is lovable."

She smiled and shook her head. "You know what I mean, Pop."

"Yes," Wally dropped his hand heavily, "I know what you mean."

"Will you? Will you do it for me?" she asked eagerly. "Will you talk to Paul? Alex says he's absolutely miserable."

"He is?" For a moment, the cherubic face lit up, and then the smile faded. "He has reason to be. If he had only been honest with me to begin with, things could have been different—"

"Honest about what?" she cried in utter frustration. "What is this all about?"

Stubbornly Wally shook his head. Much as part of him wanted to share this burden that took little pieces of him away, he couldn't. There were other people involved. "I can't talk about it yet." He looked off into space. "I just can't."

"Okay," she tried another tack. "You can't talk about it to me. But to Uncle Paul? Please?"

He chewed his lower lip, considering. He knew she wanted peace, especially now that they were all going to be one family. Slowly he nodded. "Okay, I'll give it a shot."

"Oh, Pop, you've made me so happy." She slid off the stool. If this worked, then she could tell Alex that they didn't have to pretend anymore. They would be free of each other.

And she would be alone.

Better now than later, after she got in too deep, she told herself stubbornly. The main thing was that her father and Paul would be together and that she wouldn't be hurt any more than she already was.

Paula stood up. "I'll call Uncle Paul and tell him to come over."

Wally caught her by the wrist before she had a chance to take a single step toward the phone. "Nope."

He couldn't change his mind again. He just *couldn't*. "I'll call Uncle Paul and tell him that you'll be over there?" she suggested hopefully.

"Nope."

Paula put her hand on her hip, waiting. "You propose to do this by smoke signals?"

Wally slowly, deliberately, raised himself from the stool, then took a deep breath. "I propose to do this away from you and Alex."

She didn't trust the discussion to go well without her being there. "But—"

Wally cocked an eyebrow. "You want me to go through with this?"

"Yes."

Satisfied, he nodded. At least she was letting him win one round. "Then I do it my way. Tell Paul I'll meet him at Erica's Restaurant for lunch."

She was already at the phone. "Anything you say, Pop."

He knew better. "As long as I agree with you."

Paula grinned. "Yes." And then Paul came on the line and she was busy making arrangements.

After that, she called her cousin and told her what was up, then crossed her fingers and prayed.

An eternity later, Paula saw her father return. There was fire in his eyes, and if possible, smoke coming out of his ears. Immediately there was a sinking sensation in her stomach. This didn't look good.

"How did it go?" She leaped off the sofa and met him before he had a chance to take five steps.

Wally just kept walking. He waved his hand at her question. "Don't ask."

"I *am* asking."

Wally crossed to the stairs. "Lousy. Things are worse than ever."

Paula shut her eyes. "Oh, God."

"Not even *He* could put up with Paul." He paused on the second step, turned and looked down at Paula. "Look, baby, I don't know about this special—"

Panic mounted. She couldn't let this happen. Whatever she had to endure to set it right, she couldn't let her father walk away from a twenty-seven-year friendship with a career that matched. "Oh Pop, don't say that. This special is the crowning point of both your careers. You don't want to let this go."

And maybe, just maybe, if she was there with them for the next three weeks while they taped the special, she could find a way to learn what the sore point was and bring them together. It was the only hope she had left.

"Try me."

Alarmed, she put her hand on his arm. "Pop, please."

"Don't look at me with those eyes."

"I can't help it. They're the only ones I have." She sobered. "Do it for me."

"I just did something for you."

"Consider it an early Christmas present. I'll never ask you for anything else again."

He relented. "You will, and you know it."

"Yes, but it sounds good." Her voice grew serious again. "Don't cancel the special."

"No," he considered the point. "I guess I couldn't do that to you. Okay, but I'm doing this just for you. Understood?"

She nodded her head solemnly. "Understood."

"If you weren't marrying Alex, I would have probably killed that future father-in-law of yours."

"We all appreciate that, Pop."

"See that you do."

He walked up the stairs, leaving Paula with mixed feelings. The war was still raging, and the engagement was still on. Things could be worse. But at the moment, she would have been hard-pressed to state how.

The next few days, mercifully, were filled with details, meetings and more meetings. It freed her from thinking about what was going on in her life. Those disconcerting thoughts were left to the wee hours of the morning, when she lay awake in bed, staring at the ceiling and seeing Alex's face.

This was absurd, she told herself, just her childhood infatuation playing itself out, that's all. And Alex was just a red-blooded male, taking advantage of the situation, nothing more, although she would have never thought it of him. All too soon, he'd return to his senses. His senses would tell him that she was not for him, that she could never keep him happy, could never be the type of wife that he felt was necessary for a solid estate lawyer.

When Paula finally did fall asleep, she tossed fitfully until dawn.

The pace at the studio was nothing short of chaotic. She thrived on it now more than ever. It was in her blood. She had often maintained that she thought better under pressure. The hectic pace forced her to focus her concentration on the upcoming special. It was to be taped in a little over three weeks and as of yet, basically remained unwritten except for a few sketches hastily outlined.

This was to be her shining moment. Not only was she working with her father and Paul again, but this time, she was there in the capacity of head writer. She had the additional satisfaction of having Ted and Marty working with her. Her agent had pulled it off.

The reunion was heartfelt, if brief. There wasn't much time to spare on sentiment—or extraneous thoughts, she kept reminding herself as vivid moments kept coming back to her at inopportune times.

"When do I get a chance to be head writer?" Ted pretended to pout petulantly for their benefit on their first day together. "You and Marty have had your turns."

Paula looked up from the notes she had been making. She knew how Ted felt about the responsibility that went with the role. He'd rather walk on hot coals. "When you grow up, Ted dear."

Marty walked in on the conversation. "Speaking of being all grown-up," he announced, "here's your beloved, boss lady."

"My what?" she cried, looking in his direction. Her lapboard clattered to the floor.

In the doorway stood Alex.

Marty bent down to pick it up while Paula stared at Alex. "Look who I found wandering the halls." Marty pushed the lapboard back into her hands.

Paula rose, crossing to the door. "What are you doing here?"

Alex looked around. So this was the kind of place she worked in. It seemed too crammed for someone so full of life. "I've come to take you to lunch," he said.

She was touched, and told herself that she was being juvenile. Maybe he thought this was part of the charade. Of course he did. What other reason could there be? "You don't have to do this," she said.

He looked into her eyes. "Yes, I do." He knew what she thought of him. She had told him enough times. "All basically stable, dependable men take their fiancées out to lunch."

Damn her stomach, anyway. Why did his eyes make her feel like there was a tidal wave coming on? They never had before. But then, he had never kissed her before. She turned away. "I can't get away."

"They won't let you eat?" he asked.

Ted and Marty held their hands up in protest. "Go, leave, we're dying to be left in peace," Marty told her.

"Yeah. Take a breather," Ted added.

Some support group they were, she thought. Why weren't they on her side and grumbling about her running off, leaving them to work? "We have to finish the first routine by two o'clock."

He glanced at his watch. "Okay, I'll order out." Alex crossed to the phone on the wall and began to dial. "Chinese all right with everyone?"

"Hey, I like your young man," Marty said to Paula.

She was about to say he wasn't her young man, but then realized that she couldn't. Not yet.

She moved to Alex, trying not to breathe in his cologne. It made her think of sexy things, and that wouldn't help the situation any. Besides, she was supposed to be thinking funny, not sexy. "What are you up to?"

He stopped before pressing the last button on the phone. The look he gave her was totally innocent. "I'm supposed to spend time with my fiancée and look love-struck. Wasn't that part of it?"

He was up to something. But what? Was he out to prove a point? To show her that meddling could backfire on her? She already knew that. "Everyone's convinced. You don't have to go this far."

His smile wound its way through her senses. It made her want something far more substantial than Chinese food. "Let's just say that I don't believe in half measures."

His kiss had assured her of that. She shrugged, giving in for now, knowing she liked his presence more than she should. "Make yourself comfortable."

Somehow she had a feeling that he already had.

He had to admit that he was impressed. She really was a whirlwind on two legs. And despite his feelings that her style was haphazard, he came to see that in her own unorthodox way, she was as organized as he was. At least, that was the end result, although their methods of getting there were poles apart.

He had found himself in the role of squire for a week now, dropping by at lunchtime to take her out, or more often than not, offering her some take-out food that he had had the presence of mind to pick up on his way over. There could have been reasons not to come if he had wanted to take advantage of them, but he didn't.

He had a need to see her.

Always the type to explore new developments in his life cautiously, he chose to take advantage of all opportunities to see her. Their so-called engagement had given him a ready excuse, but even if it hadn't been there he would have come. He was looking for a way out, if possible. A way out of the corner he felt he had painted himself into.

But watching her didn't give him a way out. It made him want to remain in the corner. As long as she was there with him.

What a strange development, he marveled, after all these years.

He watched her pace now, as she was thinking up an ending to the final sketch. There was no question but that she was in charge. He noted the grudging respect the other two men in the room gave her, even though of the three, she was the one who had been in the business the shortest amount of time. She was a professional, through and through.

He liked that. They had more in common than he had thought, and it pleased him.

As she moved past Alex, Paula, still talking to Marty, put out her hand. Alex put a half-wrapped tuna-fish sandwich into it. She took a bite and flashed Alex a smile that he doubted she even knew she spared. The woman was amazing. He had to give her that. Other things, he didn't want to give her, but they were coming along of their own volition, and he didn't seem to have much say about it. It was a new experience for him.

"And then," Paula concluded, "hopefully, the audience will give them a big laugh and the show'll be over. So," she leaned her posterior against the desk, looking at Ted and Marty, "what d'you think?"

"Sounds good to me," Ted agreed.

"Yeah, but instead of Wally walking out the door, why don't we try this?" And then Marty launched into his thoughts.

Paula crossed her arms before her chest and listened, then grinned. "I like it. It's better. We'll do it." She pushed herself back on the desk until she was sitting on it. "I hereby declare it lunchtime." She took a healthy bite of her sandwich this time, instead of a nibble.

Alex had sat, contemplating a thigh that had been brushed against his arm without Paula's conscious knowledge. He was now treated to a more extensive view as she dangled her legs over the edge. The pull he felt in his loins was getting more pronounced as thoughts of her intensified. He was grateful that he was seated in her chair and had the cover of the desk to maintain his dignity.

The door closed behind him as Ted and Marty filed out to get a bite to eat before they worked on the final draft. They were alone.

"How do you do it?" Alex asked.

"Do what?"

"Think in all this commotion? You shout ideas back and forth, studio people keep running in with demands or pages that need reworking—how do you do it?"

"I just do." She laughed. "I love it. The noisier it is, the better I think."

He could believe that. Alex rested a hand on her knee. "And when it's quiet? What do you think about then?"

She lowered her lids, afraid that he might see things in her eyes. "I try not to think then."

He longed to run his hands along her body, longed to know every curve, every secret. He contented himself with lightly resting his hand where it was. "Why?"

"Because." She hopped off the desk, this time aware of how close they were and how much she wanted them to be closer still. "Because then I start to feel things and my timing goes."

"Is timing so important to you?"

"In my line of work, timing is everything." Why was she so kittish around him? Alex, this is just Alex. But that was the trouble.

Alex rose and came up behind her. "You know, I have to admit, I'm really impressed."

She turned around, surprised, pleased and a little upset that it meant this much to her. "You are? I thought you hated show business."

"It's not the business I hate. It's the unpredictability about it, the nomadic type of life it represents. Nothing clear-cut, nothing in your control."

"And you like being in control."

"Don't say it with that smug little smile of yours." The one I'd like to nibble on. "You do, too," he pointed out.

Paula tossed her hair over her shoulder. "Yes, I suppose I do at that. I guess we just have different ways of getting there." His eyes were drawing her to him as surely as if he were a magnet and she, a small iron filing. She didn't like feeling as if she had no choice. But she didn't.

"Different, but the same."

"We're not the same," Paula said stubbornly. That was just the problem. They were different, very, very different. Too different. She remembered her conversation with her mother the night of the engagement party. "A world of differences that laughter couldn't bridge." That's what they had between them here.

"No, we're not," he agreed easily. He loved the way she raised her chin when she was arguing. "I'd hate to think I was having these kinds of thoughts about a guy."

She was about to render a dry retort, but her curiosity got the better of her. "What kind of thoughts?"

He took her into his arms. "Guess."

"What do I get if I do?"

"I'd say a prize, but I'd be leaving myself wide open to that sharp tongue of yours."

"It's not so sharp," she murmured as his lips came down on hers.

It wasn't. Her tongue was sweet and stirred up agonizing desires within him. She tightened her hold on his arms, lifting herself on her toes, as the full thrust of excitement swept through her. His hands brushed against the sensitive swell of her breasts, and though there were clothes in the way, his touch seared through, branding her.

It was only going to be a matter of time, and she knew it. This couldn't go on brewing and brewing without something spilling forth.

The telephone jangled insistently for several rings before she even heard it. "You're very good," she said breathlessly. "I even hear bells."

"That's the telephone." He nodded behind her, toward her desk.

"Realist," she murmured teasingly. She wasn't fooling him. She was shaken, and he knew that he was responsible.

Taking a deep breath, she put her hand on the receiver.

"I have to be going," he told her.

She merely nodded, still trying to get her breathing under control. By the time she picked up the phone, there was no one there.

Chapter Thirteen

Feeling the need to talk and unwind, Paula paid a quick visit to Erica's place of business during her lunch break the next day.

Erica's restaurant was tastefully done in a tropical motif. The outside had been designed to look like a peaceful hut perched on a Hawaiian Beach. Inside, Erica had worked hard to emulate the best in island decor.

Paula hurried in, then stopped. She let her eyes become accustomed to the dim atmospheric lighting before charging forward. She spied Hugo taking an order from three executives at a back table. Then she found Erica. The tall, willowy woman dressed in vivid colors and wearing an orchid in her hair was seating a couple. Not standing on ceremony, Paula entered the main dining area, bypassing the "Please Wait to Be Seated" sign and tapped Erica on the shoulder.

Erica turned around, a cheery smile on her lips. When she looked at Paula, the smile froze, and a look that Paula could only describe as panicky came into her eyes.

Instinctively Paula looked over her shoulder. There was no one there. She turned to look at her cousin. "Erica, you look like you've seen a ghost. What's the matter?"

Instead of answering, Erica quickly took hold of Paula's arm and led her over to an empty table. She looked at her cousin uneasily. "Is this all right?"

"*This* is fine. It's you who don't seem to be all right. Erica, what's wrong?"

"Nothing, nothing really. But you know how it is, the first of the month and all." She fidgeted with her lei, looking one way and then the other, as if searching for a way to make a fast escape.

Paula sat down, still looking at her cousin curiously. This was supposed to be the stable one in the family. So much for family myths.

"No, I don't know how it is. I know that there are usually a lot of days that follow the first of the month with increasing numbers. Is there something particularly scary about that?" Erica was acting positively weird, Paula thought.

"No, but the first of the month I have inventories to make, supplies to order, parties to juggle, things like that." The statement was delivered breathlessly. Totally unlike Erica. Erica always took everything at a much calmer pace than she did.

Everyone was behaving against type these days, Paula decided. Look at her. Look at Alex. She stopped. She didn't *want* to look at Alex. That was just the trouble. "I take it that means you can't talk."

"No, not now."

Paula could have sworn there was relief in Erica's voice and in her eyes. Why? Was she that anxious to get to her inventory?

Erica began to move away, then looked at Paula guiltily. "Um, was it anything important?"

Paula shook her head. "No, just life and death, love, my pending insanity. Nothing important."

Erica nodded. "Oh, well then, if you'll excuse me." She turned and all but ran off.

Paula sat staring after her. Now what had all that been about? Hugo sauntered by her line of vision, and Paula signaled for him to stop at her table.

The tall, thin man looked down his long, prominent nose at her then deigned to offer up a smile or what passed for one in his book. "Hello, Paula. Something to drink this afternoon?" Having a mind that committed every detail to memory, Hugo eschewed the standard pad and pencil of his trade.

Paula put down the wine list she'd been toying with. "Amid other things."

Hugo struck a pose as he waited, one hand on his near-to-nonexistent hip. Hugo was an artist who hadn't quite found his art form yet. He specialized in just being Hugo, which was a full-time occupation. "Food?"

She shook her head and lowered her voice. "Information."

"Gossip?" he asked hopefully.

"Of a sort." She leaned back in her chair and looked in the direction that Erica had disappeared. "Has everyone gone crazy?"

He seemed to give her question a moment's thought. "As far as I know, yes."

She had forgotten that the man was a lay philosopher. She made her next question more specific. "Why is Erica behaving so oddly?"

He looked chagrined, as if the detail had escaped him. Hugo turned and looked off in Erica's direction, then turned to face Paula again. "I'm ashamed to say I have no idea."

Paula thought of her cousin's flimsy excuse. "Does she act like this on the first of every month?"

Hugo looked at her blankly.

"Inventory," Paula prodded. "Erica said that she was harried because she had to complete the inventory, among other things."

"Simon and I do the inventory," Hugo informed her with a touch of pride and haughtiness. "And an outstanding job we do, I might add. Of course Simon's figures could be a little clearer. The man does have the most atrocious handwriting, but that's neither here nor there." He shrugged carelessly.

Paula looked into her water glass. The light behind her was caught up in it and shimmered hypnotically. "I see." Odd. Very odd. "Bring me a glass of wine, please, Hugo." She glanced up and saw that he was about to ask a question. "White."

"Very good." He took her wine list with him when he left.

Paula had one drink, a light salad and marched herself back to work. It was, she told herself, what she was being paid for. She wasn't being paid to wonder what had gotten into her cousin, or her father, or herself, or Alex.

Besides, she thought as she maneuvered her annoyingly sluggish car through slow-moving traffic, work was good for the soul and the mind.

Work might be good for some people, but it did her absolutely no good.

Alex stayed in her thoughts for the rest of the day. With the script completed and only rewrites to worry about, the pace had slowed down a little. That left her time to think. And feel. And she did plenty of both. There was no solution in sight. She couldn't let herself feel anything for Alex, no matter what every part of her body said to the contrary. Alex needed a sedate, cool woman who'd complement his life-style, who could be the hostess for his parties, who wouldn't yawn two hours into a boring conversation. He was set on "play" while she was going to play out the rest of her life on "fast forward." Incompatible. There was no getting away from that. The best thing she could do for the two of them was just walk away from all this.

And yet she couldn't put it to rest.

With a measure of relief, she saw the end of the day arrive. But just as she and the others were about to leave, Harold Groggins, the assistant director threw open the door to their small office.

"Cassidy wants a rewrite on the second sketch," he announced in a deep voice that did not fit the rest of him. "He says the middle doesn't work."

Paula, weary, aggravated, and battling a very annoying case of nerves, was tempted to say that Cassidy didn't work. But calling the director names wasn't going to get her anywhere.

Besides, it was only her frustration talking. Philip Cassidy was a prize, a man whose comedic timing was excellent, and she darn well knew it.

She exchanged glances with Ted and Marty. Both men looked dejected at the announcement.

"My kid's got a play tonight. Can't this wait until morning? Sheila'll kill me if I miss another school function," Marty complained to the lanky man in the doorway.

Ted took out tickets from his coat pocket and kissed them dramatically. "Goodbye theater, goodbye Stephanie, hello celibacy." He sighed loudly.

Paula took the script pages out of Harold's hand and glanced at them. "Okay, you two, there's nothing here that I can't handle. Go." She waved them out the door with the script.

"Thanks, Paulie." Marty gave her a quick peck on the cheek. "I'll remember you in my will," he promised as he hurried out the door.

"Thanks. I'll use the nickel and buy a condo," she murmured, flipping through the pages again.

"How about your intended?" Ted asked, raising and lowering his eyebrows in an exaggerated motion. "Don't you have something hot planned for tonight?"

"The only hot thing I have planned is a shower," she assured them.

"Alone?" Ted peered at her face intently.

She pushed him out the door. "Yes, alone. You get cleaner that way."

"That's our Paula." He patted her head affectionately. It wasn't difficult. He towered over her by a good foot. "You're a brick."

"God, I hope not. I've been trying to watch my weight." And then she grinned. "Go ahead. If I need help, I'll call early in the morning." She turned to look at Harold. "That satisfy you, Mr. Assistant Director, sir?"

The lanky man spread his hands wide. "Hey, don't get on my case. I just follow orders." He backed out.

Paula sat down at her desk. She switched on her computer again. The low hum was the only noise in the room. It was almost eerie. She reached over to Ted's desk and turned up the radio. She couldn't work in a quiet atmosphere.

It took her two more hours before she deciphered the director's notes in the margins and came up with something fresh. By that time it was quarter to seven and she was exhausted. The shower she had promised herself was sounding better and better.

"If I don't fall asleep and drown," she said with a sigh as she locked the office behind her.

Her car was one of the last in the parking lot. She got in and started the engine, only to hear it complain, whine and then sputter.

"Turn over, damn it, this is no time to play games."

The game was over. The car gave her the silent treatment. Frustrated, she hit the dashboard. "Great, now what?"

She was thirty miles from home. The cab ride would be a king's ransom, and she was in no mood to ransom a king. She thought of Alex. He lived close by. It would take her a bit of time, but she could walk there, and he'd take her home.

The thought brought her immediately to life. Suddenly she wasn't tired anymore. "It's just the logical thing to do," she told herself as she got out again. She shook her head, amused. "Since when were you such a big fan of logic?"

"Since I fell for a lawyer, that's when," she answered herself. There was no use denying it.

Paula began to walk off the lot.

She felt a smile forming, not just on her lips but all over. A sense of relief was spreading over her. She felt good for the first time today. She told herself that it was just because she had come up with a simple solution to her car problem, but she knew she was lying. It didn't seem to matter right now.

She had fallen for Alex. Maybe it had always been there, but she had masked it. That's why she had always been so picky about the men she went out with. She always kept it light, fun. Nothing serious. They never quite managed to measure up to some unknown standard of hers. Now she wasn't measuring anymore. She was just reacting.

As she crossed the street two blocks away from Alex's apartment, her feet aching in her high heels, a sudden cloudburst engulfed the area. Within a matter of three minutes, she was soaked.

Terrific, I'm going to walk in on him looking like a drowned chicken. Why couldn't he have lived three blocks closer? It seemed to her that nothing concerning Alex was simple, not even his address.

Alex heard the doorbell and cleared his throat. She was early. He was still rather stunned how everything had evolved. Corbett had walked into his office, saying that he was giving Diana tickets to see a limited engagement of *Brigadoon* currently playing at the Dorothy Chandler Pavilion and he had thought that having Alex escort her to the program was a good idea. Springing the invitation on him so suddenly, there had been no room for refusal. With nothing planned for the evening, Alex had agreed, vowing that he was going to make the state of their relationship very clear to Diana. There *wasn't* one.

Diana had called immediately after that, to confirm the situation. Since he lived closer to the Pavilion than she did, Diana had volunteered to pick him up. Though he didn't like the arrangements, Alex couldn't come up with a viable excuse. He agreed and gave her his address. Not, he knew, that that was necessary. He was certain Diana had already gotten it from her father.

Well, no time like the present to get this squared away, Alex told himself as he crossed to the door. He opened it and then stopped. Instead of a richly dressed socialite, he was looking at a redhead who was wet to the bone. "You're not Diana."

It was only through extreme control that Paula kept her face from registering the sudden salvo of pain his words had created. He was waiting for Diana, was he? Your timing is terrific, Paula.

"No, and I'm not Glinda, the Good Witch of the North, either. Can I come in, anyway?" she asked sharply.

Taken aback by her appearance, he stepped away from the doorway. "Sure." He looked her over. "Is it raining outside?"

"No, I was taking a shower with my clothes on when I suddenly decided to pop over. Yes, it's raining outside." She pushed the wet hair out of her face and tossed her head. "My car died, and I was going to ask you to drive me home. But if that's too much trouble—"

She turned, ready to leave. He was going to have *her* here. After the way he held her and danced with her and *kissed* her, he was going to spend the night with that—*that*—*boss's daughter*. Paula felt like throwing something. Instead she yanked at the doorknob.

Alex put his hand over hers and kept her from opening the door. She glared at him, feeling like a fool. A wet fool.

"I didn't say it was too much trouble. You never let me finish a single thought, a single statement. Let me talk for once. Besides," he let a smile slip over his face as his gaze skimmed her body, "it's raining out there." Her dress clung to her body like plastic wrap and left little to the imagination, although his seemed to take flight. He felt familiar stirrings.

She pressed her lips together. The degree of the hurt she felt stunned her. "You're very astute."

"Graduated at the top of my class. Listen, I have a robe in the master bath." He took her arm, intent on escorting her toward it.

Paula refused to move. "Good for you. Everyone should have a bathrobe."

Why was she always so difficult? And why did he have this overwhelming desire to peel that wet dress from her himself? "Why don't you stop being the comedy writer and put it on?"

Paula lifted her chin. "Why?"

"Because you're dripping on my rug."

She glanced down contemptuously. "It's only a few drops."

"More like a puddle." He pointed her toward the bedroom. "I'll take your clothes down to the laundry room and dry them. There's no use in you streaking the upholstery in my Mercedes."

"We can take your BMW. I'm sure that's already streaked from the other night at the Dorothy Chandler Pavilion." *When you first kissed me,* she added silently.

"It's in the shop, and the Mercedes has custom sheepskin seat covers."

"It figures." She walked into the bathroom.

Quickly she stripped off her wet clothes. Within a couple of minutes she was back out, wearing a brazen smile to hide the sudden nervousness that was taking hold of her.

Alex turned with the glass of brandy he had poured for her, and then began to laugh.

"What's so funny?" Paula asked defensively.

He crossed over to her and handed her the glass. "Here, it'll warm you up."

She looked at the glass warily. *I don't want to be warmed up. Not any more than I already am.*

What was she doing here? Simple, playing a game of Russian roulette.

Alex stood back and appraised her. "You look like a lost waif. I never thought of you as a waif."

"Don't." She cupped the glass in two hands and drained it. The liquid was hot and burned a hole in her stomach, but she felt better. Stronger. Her nerves stopped dancing on end, and she felt alert, ready to take on anything. Or was that just an illusion?

Alex looked at the empty glass in her hands. He hadn't thought of her as a drinker. "More?"

She held it toward him. "Why not?"

She knew why not very shortly. The alcohol, meant merely to take the chill out of her bones, put fire into them instead. Fire and longing. She wanted to say things to him, but didn't know what, wanted to be with him and knew that she shouldn't.

It was all there in her eyes for him to see.

He had never seen her looking so vulnerable before. The feelings of desire that had been smoldering so close to the surface moved that much closer.

"Hadn't you better take those things down to be dried?" she asked, nodding at the bundle she had brought out of the bathroom.

"In a minute." Slowly, deliberately, he took the glass out of her hand.

"I don't think you should do this." Why, oh, why couldn't she stop this trembling?

He grazed her cheek with his knuckles. Soft, so soft.

This is Paula here with me, isn't it?

And yet it was a Paula he had never known. "Why?" he asked.

It was hard to form words. She had never had that problem before. What was it about him now that made her tongue-tied. "Do you have to have a reason for everything?"

"Yes."

She didn't know who kissed whom. It wasn't important. What was important was that his lips were on hers and the whole world was swimming beyond her reach in an amazingly short time. She dug her fingers into his shirt as he gathered her closer to him, his mouth taking everything she had to offer.

"Bells again," she murmured against his mouth, her breath gone.

"Omigod, Diana."

Paula went cold inside. "Nice to be the opening act." Angrily she jumped to her feet and snatched up the bundle of clothing.

Already striding toward the door, he looked over his shoulder at Paula. How in heaven's name had things gotten so complicated? He pointed an authoritative finger at her. "Stay where you are."

"Don't you order me around, Alex Hamilton!" she snapped, glad of her anger. If she was angry, she wasn't going to cry. Oh God, she couldn't cry. Too late, she remembered that tears came to her when she was angry, as well.

"Shut up and stay put." He threw open the door.

Diana was a vision in pink. Her wide, inviting smile turned brittle as she looked from Paula's state of disarray to Alex's mussed appearance.

"Am I interrupting something?"

"Just dress rehearsal," Paula retorted, clothes in hand, on her way to the bathroom.

"More like undress rehearsal." Diana's mouth was cold, her eyes accusing.

Paula was all set to bounce into that one, all her frustration and hurt rising up, but Alex restrained her with a glance. He took Diana by the arm and led her out into the hallway, closing the door behind them.

"That's right, beg for her forgiveness," Paula called after him, blinking so that the hot tears wouldn't fall down her cheeks. "Damn it, what's wrong with you?" she cried to herself. "This isn't your first time. You're not some trembling virgin who's been betrayed by her lover. He's not your lover, for pity sake. You knew what it was all about." But knowing didn't help.

She hurried to the bathroom, wanting to be dressed and out before he had a chance to return. She'd take the stairs.

"I should have called a cab," she told herself. "I should have never come up with this stupid idea. I should have—"

"Paula?"

She jerked at the sound of his voice. Her clothes all fell on the floor in a wet heap. "Leave me alone, I'm getting dressed."

Curbing his impatience, he knocked on the door again. "Paula, open the door. I have to talk to you."

"No. Go back and talk to Diana."

"Diana's gone."

"If you grovel, you can get her back."

She was pushing him over the edge. "Damn it, woman, why can't you ever listen to reason?"

"Because I don't like reason, that's why!"

It was the last straw.

Suddenly she heard him hit the door with his shoulder and it flew open. Paula jumped back.

Alex stopped short. She was standing totally nude except for the silk panties she held in her hand.

Paula grabbed for a towel and held it up in front of her. "You can put your eyes back in your head, now, Superman."

Defenseless, she grabbed for the only weapon at her disposal. Her tongue. "Alex, I know that this is your bathroom, but when someone else is in it you should knock." Somehow she managed to hold herself steady.

God, she was beautiful. His mouth felt dry. "I did knock."

She looked at the door. It was no longer hanging quite right. "That's called breaking the door down."

"Sorry." He looked away, though he didn't want to. "Um, you've changed since we went skinny-dipping, Paula."

Her throat felt achy, as if she had been crying. Well, she wasn't going to, damn it. Why didn't he just leave her alone? Why couldn't he have let her go in peace? Better yet, why had he ever been born? "People do that in twenty years."

He turned and saw her reaching for the fallen robe. "What are you doing?"

She glared at him. "Putting on your bathrobe."

He took it out of her hands gently and let it drop to the floor again. "I don't want you to." He slipped his arms around her, drawing her against his hips.

She was aware of his growing desire. It flared her own. Her heart was hammering so hard that it hurt to feel it. "Then what do you suggest I wear while my clothes dry?"

He touched the necklace around her throat. In fascination, he saw the pulse there jump. For him. It was jumping for him. He had never been so glad of anything in his life. "Your pearl necklace."

She couldn't draw her eyes away from his face, couldn't draw her body away from his, even though common sense told her to flee. "It's not very warm."

He let his finger sift through her hair. "I'll keep you warm, Paula."

"I know that," she whispered.

His lips came down on hers, and then it was past the time for words, past the time for running, for logic, for common sense. Now it was time to feel, to taste, to experience and let the rest of the world be damned. At the end of the road, she knew there was a price to pay. So be it. Right now she wanted nothing more than to be made love to by Alex.

It was like nothing she had ever expected.

If he was impatient, he kept it bridled well. There was nothing but gentleness, tenderness in his every movement. If she had been a little in love with him before, she was more so now, achingly so.

He kissed her over and over, each kiss deepening, making the one before pale by comparison. Her head was swimming, a rushing noise in her ears was drowning out everything else but the beating of her heart. And she was drowning, drowning in desire, in sensations she had only fantasized about before.

When his lips left hers, she moaned involuntarily, then moaned again as they moved to the hollow of her throat. Paula curled her fingers in his hair, pressing his head against her as she arched into the magic his mouth was creating. His tongue encircled one nipple, then the other, making them hard. She was certain her own desire was going to make her explode.

When she opened her eyes, she saw everything in a haze.

"You're still dressed," she whispered hoarsely, barely getting the words out. "Is this going to be a formal affair?"

When he laughed softly, she felt delighted. "I don't want to stop kissing you long enough to take the time to undress."

"Let me," she offered, her fingers gliding along the outline of his body until they found their mark. "Don't stop what you're doing on my account."

"I won't," he promised.

It was hard getting buttons out of their holes and the belt from its loop when her head was swirling and her liquefied limbs were on fire. But she managed. Somehow she managed.

Tugging hard, she pulled off his shirt, interrupting his hands briefly as they encompassed her breasts, filling themselves, kneading her soft, pliant skin.

"You're going to have to do the rest yourself," she breathed. "I . . . can't seem to . . . concentrate."

With a quick jerk, he shucked his trousers off. But as his hand went to the waistband of his briefs, Paula stopped him. "What?"

Mischief danced in her eyes. "I've gotten my second wind."
With the flat of her hands on his taut hips, she slid them under
his briefs and moved them slowly down the length of his body.

"Paula," he groaned, "won't you ever stop torturing me?"

She stopped when she reached his thighs, withdrew her hands
and let the briefs drop. "Make me," she challenged. She drew
close against him again.

She was a she-devil, a vixen, and the only one he had ever
truly wanted. "You're on." He pulled her into his arms so
quickly that air whooshed from her.

The stolen breath was not replaced.

Suddenly she felt herself being lifted in his arms. "Where?"

"The floor's too crammed," he told her before he kissed her
again. And again, and again.

The bedspread whispered against her skin as he placed her
down. It was the last sound she heard as she was enfolded in his
arms.

So this was heaven. The thought vibrated through her mind
as his mouth, his wonderful mouth kissed her, teased her, made
her desire mount to an incredible high as he touched upon each
and every one of her pulse points.

He couldn't get enough of her. Not now, not ever. The more
he kissed her, the more he touched, caressed, explored, the
more he wanted. Every fiber in his body begged to have him
reach fulfillment, but he didn't want it to be over yet, not this
first time. He wanted to savor it, to drink in her sweetness, to
bury himself in her scents, to brand himself with all that was
hers. Nothing had ever pleased him more than the way her eyes
dilated when his hands touched her in secret places, making her
his.

"Alex, I give up. Now, please, now."

She clutched at his shoulder, her fingers white. She was going to die if he didn't take her to the final brink. The peaks he
had been creating within her were crescendoing, crashing into
one another until she thought she'd go mad with ecstasy.

He raised himself over her, pivoting on his elbows. He smiled
down into her feverish face. When had lovemaking ever been

like this? Never. Everything before had been only simple tunes, carelessly hummed. She was a symphony of sights and sounds.

"Always giving directions."

She encircled her arms around him. "Only when necessary," she breathed, adoring the way his skin felt against hers as she moved beneath him.

When he entered her, it was with incredible gentleness, as if he didn't want to hurt her or shatter the moment. She tightened her hold on him, anticipating the whirlwind ride they were both about to undertake.

She didn't anticipate enough. Joined, they rose on a wave of mutual passion she couldn't hope to describe. As they moved faster and faster, they became one in far more than the physical sense. He took her up, up, up, beyond plateaus that she had ever reached. Beyond pleasure. Flashes of lights echoed through her brain.

With one final thrust paradise flowered and billowed around her.

Crying out his name, Paula knew there'd never be anyone else.

Chapter Fourteen

Paula shifted sleepily in bed. Stretching out her arm, she turned and felt something warm next to her. Warm and breathing. She opened her eyes inches away from Alex's sleeping face.

Omigod!

She was certain she had practically shouted the words out loud. But Alex went on sleeping, so she knew she couldn't have.

Okay, calm down, Paula, she ordered herself.

She lay perfectly still for a moment, utterly paralyzed, her mind totally blank. Her heart was pounding so hard, she was positive that it was echoing within the quiet room.

What had she gone and done? More importantly, what had she gone and done with Alex? Was she completely out of her mind? And if she was, could she use that in her own defense in a court of law?

This was no time for jokes.

She tried to clear the fog from her brain as a hundred different emotions came at her all at once. Disbelief, wonder, fear and happiness. Beneath the jumble of thoughts and emotions was an underlying layer of happiness, a warm, silky contentment that all the nerves and anxiety attacks couldn't dislodge. Whatever else happened after this, she had last night, an absolutely incredible experience that left her feeling soft and tender and very womanly.

And very nude, she realized, glancing down suddenly.

Chewing on her lower lip, Paula slowly eased herself into a sitting position. She looked at Alex's face. Nothing. He was still asleep. One thing in her favor. Letting a small sigh of relief escape, she went on with her attempt to successfully slip out of bed and away without waking Alex. One toe made it to the rug. Others were stretching to join it.

She felt a hand encircle her wrist firmly and she stiffened.

"You left them in the bathroom."

"Left what?" She knew her voice sounded far too innocent for the situation she was in.

She heard the grin in his voice. "Your clothes." At least he was handling this better than she was. He wasn't laughing at her, was he? She swore at herself for the self-conscious thought.

She sagged a little, pulling the sheet up against her chest. Only then did she venture to look at him again. He *was* grinning. She felt her own lips curve upward. "And my courage."

"No, that you always wear like armor." He raised himself up on his elbow. He felt her nervousness. Was she having second thoughts? Was last night just something that she let happen? Or did it mean something to her, as well? As well? Just what did it mean to him, he asked himself. Perhaps too much.

"Look, Paula," he began, feeling a bit awkward. He really didn't know how to approach this. "I'm sorry."

Sorry? The most beautiful night of her life and he was sorry??? Well, what did she expect? It was daylight, and the madness had passed. He was Alex again. "Are you?" She sounded very calm, very sophisticated, almost disinterested. She congratulated herself. Inside, she was shaking with anger and with hurt.

"If you are."

She dragged her hand through her hair. It fell like a shower of flames about her bare shoulders. Alex couldn't help himself. He reached out and touched it.

Which way did he want it? Which way did *she* want it? "I don't know *what* I am."

He let his hand glide down along her back. "Beautiful," he told her.

"Confused." She leaned her cheek against the pyramid created by her raised legs. She hugged them to her, but she kept her eyes on Alex.

"A lot of that going around."

"You, too?" she cried in wonder. The unshakable, unflappable Alex Hamilton? Was it possible that he was as confused about all this as she was?

"Me, too." He had places to go, things to do. Why was it that all he wanted at this very moment was to pull her into his arms and make love to her?

She sighed and hugged her knees even closer. "It'll never work, you know."

"I know." It wouldn't. She was right. They were worlds apart, destinies apart. That didn't change the ache in his gut or the desire that flared through every part of him.

She cocked her head and looked at him, a bittersweet feeling playing through her. "What are we going to do about it?"

He reached over and wound a lock of her hair around his finger. "I have an idea."

"So do I," she flashed a grin. "But we'll be late for work."

Her grin faded into almost a shy smile. He would have never thought she was capable of being shy. There were sides to Paula that intrigued him. One could spend a lifetime learning all about her. He didn't have a lifetime to spare, he reminded himself.

So what was he doing with his life that was so very important?

"Alex?" Paula hesitated for a moment.

"Yes?"

"It was very nice."

"Yes." His tone matched hers although he wasn't certain how she felt. "Yes, it was." It was beyond nice. It was exquisite. He had never felt so alive, so free in his whole life.

Time to make a run for it, she thought. Play it casual. He can't know what this *really* meant. She didn't want him to have the upper hand in this, whatever "this" was. "Um, Alex, how do you usually work this?" She nodded toward the bathroom.

There was no point in telling her that there was no "usual" about this. An unending supply of women did not parade through his apartment, offering momentary love and then leaving. This was a very *un*usual situation, as far as he was concerned. "I've never come up with a standard approach."

She swung her legs off the bed and rose with the sheet wrapped around her. The end fell on the floor like a train behind her. "Alex, I'm surprised at you. I thought you had every detail of your life mapped out. You're slacking off. If you're not careful, you're going to sound like you're positively human."

He was having very human thoughts about the shape that was haphazardly draped in the sheet. "Since you're already on your feet, you go first."

Throwing the end of the sheet over her bare shoulder like a Roman toga, Paula marched off to his bathroom. There was absolutely no indication that her knees were shaking as she made her exit.

It was a game to her, Alex thought as he lay back in bed and stared at the closed bathroom door. Nothing more, just a game. That was Paula for you, never serious. She didn't feel about what had happened between them the way he did.

What *did* he feel? he asked himself impatiently.

Was it just curiosity? A natural outlet for the years of hidden affection? Or what?

The only thing he did know was that she had effectively thrown his world into chaos. Maybe it was better that she was so flip about the situation. After all, he had no business in her world or she in his. They had different temperaments, different goals, different *everything*. It would never work, just as she said.

So why did it bother him when she acted so glib? He'd be damned if he understood.

Paula leaned against the bathroom door and nearly collapsed. Her legs felt like rubber. She slid down until she was sitting on the floor. What had all that been about out there? How could she have *let* this happen? How could she have allowed herself to lose total control and make love with Alex? Now she had no defenses left. Things had gotten very, very complicated. What was going on in his mind? Had he liked what happened between them? Would he be back for more just to have more, or because all this meant something to him? Or wouldn't he be back? What if he hadn't liked it?

Oh God, this made her life even more confused than it already was. She hadn't thought that was possible.

She had to calm down, she told herself. She was getting carried away. Last night was just a wonderful interlude; that was all it was, that was all it could be. Alex couldn't give her what she needed. She needed to be free. And he wanted a little corporate wife who could help him with his career. He wanted Diana and all that she could give him. Last night was a fluke, and he was probably out there right now regretting that it ever happened. Or putting another notch on his belt.

So what? she thought, annoyed. Who needed him?

Something small within her ached and echoed, You do, but she shut it out. She didn't want to dwell on her feelings. After all, *he* wasn't feeling anything, not if she knew Alex.

The ache grew.

"I'll get a cab," Paula announced when Alex walked into the kitchen after his shower. "It's what I should have done last night."

Fresh out of the shower, Alex was still dressed in his bathrobe. He slung both ends of his towel around his neck and held them tightly in his hands. Too tightly. "Is that how you feel?" he asked slowly.

"Since when are you interested in feelings?" she retorted too quickly.

"Sorry." He held up his hands in surrender. "Don't know what came over me."

That's probably how he thinks of last night, as well, Paula thought bitterly.

"What's that?" He nodded at the plate she was placing on the table.

"Some call it breakfast. It's my way of saying—" What *was* it her way of saying? She wasn't certain. "Just eat it while it's hot."

He sat down and picked up his fork, but he didn't eat. He had no appetite. "What's bothering you, Paula?"

She grabbed up her purse and slung it on her shoulder. "I don't like being late, and I will be if I stand here, watching you eat breakfast."

He looked at the large clock that hung on the wall just behind her. "You start work at six-thirty?"

"Creative people don't keep regular hours."

"Then how can you be late?"

"Don't nitpick."

"I wouldn't dream of it."

He knew better than to stand in her way. Life had trained him early to step aside when he saw a runaway steam roller. And Paula had all the signs of being ready to roll right over him.

"I'll see you around," she said, a bit too breezily.

"Until the charade is over," he countered.

"Yes, until the charade is over," she echoed. And then she was gone.

Alex pushed his plate away angrily. He'd never understand her, not if he lived to be older than Methuselah.

She was driving him crazy. He had purposely not shown up to take her out to lunch for the last two days, hoping that he could get his life back into order. All he accomplished, instead, was basically nothing. His work was suffering. Paula was preying on his mind. Telling himself that it was no good, that any relationship between them didn't have a prayer of surviving, that she didn't care, didn't work. Nothing worked.

He needed to see her. There was something about her that called to him, something he wanted to leave buried, something he *couldn't* leave buried when he was around her. She mixed up all the rules, destroyed everything he believed in. He was a controlled person, but she made him want to do things spontaneously. He *hated* spontaneity, she lived and breathed it.

She made him want to run barefoot on the beach.

He had never had trouble concentrating before. No matter what the crisis, he could always gather his thoughts together. She made his mind wander.

She was absolutely no good for him.

So why did he want her so badly?

"Hey, Paulie? You and your three-piece-suit Romeo have a misunderstanding?" Marty asked kindly on the third day that Alex didn't show up.

She knew Marty was only trying to be nice, but she wished he'd mind his own business. That wasn't like her. It was getting to the point that she didn't know who she was anymore. "No, why?"

"Well," Marty spread his hands wide, "he's not here to take you to lunch."

Paula pretended to jot down a note about the script changes. "I'm perfectly able to eat lunch on my own. He's busy."

"Has to be pretty busy to keep away from you." Ted leaned over her desk, giving her a wide leer. "If you were mine, I'd be eating out of your slipper."

"If I was yours, you'd starve to death." She pushed back from her desk and raised her foot slightly for his examination. "I wear open-toe high-heeled sandals."

"Could use the diet." He patted his slightly thickening waist, then leered again. "How about it?"

Paula pointed at his paper-laden desk. "Back to work, Hammerstein."

Ted pretended to sulk as he retraced his steps. "Slave driver."

Paula laughed. "And don't you forget it."

* * *

Paula tried to concentrate on her work, but nothing was jelling. She missed seeing him, missed having lunch with him. Missed him, period. She hadn't seen him since the morning after her disastrous slip.

Her glorious, disastrous slip, she thought dreamily, recalling every fiery moment spent in his arms.

So where was he?

Simple, he didn't care, remember? This was all make-believe, right?

But he had made love to her.

So what did you expect him to do with a naked woman? Crochet her a dress? He's only human, after all.

Paula sighed and ran her hand through her hair, then stuck a clip in it to keep it back from her face.

He was probably having lunch with Diana these days, she told herself. Undoubtedly he was trying to patch things up with her. That was where his future lay. That was where his future *should* lay. What was the matter with her? She was a big girl. It wasn't as if this had been her first time. She was old enough to know that fairy tales were just that. Of all people, Alex was not qualified to take on the role of her knight in shining armor. It was good, very good, that reality had set in so soon, before she had a chance to let her delusions get the better of her.

He wasn't right for her. He wasn't. He wasn't.

So why was she so miserable? Why did she want him so badly?

Paula pressed the wrong key on the computer, and her screen disappeared, taking all her work with it. She screamed.

She didn't know what to think when she saw him standing there on her doorstep with a single rose in his hand, at eleven o'clock at night. She didn't want to think anything. She just wanted him to kiss her. But she forced herself to stay calm. The last thing in the world she wanted him to know was how much she had missed him.

"Business bad, Alex?" She leaned against the doorjamb, her arms crossed before her. "Are you selling roses door-to-door?"

He felt ill-at-ease. Part of him hadn't wanted to come. But it couldn't hold out against the rest of him. "Not selling, giving."

No calls for three days, and now this? "Why?" she asked suspiciously, seeking refuge in the hurt anger that was beginning to rise.

He peered in behind her. "Is your father home?" He hoped not. He wanted to make love to her, wanted it so bad he could taste it.

"You want to give the rose to him?" Alex shook his head, then grinned. Paula nodded toward the stairs. "Pop's asleep. It's been a long, brutal day."

"Yes, so my father says." He felt ill-at-ease, but he couldn't make himself leave. He offered her the rose.

Paula accepted it hesitantly. What was he doing here? "Would you like to come in?"

"Yes," he admitted. "I shouldn't, but I want to."

She stepped back. "Never let it be said I didn't encourage you to do the wrong thing."

She shouldn't be this happy to see him. But she was. She tried to remind herself of all the reasons having a relationship with Alex was wrong for her. She couldn't remember a single one. "Diana busy tonight?"

He got no farther than the threshold. "I didn't come to talk about Diana."

To keep from touching him, Paula shoved her free hand into the pocket of her robe. "What did you come to talk about?"

"That I want you, and I'll be damned if I know what to do about it."

He hadn't taken a step toward her, yet she felt herself melting, felt her desire growing, begging to be freed.

"That makes two of us."

"What? That you want me, too, or that you don't know what to do about my problem?"

"I plead the Fifth." But her eyes gave her away.

Paula cast about for something to say. "Do you want to sit down?" She took a step toward the living room.

He stopped her by the mere touch of his hand on her shoulder. "No. I want to make love to you. That's all I've thought about for two days and two nights."

She turned to look at him. She saw his words reflected in his eyes. "The lawyering business must be slow these days."

"I wouldn't know." He brushed her hair away from her neck and pressed his lips to it. "My mind hasn't been there."

She felt everything within her turning to hot liquid. "What are you doing?"

His tongue traced the outline of her ear. "I thought you knew."

Slipping, she was slipping badly. "Of course I know."

He loosened the tie about her waist and her robe hung open. "Then why are you asking?"

She meant to stop him, but all she could do was place her hand on his. "Because I can't believe you're doing this."

As his lips skimmed her neck again, he sought out the softness of her breasts, gently massaging them with his hands. "Why? Am I doing it wrong?"

Paula pulled in a breath. "No." Oh God, no. He was doing it just right. It was too exquisite for words. Her eyes fluttered shut for a moment, savoring the sweet, hot feeling.

The need within him was growing, aching for a release, aching for her. "Then, what's the problem?"

She opened her eyes and looked at him. "You, you're the problem. You have no business doing this to me—"

He slipped his other hand inside her robe, holding her by the waist. "But I mean business."

As if her body were on automatic pilot, she leaned into him, eager for the feel of him. "Easy for you to say."

"Easier to do." He raised his head until his mouth was just a hair's breadth away from hers. "Can you stop talking long enough for me to kiss you?"

"I think so. Why don't you try and see?"

He did.

The rose fell from her hand. Everything else disappeared. This, this was what she had needed for the last few days to make her feel whole again.

Alex swept her up in his arms and carried her up the stairs.

"My father," she whispered against his neck.

He felt heat flame where her breath had touched him. Was it possible to burn with such longing and still remain sane? He doubted it. "Sleeps like a rock. My father told me so."

"I suppose I'm doomed, then." She wrapped her arms around his neck.

"I suppose so."

He entered her room and pushed the door closed with his shoulder. Setting her down, he framed her face in his hands and kissed her deeply.

Paula moaned. Alive, she felt alive again, the way she hadn't felt in three agonizingly long days. Three days without sunlight. Three days without him. How could it be possible that he could become the center of her universe so quickly?

He wanted to tear her nightgown off, but he held himself in check as he slid the gauzy robe from her shoulders. She stood dressed in only his warm gaze. He wanted to lose himself in her trim, athletic body.

She shivered, but not from the cold. He made her feel beautiful. "I never realized what a fast worker you were, Alex."

"There are a lot of things," he whispered against her bare shoulder just before he kissed it, "that you never realized about me." *That I never realized about me,* he added silently, and then ceased to think coherently, at all.

She wanted to touch him, to feel his hard, lean body, to pretend, just for a moment, that he was hers and that a myriad of complications didn't exist. That there was no "his" world and "her" world, only "their" world, and they were the only two people in it.

With anxious movements, Paula tugged at his sweater and pulled it over his head, then tossed it aside. "You always overdress for these occasions, Alex," she whispered.

"Maybe I just like having you undress me." And he did. He liked the feel of her cool fingers as they glided along his skin, stripping him of encumbering clothing until they were both free.

Clothes strewn in a heap on the floor, there were no more barriers, real or otherwise. At least not for now. His lips covering hers, he gently pushed her onto the bed. And then his body covered hers.

Paula thrilled to the feel of his skin against her, the soft, downy sprinkling of hair on his chest rubbing against the sensitive areas of her breasts, his hips fitting against hers as if that was what they were created to do.

This time the kisses flared into an intensity that drew her breath away and kept it away. This time his passion was more raw, more demanding. Something within her rose up to meet it, demand for demand, storm for storm. It was wild and twisting, and if she died this instant it would have been only fair, Paula thought, gripping him to her even closer.

She felt him move from her, and then she felt the warm imprint of his tongue and lips as his mouth moved along her body, grazing, teasing, loving, making her his. Her stomach muscles contracted and quivered as he dipped lower, touching her navel, moving lower, even lower, questing to find her secrets, to make her pulses sing, to make her unquestionably his. His tongue moved deep into her.

Paula dug her fingers into his shoulders as the first peak came to claim her, leaving her gasping, leaving her wanting more. More came. It was ecstasy of a kind she didn't think she could contain without screaming out. She grabbed handfuls of her bedspread, jerking them up as she moved.

"Alex, Alex—I—"

Suddenly, he rose up over her, his mouth covering hers, his body blending with hers. Passion exploded as the final climax came to them.

It felt so right. It shouldn't, but it did. So very right to be there, in her bed, lying next to him. She didn't want it to ever end. "What made you come here tonight?"

He smiled at his own foolishness. No one he knew would have believed this of him, sneaking around into a woman's bedroom while her father lay sleeping down the hall. "Madness."

She let her hands trail along his chest, playing with the soft swirls of dark hair. "That would explain it, yes."

Alex kissed the top of her head. It was a purely affectionate gesture that warmed her very soul. "I missed you, you know."

"Did you?" he asked, pleased.

She rested her hand on his chest, leaning her chin on the small perch. "There was no one to tease."

He stroked her hair. It was so fine, so silky. "Nice to know I have a purpose in life."

"A very big purpose." She inclined her head toward him. "Alex?"

"Yes?"

"Tell me something about yourself, something personal." She had a need to know, to clutch a piece of him that he hadn't shared before. She thought, then smiled. "Like what was it like, traveling around with your father?"

He closed his eyes and remembered. Remembered everything. The sounds, the smells, the lonely hours. "Awful."

She couldn't believe that. "But you got to see all those different places, meet all those different, interesting people."

He looked down at her. Yes, she would see it that way. Maybe if she had been there with him, he would have, too. But there had been no one for him to talk to, to share his thoughts with. "The places all looked alike. One hotel room is pretty much the same as the next. And the people, well, I've never been very good with people."

"Oh, I don't know." She grinned at him, touching his cheek with her fingertips. "You're pretty good with me."

"That's because I've always known you. I can't remember a time when you weren't there, somewhere." He moved his head so that he could see her more clearly. "Do you know that I even looked forward to seeing you again, when I was on the road? That was how desperate I was to come home again."

She laughed. "I'm touched."

He slid his finger along her nose. "I always said that."

Paula grew serious as she digested his feelings. "I never thought about how hard it was on you. I always envied you."

And he had always envied her, he thought, envied her the gift for making friends, her being able to have friends around her. "There wasn't anything to envy. I spent a lot of time alone, with my bear."

Her eyes opened wide. "You had a bear?"

"A stuffed bear," he clarified.

The revelation fascinated her. She couldn't visualize it. "What did you call him?"

"Bear."

Paula laughed. "Sounds like you. I can't seem to picture you traveling around the countryside with a teddy bear tucked under your arm, even if you were seven."

"Six," he corrected. "Bear was gone by the time I was seven."

"Cast him aside, did you?"

"No, I lost him."

Something in his voice told her that this was more important than he was letting on. "How?"

"We had to leave in a hurry, and Bear was accidentally left behind. When I found out he was gone, I was pretty upset. At the time, I thought of him as my only friend. But we couldn't turn back to get him. There was no time. Dad and Wally had a booking to get to. By the time we could get back, Bear was gone." He remembered how heartbroken he had been. At the time, to a child of six, it had brought into focus how much he hated the nomadic, rootless life he was forced to lead. Even his silent friend had been lost to him.

Silly thoughts. A child's thoughts. Yet he wondered, as he told the story to her now, if the small incident hadn't somehow laid the foundations of what he was to become.

"Oh Alex, I'm sorry."

He shouldn't have told her. He didn't know what made him tell her. He hadn't even admitted his need to his own mother at the time. And no one had seen him cry, alone in his bed, after the lights were out. Why had he shared it with her now?

Embarrassed, he tried to make light of it.

"Hey." He lifted her chin so that her eyes met his. There were tears there. It surprised him. He had never seen her cry. "It was just a stuffed animal, Paula. I got over it fast enough."

But it wasn't just a stuffed animal, she realized. It was a key. A key to the man he had become. Her heart went out to the lonely boy in the hotel room who had lost his only friend.

Paula raised her lips to his and loved him all the more.

Chapter Fifteen

Alex left shortly before dawn. "Engagement" or not, he didn't want to run the risk of having Wally wake up early and find him in bed with Paula. Alex kissed her lips softly and let himself out.

In his wake he left more than just an empty, warm space in Paula's bed. He left Paula with a great deal to think about. Too much. Her thoughts were jumbled together, wavering between utter, never-ending surprise at the depth of her reaction to Alex and a nagging, growing guilt. Her reaction, she knew, could no longer be labeled as anything but what it was. She was in love with Alex. For whatever that meant and wherever that led, she was in love with him. The guilt came from her suspicions that she was somehow responsible for all this, that perhaps her intense feelings had in some way pulled an unwilling Alex into the vortex of the hurricane, as well.

And to what end? Because of her, he was behaving in a way that could jeopardize his position at work. Or was it all due to her? Maybe she was actually being overconfident. Could she, did she actually have this kind of power over him? Did she want that? Or could it be that Alex wasn't what he seemed to be? That somehow she had brought out the real Alex?

Or was that wishful thinking on her part?

She needed to untangle her thoughts. Human relationships were so much more difficult in real life than on paper. On paper, she could make people behave any way she wanted to. She was assured of a happy ending. There were no assurances in real life. No guarantees that she was doing the right thing. What *was* the right thing?

Restless, she rose and went to the kitchen to fix a strong cup of coffee. Maybe some caffeine would help.

She wasn't vain enough to think that she was worth any kind of sacrifice on Alex's part. Sure, she might have laughingly suggested as much to Alex, but she didn't believe it herself. If he sacrificed what he wanted, his future, his vision of what life should be like for him because of her, would he someday turn to her with anger in his eyes, saying she had cost him his dream? In drawing him away from Diana, was she doing something to hurt Alex?

She couldn't risk that chance.

He had appeared on her doorstep thirty miles out of his way with a single rose. Very un-Alex-like. That was something she might have done, given half a chance. He was meeting her on her grounds. But could he stay? And if he couldn't, could she cross to his? Could she be the wife he needed, to maintain his corner of the world? She was afraid that the answer would eventually be no.

They were wrong for each other, totally, utterly hopelessly wrong. It was best to end it here, end it now.

But oh, what, she thought as she aimlessly milled around the kitchen, would she do without him?

Simple. Die by inches.

Life went on. Taping went on. And the feud, when she paid attention to it, also went on. It seemed to Paula that when she was on the set, her father and his partner had more than their share of professional differences. Marty observed that when she wasn't on the set, the two men seemed to get along much better. Perhaps not quite sharing the camaraderie that they always had, but neither were they arch enemies. He told her as much.

Something wasn't quite right here. If her own life wasn't such an emotional mess, she might have had the sense and strength to untangle the skein. But as it was, she could only make note of it and wonder. She had little energy for anything more, beyond her work.

She tried, successfully to an extent, to block out her problems when she worked. But the enthusiasm that she usually exhibited just wasn't there. And everyone noticed.

"Can't you punch this sketch up just a little more?" Harold asked, when he dropped off five pages on her desk. It wasn't the first time the assistant director had made the request.

She raised her eyes to meet his, contemplating punching up something else. But she murmured, "We'll see what we can do."

Harold pulled the baseball cap that he wore to hide his bald spot low over his eyes. "By four o'clock."

Paula pursed her lips. "Have you looked in the yellow pages under *M* for miracles?" she called after Harold as he left the room.

He paused momentarily in the doorway. "If anyone can do it, you can, Paula."

"Great words to fail by," she muttered. With a sigh, she blew her bangs out of her eyes and looked at the two other men in the room. Both Ted and Marty were oddly quiet these days, as if they were waiting for a volcano to erupt. One whose first initial was *P*. She tried not to notice. "Okay, guys, we're on."

When the pages were sufficiently polished to everyone's weary satisfaction, Paula decided that she needed to clear her head. Instead of sending the pages to the set by messenger she opted to walk them over herself.

As she approached the darkened soundstage, she saw her father and Paul deep in conference.

"Finally," she muttered. At least this was going right. Her father looked over in her direction, and Paula saw his body straighten, like a funny little teddy bear on the alert.

Teddy bear. She suddenly thought of the story that Alex had told her.

No, no thoughts about Alex during working hours, she reminded herself. She was just too confused over what to do about all this. Mercifully he hadn't showed up at lunch. She had to keep him out of her mind until at least quitting time, if she was to remain functioning.

Wally stood on his toes, shouting into Paul's aristocratic, stubbornly set face. "And I say she'll want the tickets. I ought to know."

Paul gave him a cool, pitying look. "You know very little, Wallace."

Despite the situation, a smile curved her lips. Only Paul called her father Wallace. But then she wondered what was real and what was illusion. Was this, for some reason, a ruse on their part? She couldn't even begin to think of a reason why they would pretend to be feuding. If they weren't pretending, then the war was still on despite everything that she had tried. Despite the fact that they had been working side by side now for almost three weeks. That didn't bode well. Would it never be resolved? She felt a heavy sadness overtake her when she thought of that.

Wally whirled around and took her by the arm. "You settle this, baby."

"I have your sketch reworked—a third time," she said, looking over her shoulder at the smiling black-bearded director. Phil Cassidy merely gave her an innocent look and held out his hand.

Smiling back, she slapped the pages into his hand. He began to read immediately.

"Forget the sketch," Wally told her. "What kind of a wedding do you want?"

She looked from one man to the other. "A peaceful one." And it was beginning to seem as if that were never going to happen.

"See," Wally snapped at Paul.

Maybe Paul did, but she didn't. "Hold it." She held up a warning hand. "What argument have I just fueled this time?" She waited for an explanation.

"I told this old so-and-so that you'd want to go to Vegas and elope." Wally jerked a thumb at Paul but refused to look at the man, even though he was standing right next to him. "*He* claims you'd want a church wedding with all the trimmings."

For a moment Paula forgot it was all a charade and let herself envision a lavish church wedding. Alex, dressed in a formal tuxedo, waiting for her to approach. Something fluttered in her stomach, and she involuntarily put her hand to it.

"Well?" Wally demanded.

Paula blinked. "What?"

"We're waiting for your decision, baby. What kind of a wedding do you want? A three-ring circus or something romantic?"

Paul frowned at Wally's terminology. "You're just trying to get out of paying for the wedding."

"I'm paying for the tickets, aren't I?" He thrust them at Paula.

She took them in hand. "Very nice, Pop. I'll talk to Alex. Now would you please do me and everyone else a favor, and talk to each other without a whip and a chair in between you?"

They walked away from her, still bickering.

"Vegas."

"Church."

Paula shook her head as she crossed her arms before her.

"What was all that about?"

She turned, startled. Alex was behind her. She should have sensed it. Her body suddenly became taut, like a violin about to be played. She told herself to calm down. "Our wedding, it seems."

He took her arm, guiding her away from the dark corner. "They want to come along on the honeymoon?"

"No, they're having a difference of opinion as to where we should do the dastardly deed." She tossed the term carelessly about, not wanting him to know that suddenly, she wanted the dastardly deed to come to pass very, very much. "What are you doing here?"

He shrugged, not fully ready to admit to her that she was all he could think about all day. Right now he should be dressing for a dinner party that Corbett fully expected him to attend. But he wasn't getting ready, he was here, looking at Paula, drowning in her eyes and wishing he had a lifeline tied to his waist. What a quantum leap away from the man he had been a month ago.

"I ran out of work," he lied. "So like a dutiful fiancé, I thought I'd drop by and take you out for a drink."

Lunch, a drink, running in the rain—it was all the same to her, as long as she could do it with him. But a shred of common sense reminded her that it wasn't wise, that it was foolhardy to keep going on this way. Foolhardy for her. Foolhardy for him.

She tried to pull back, but her heart wasn't in it. "Alex, I've still got—"

"Marty and Ted said that they owed you a few hours and also their first-born."

"That would be Marty. He's been trying to palm off Roberta for years." She laughed, seeking shelter in what she was familiar with.

He put his arm around her, leading her out of the building. "They said you could leave early. That they were quite capable of keeping the ship afloat until tomorrow."

"Well..." She looked dubious. "I don't know." But she did. She did know. She wanted to run off with him no matter what called her back.

"Now you're beginning to sound like me," he observed. He knew that would do it.

"Can't have that. Just let me get my purse and we'll—" Alex retrieved it from the chair where he had placed it. "My," Paula said, impressed as she took it from him, "you are eager, aren't you?"

He grinned and held the exit door open for her. Sunlight streamed in, momentarily blinding her. She held onto his arm and crossed over the threshold. She looked around for his car and didn't see it.

He wore a strange expression as he looked at her. "We need to talk." Taking her arm, he led her across the street.

With effort, she kept her voice light. "About what, counselor?"

"About us."

She became nervous. Do the right thing, Paula. The right thing. Don't let him think you really care. Don't ruin his life.

But what of mine? she wanted to cry.

"There is no 'us' away from your father and mine, remember?" Who said she couldn't act? she thought, remembering a tiny review in a forgotten newspaper that had made mincemeat of her abilities.

She wasn't fooling him this time. She had communicated things to him with her body last night that her words couldn't erase. "I don't remember your father being in your bedroom last night."

"Lucky for you. He'd like nothing better than to play the irate father. Be his first serious role. No, his second," she amended, remembering how he looked when he told her that he was never going to speak to Paul again.

People got in his way on the sidewalk. He saw no one else but her. "Don't hide behind words, Paula."

"Then how do you expect us to talk?"

He left it alone for now. "The Velvet Turtle suit you?"

She nodded, not really hearing him. "Fine."

"First time we've agreed on a subject in a while." He couldn't help the sarcasm that rose in his voice.

She had hurt him by saying that there was nothing between them. Oh, she hadn't meant to do that. Wasn't there a way out of this mess without hurting? She turned to him and smiled. "Oh, I think we agree on more things than we'd like to admit."

He stopped short before a Chinese restaurant. To hell with Corbett and the party tonight, he thought suddenly. He was going to do what he wanted to do.

Paula came to an abrupt halt next to him. Her breast brushed against his arm. It was enough to make her remember. And yearn. "Forget where you parked your car?"

"How about take-home?"

Light. Keep it light. She'd done it a thousand times. No big deal. "What, food, or me?"

"Both. Instead of going to a bar." He was acting so much against type that he was beginning to think that perhaps this was who he really was, this, not the man he had been a few short weeks ago, was the real Alex.

She bit her lower lip. She knew she shouldn't accept. It was only making a big mistake bigger. "Sounds good to me." Damn, how had those words slipped out?

Because she wanted them to.

"You order. I'll get my car and follow you home." He grinned at her words. She couldn't resist him when he grinned. "What?"

"As a kid, I always wanted to tell my mother something followed me home and then convince her to let me keep it as a pet."

"Do I qualify as a pet?"

He touched her hair lightly. She saw the passion there. "You qualify as a hell of a lot of things, Paula. I just have to sort it all out."

"Me, too. See you at your place."

He watched her disappear before entering the restaurant.

They ate on paper plates and sat on the floor before his fireplace. It was one of those chilly evenings that happened inexplicably after a warm spell, and Alex had started a fire going. In the hearth and in her blood.

Paula slipped out of her shoes and then laughed. "You're only supposed to have your shoes off in a Japanese restaurant."

He had no idea what he was eating. The only thing he did know was that he wanted to touch her, to make love to her. She was quickly eroding everything else inside of him and filling it with thoughts of her. He couldn't seem to get enough. Each time they made love, he thought this was it, this was the peak, but it wasn't. It just made him want her all the more.

"What are you supposed to take off when you're eating on the floor?"

She pretended to think that one over. "Depends." The smile began in her eyes and lit up her whole face.

"On what?"

She turned her face up to his, food, promises to herself, everything else forgotten. Everything but Alex. "On who you're eating with."

Things were happening again. No, they had been happening all along. They were just intensifying now. He leaned over and kissed her shoulder through the light material of her dress. Paula closed her eyes, feeling the heat singe her.

Stop it. Stop it now. Once is for curiosity, two is for pleasure, three is madness. People get hooked after three.

Who was she kidding? She *was* hooked.

She began to unbutton his shirt, eager for the feel of his skin. "You haven't even had the main course."

He skimmed his tongue on the shell of her ear and sent shivers throughout her body. "I'm working on it."

"And doing a fine job of it, too." How could she have *ever* said he was a stuffed shirt? A stick in the mud? "Alex . . . you said . . . you wanted to talk. . . ." she said with effort.

As he slowly, sensuously kissed the side of her neck, she felt the zipper on her dress slip down. Any second now, she was going to dissolve into nothingness.

"Since when have you ever listened to what I said?"

She bent forward to let him slip the dress from her shoulders and down her arms. "I thought I'd turn over a new leaf."

Alex kissed the hollow of her throat, savoring the taste of her. There were so many different tastes to her, and he wanted to sample them all over and over again. "Later."

Her eyes closed, her head swimming, she managed to drag his shirt from him. "Whatever you say."

The thin camisole she wore could have been dispensed with quickly, but he wanted to do it all slowly, to bring her to the peaks slowly and enjoy the light of glowing passion in her eyes.

"I like the sound of that." The palms of his hands touched only the tips of her breasts. He felt her nipples harden against them before he filled his hands, caressing her.

She had to concentrate to find words. He took it all away from her. "Don't get used to it."

He laughed, and she opened her eyes. "Paula, with you there's very little I could ever get used to. Everything keeps changing." With a little tug at the hem, the camisole fell to her waist. "It's like I'm trapped in a giant, rolling kaleidoscope."

She saw desire flare in his eyes as he looked at her. Impatiently she pulled open his belt and fumbled with the zipper. "Thank you—I think."

He covered her hands with his own and helped her. The heat of his body warmed her fingertips. "Don't."

Paula swallowed. It was so hard to pretend that this was all just an act, that it meant nothing to her. That he meant nothing more to her than he ever had. He meant the whole world to her. "Don't what?"

He made her raise her hips slightly and then the dress was gone. And so was the wispy scrap of material she wore below it. A twist of his wrist had torn it away. "Think," he whispered against her flesh as he pushed her back on the soft plush rug.

She opened her arms to him. Her heart had long ago done the same. "Is that a new leaf you've turned over?"

"That's my motto, when I'm with you, it seems." With a quick tug, he freed himself of his clothing and then melted against her, hot, pulsating skin against hot, pulsating skin. His hands took on a familiarity as they caressed her body. She was his, and he knew it, even if he knew nothing else anymore.

Their differences and the impossibility of the match were pushed aside, as they sought shelter in each other's arms. Shelter and their own private heaven.

Chapter Sixteen

Even she couldn't escape reality forever. It was there, waiting for her, once the magic of their lovemaking had softly taken its leave, waiting like a dour headmistress for a tardy student.

She didn't want to face it.

Paula rested her cheek on Alex's chest. She felt his heartbeat beneath it. How could being with him like this feel so right and yet be so wrong? It didn't seem possible.

But it was, it was wrong for her, wrong for him. The sooner they stopped seeing each other this way, the better. Besides, this was really all just make-believe, right? They had gotten caught up in it, that was all.

Liar.

Paula spread her fingers along the taut, hard muscles along Alex's abdomen and felt them quiver in response. She didn't want to talk, to think. She just wanted to make love with him until she died, never mind logic. But that was running and hiding from the truth. And tomorrow. And for some reason, tomorrows always had a nasty habit of arriving, especially when they weren't wanted.

"We have to talk," she whispered sadly. The words rippled against his chest.

He stroked her hair. Something within him knew what was coming. For the first time in his life, he didn't want to meet something head on, didn't want things neat and tidy and orderly. He wanted to stay lost in the chaos they had created, no, that *she* had created within him.

"I've never known you not to talk when you wanted to." Her hair sifted through his fingers like shimmering tongues of fire.

There was only silence.

Was she as afraid to verbalize what was bothering her as he was? Were they agonizing over the same thing? Did she know what was going on in his mind? No, he doubted it. There were times he doubted that *he* knew what was going on in there now. He felt cornered, trapped not by her but by his own emotions. He was angry at himself for losing control, for acting impulsively, irrationally. All the things, he suddenly realized, that he had always accused her of doing. For a moment, he wondered if his feelings were truly his own or an echo of hers. Was she making him see things more clearly, or was she clouding his vision, making him see things through her eyes? He didn't know.

She was turning him inside out. And yet he couldn't let her go.

"Maybe this is a first," she said finally.

"What is?"

"My not talking."

He laughed softly. "It'll never last." When she raised her head to look at him, her eyes were serious. And sad. He had never seen her sad before. Angry, yes, with fire in her eyes, but never sad. That was for other mortals, not for Paula.

"You said you wanted to talk when you came to the set, Alex. You have all the answers. You go first."

His stomach tightened. Was it fear? "I don't have answers anymore, just chaos."

His voice sounded bewildered, maybe angry. She tried not to dwell on the latter. Did he blame her? How could he help it? "I've done that to you, haven't I?"

"Yes." It wasn't quite an accusation. But she was to blame.

Paula sat up, turning away from him. "Funny, three weeks ago, I would have flippantly said 'I'm glad.' Now," she sighed, running her hands through her hair, "I don't know anymore. Nothing is the way it was. Being with you has thrown everything out of whack." She didn't need Alex in her life, complicating everything. But he was there, whether or not she wanted him. And she did, which made it that much worse.

He detected a hint of resentfulness. It hurt. Didn't she know how much of himself he had given away? Didn't she realize how much it was costing him? "You make it sound like it's my fault."

An edge of aloofness, of distance, seeped into his voice. Paula suddenly felt not nude, but naked. There was a world of difference. Just like there was between them. She reached for her dress and shoved her arms through the sleeves. "Well, it is." She kept the hurt out of her voice and covered it with anger.

He saw the flare of anger and couldn't contain his hurt. A hurt that quickly transformed into anger, as well. What was the matter with her? "I'm not the one who came up with this little gem of a plan."

She pulled her dress down about her hips and thighs with an angry jerk. "That's right, get sarcastic." She rose from her knees to her feet and glared down at him. "I didn't exactly tie you up and drag you into this." She tugged at the zipper. It was stuck on a piece of material. So much for a dramatic exit. She tried again. Finally, with a jerk, it moved.

Damn it, how could she make him so angry and arouse him so much at the same time? She was getting dressed, for heaven's sake, not undressed. She *had* made him crazy. He was getting what he deserved for getting involved with her in the first place. He wasn't even certain what it was that they were arguing about. Only that they were arguing, and hurt feelings were spilling out. "Now who's sarcastic?"

She grabbed her camisole and panties and looked around for her purse. It was on the floor a few feet away. She dragged it over to her. "Damn right I'm being sarcastic. If I had stayed sarcastic, I wouldn't be in this mess." Fighting tears, she stuffed the undergarments into her shoulder bag.

He couldn't believe what he was hearing. "Is that what this is to you, a mess?"

Any minute now, she was going to cry. She had to get out of here. She couldn't let him see her cry. "I call them as I see them."

His voice was cold, brittle. "Then I suggest you get glasses."

Summoning control from somewhere, Paula drew herself up regally. "Maybe while I'm at it, I should have my head examined." For ever having believed I loved you, she added silently.

"What for?" he shouted. "They'll only tell you it's empty."

She swallowed. Hard. "Like your heart."

There was no expression on his face. Though he wanted to take her, to crush her in his arms, to shout that no matter how much they argued, it didn't erase what he felt for her, he remained where he was. "So, I guess it's a standoff."

"Yes. And my side would like to go home now."

"You know where the door is." His voice was dangerously low. He was daring her to take it, not believing she would, not like this.

The slam of the front door vibrated through his body. She had taken the dare. Would she have been Paula if she hadn't?

"Yes," he said softly, "you do know where the door is." He leaned on something and realized that it was her shoes. Paula had left barefoot. Somehow, it seemed to fit.

Paula saw the security guard looking at her oddly as she stepped out of the elevator. She glanced down and realized, too late, that she was barefoot. She'd be damned if she'd turn around and go back to retrieve her shoes. Alex knew where he could put them.

"Haven't you ever seen a woman barefoot before?" she inquired in a cool, unflappable voice as she walked by the gaping man, every inch the princess.

"Yes, ma'am," he muttered.

She walked down the long block to her car, calling Alex every name in the book. It didn't help. It didn't make the ache go away. It didn't make her heart hurt any less.

By the time she reached her car, the bottoms of her feet were scraped. That, too, was Alex's fault, she sniffed, blinking madly to keep the tears at bay. This wasn't the way love was supposed to be. When she had dreamed about falling in love, she had thought it was going to be all blue skies and pinwheels. She would *make* it that way. A happy ending was to be waiting for her at the end of the whirlwind ride on the merry-go-round.

But there were no blue skies, no pinwheels and no happy ending waiting for her. No rides on the merry-go-round. It had turned out to be a wild ride on a roller coaster, filled with rockets and surges of inexplicable joy. And pain. Lots of pain.

She didn't like the downside of love. And she didn't know what she was going to do about it.

"Where are your shoes?" Wally wanted to know when she walked through the front door.

"Alex has them."

Wally followed her to the stairs. "I never knew Alex had a foot fetish."

She wanted to go to her room, to be alone. Maybe for the next twenty years or so. "He doesn't. They're a souvenir."

The shaggy rust-colored brows drew together as Wally looked at her in confusion. "Of what?"

"Of a moment of madness." Paula took a deep breath. "Daddy, I don't want to talk right now." Her voice caught, and she turned away, afraid that her tears were going to start again. She had cried all the way home. Thirty miles of crying had taken a lot out of her.

She coughed to mask her distress. "I've got a cold coming on."

But Wally didn't let her escape. He wasn't fooled so easily. He put his hand over hers on the banister. Paula stopped, though she didn't turn to look at him. "Sounds like you have a lot worse than that coming on. You haven't called me Daddy since you were five years old."

She bit her upper lip. "I'm going through my second childhood."

Wally took two steps until he was standing directly above her and could look down into her face. He took her chin in his hand. "Sounds like you're going through your first really big heartbreak."

Her shoulders sagged. "Never could put anything over on you, could I?"

"Oh, I don't know. This thing with Alex had me going for a little while."

Her eyes opened wide, stunned. Then this had all been for nothing? Her heart getting caught in a vise was for nothing? "You knew?"

There was no sign of gloating. Only a soft, gentle smile. "Yes."

"From the beginning?" She was even a worse actress than he had thought.

"No, not from the beginning. I told you, you had me going for a while." He chuckled. Placing his hand on her shoulder, he urged her to come down.

Paula walked down the steps, then stopped at the landing. "When did you find out? *How* did you find out?"

He took her hand and walked into the family room, then sat down on the floral sofa. "Erica."

Paula was too keyed up to sit. "She came and told you?" Paula asked, stunned. Couldn't she trust anyone anymore? No, she couldn't. She couldn't even trust herself to act normally, so why did she expect to trust anyone else?

Wally shook his head. "Not exactly. Remember that day you sent me off to talk to Paul?"

"Yes?"

"Well, we did iron things out, then."

This wasn't making any sense to her. "But you didn't tell—"

He raised a reprimanding brow. "Who's telling the story?"

Paula sank down on the sofa. "You." She knotted her fingers together to keep from clutching his arm and pumping the story out of him at a faster pace.

"Then let me tell it."

She pressed her lips together, searching for strength. Her father was a born storyteller, but there was a time and a place for long, drawn-out tales. Right now, all she wanted were some quick answers. But she knew that asking for them wouldn't get her anywhere. "Sorry."

"Just like your mother, never letting me finish." But he said it with a fond, faraway affection that made Paula wonder. She knew that the only way she was going to get any answers was to let him continue in his own fashion.

"When Paul and I finally resolved our differences, Erica came over and laughed, saying that now you and Alex wouldn't have to go on with that ridiculous charade of yours." He saw the stubborn set of his daughter's jaw. "Anyway, we couldn't let her get away with that, so we pumped her. That girl wouldn't make much of a secret agent. She told us everything in a matter of minutes, though she did mumble something about leaving town once you found out that she told us."

So that was why Erica had looked so nervous the day she had stopped by her restaurant, Paula thought. The rat.

"Paul and I thought it might be a good idea if we continued to pretend that we were still angry with each other, so that you and Alex could go on with your charade."

Now that made the least sense of all. "Why would you do that?"

Wally grinned from ear to ear as he leaned back. The thick cushions absorbed him the way a bun absorbed a hot dog. "Because I've always wanted you to get together with Alex. We were hoping that the pretense might lead to the real thing."

A lie within a lie, she thought dryly. "Well, you hoped wrong."

Wally closed one eye slightly and peered at her. "Did I?"

"You did. Alex hates me. He hates everything I stand for."

The look on Wally's face told her that he wasn't buying it, even if she was. "That's why he kept your shoes? To remind him how much he hated you?"

"You don't understand." What was the use? she didn't understand, either.

"Oh, I might," Wally told her loftily. He laced his hands behind his head as he leaned back even farther. "I might understand more than you think. Now I'm no expert, but it seems to me that when you really love someone—"

"I—" she began to deny it.

"You're interrupting again." He eyed her, and she fell silent. "When you really love someone, you should be able to make some compromises. As long as you're not the only one doing the compromising."

"It's no use." She shifted restlessly on the sofa. It was a restlessness that had no relief in sight.

Wally placed a hand to his heart as his eyes bugged out in shock. "Is this Paula? My Paula? I'd like to see some ID please. My Paula would never give up."

Paula laughed, but the laugh was tinged in bitterness. "Your Paula was never in love."

"So you admit it." He seemed content with the admission.

She shrugged, trapped. "A lot of good it does me now."

"Not one whit of good, admitting it to me. Go tell Alex."

She shook her head. No, not in a million years. "He thinks I've ruined his life."

"Did he say that?"

"Not in so many words."

"Oh, I see." Wally folded his hands across his stomach and studied them. "So just when did you take up mind reading?"

She didn't want to talk about it anymore. Talking wasn't going to do any good. Nothing was going to do any good. Besides, there was something her father hadn't cleared up yet. Something she just had to know. Paula leaned over, tucking one leg under her. "Pop, what was between you and Uncle Paul?"

Wally looked a little uncomfortable, but he didn't avoid her gaze. "A lot of years and a cloud I never knew existed."

"Does it get any clearer than this?"

"C'mere."

He held out his arm to her. Paula leaned against him, wishing she could feel as safe and warm here now as she had when she was a little girl. But that had long since passed. She couldn't hide in the shelter of her father's arm any longer. The world had found her out.

"I guess after what you've been through, I owe you the truth. I can't hold a grudge against Paul for not telling me the truth, if I can't do the same with my own daughter." He took a deep breath. "I found out, quite by accident, that Paul had slept with your mother."

Paula bolted upright. "What?"

"Get your eyes back in your head, baby." He pressed her head back against his shoulder. "Your generation didn't invent lovemaking. Mine did. Anyway, it happened long before I became serious about her. Just one of those things, I guess. What hurt me wasn't that they had slept together. I could have understood that. It was that Paul kept it from me all these years. I loved him like a brother, trusted him with my soul, and he had kept this secret from me. That hurt."

She could just imagine the anguish Paul had gone through, keeping the secret all these years. She raised her head to look at her father. "But he probably didn't want to hurt you."

"That's right. That was the point I had to get through my thick skull. He kept it from me for my own good, not because he enjoyed having a secret on me. But after I found out, I blamed him for our breakup, your mother's and mine. I thought that maybe we broke up because she was always comparing me to Paul and finding me lacking. But then I remembered. I'm a great lover, so it couldn't have been that." There was humor dancing in his eyes as he said it. "No, the problems your mother and I had had nothing to do with Paul." He grew more serious as he took Paula's hands into his. "People are complicated creatures, baby. Don't make things worse by not communicating. Don't make my mistake."

"I've already made a huge one of my own, Pop."

"I don't know about that, but I'd say that losing Alex would qualify under that heading."

"You can't lose what you don't have, Pop."

But he wasn't listening to her excuses. That's all they were to him, just flimsy excuses. "You lost your shoes. Why don't you go back to Alex's apartment and get them back?"

Paula sighed and shook her head. "It's not that simple, Pop."

"It's not that complicated, baby. Not unless you make it that way."

She kissed his cheek and rose to her feet. "I'm glad you and Uncle Paul are back together again. That's all I ever wanted. Now there's no more need to pretend anything anymore. Good night, Pop. It's been a long day, and I'm really very, very tired."

He had given her all the help he could. The rest was up to her. Wally watched his daughter leave the room, hoping that he wasn't wrong about her.

Chapter Seventeen

It was a day for endings. The taping of the special was in its final moments. It was past the point of rewrites and script tinkering. The writers' job was over.

A lot of things, Paula thought, were over.

She tried to keep her hands, if not her mind, occupied by packing up. After today she was unemployed again. She had absolutely no idea what tomorrow would bring. Once that had been exciting. Now all it brought was an uneasy restlessness racing through her. The unknown had lost some of its flash. That was, she knew, Alex's influence on her.

"C'mon, Paulie, do that later." Marty took the pad out of her hands and put it back on her desk. "There's a big party being held on the soundstage. The producers have gone all out because the special looks like such a hit."

"It *is* such a hit," Paula corrected, making a stab at playfulness. She didn't want any sympathy aimed in her direction. She wasn't up to it. "I'd rather make sure everything's packed up first. You know how grumpy I get when I can't find something." She resumed stacking the notes she had decided to keep for future reference. "You and Ted go. I'll be there in a little while."

"Sure thing." Ted was already at the door, smoothing down his unruly hair. "Think I can get to first base with that cute little blonde from casting?"

Paula pretended to consider the question. "Only with a baseball bat. But what the heck, try." Paula winked her encouragement. Ted disappeared down the hall, ready to take on the challenge. Paula listlessly picked up a handful of pencils.

"There were about two hundred and fifty watts missing from that wink."

Paula turned to look at Marty who was still standing in the doorway, his hands shoved into his pockets. He was silently studying her.

"What?"

Marty straightened. "I've known you close to two years now, Paulie. I've never seen you like this."

She shrugged and deposited the pencils into the cardboard box. They clattered noisily against the various things that were already in there. "I'm just a little tired, that's all."

He wasn't convinced. "The Paula I know never gets tired. She hardly eats, doesn't sleep—"

Paula turned, a self-deprecating smile on her lips. "—Bends steel in her bare hands—"

Marty pointed a finger at her. "Bingo, that's her. Know her?"

Paula dragged her hand through her hair. "I used to." She crossed to him. "Marty." She touched his cheek, affected. "Thanks."

Marty looked at her, confused. "For what?"

"For caring."

"Is it doing any good?"

She inclined her head slightly. Nothing was going to do any good, but she didn't have to tell him. It wasn't his fault that her life wasn't destined toward a happy ending. "It's nice to know it's there."

"Okay. I guess I'll move along."

"See you later."

"Sure." He waved as he left. "Thanks for recommending me for this job."

"I always like having the best around." She raised her voice so that he could hear.

"You deserve it," he called back, his words echoing down the hall.

Alone again, Paula threw her PC into its leather carrying case and went through the motions of securing it. The zipper was left hanging half opened.

"You pick that thing up that way and it's going to fall out and break."

Paula swung around to see her father standing in the doorway. Was the whole world planning to pass by and comment on her activities? On her life? She knew her reaction was unreasonable and banked it down. After all, people were just expressing their concern. They cared about her.

But the most important person didn't, she thought miserably.

She raised her eyes to her father. "You startled me, Pop."

He crossed into the room. "I was hoping to shake you up." Wally took hold of her arm and pulled her away from the desk and the half-filled carton. "C'mon, baby. There's a great party going on to celebrate our hit."

There was no use pretending with her father. "I don't much feel like celebrating." She grabbed an armload of books.

He took the books out of her hands and leaned against the desk. Paula sat down listlessly on her chair. "We couldn't have done this special without you."

"Sure you could have," Paula said without much feeling.

"You were the one who got us back together."

"That would have happened eventually, too."

Wally cupped her chin in his hand. "You don't believe that." A smile began to rise. "No."

"Neither do I. C'mon." He rose again, nodding toward the door and the party that lay just beyond. "I hate seeing you like this."

"I hate seeing me like this, too. But there doesn't seem to be much I can do about it right now except to ride it out." She saw the look of concern etch deeper on her father's face. She leaned forward and kissed his cheek. "I'll be fine, Pop, honest. I just need a little time to pull myself together, that's all. Here." She handed him the tickets to Vegas.

Wally stared down at them. "What's this?"

"Oh, how soon they forget," she quipped. It was a half-hearted attempt, but at least it was a start. "They're the tickets you gave me for my elopement. I don't seem to be needing them anymore."

He pressed them back into her hand. "Well, I can't use them. Paul and I are going on a tour."

Her eyes grew wide. Finally some good news. "Really?"

"Yeah, we're having a twenty-fifth-anniversary celebration through twenty-five big cities."

Something didn't click. "But you've been together for twenty-*seven* years."

He laughed. "So who's counting? Twenty-five sounds better. Besides, the first two years were so bad we had to bribe the audience to come. They don't count."

She threw her arms around him and hugged hard. "Oh, Pop, I'm so glad for you."

Wally patted her arm. He wished that he could take the pain from her. But some things people had to go through themselves, no matter how unfair that was, he thought. "Yeah, me, too. Listen, keep the tickets. Maybe you can use them to get away for a little while."

She turned them over in her hand, not really seeing them. "Yes, maybe I will." She barely noticed her father leaving.

Paula settled down in her chair. She was alone again. More alone than she could ever remember. Drifting in through the open door were the sounds of the ongoing celebration. It seemed unreal, as if it were happening in another world.

No, that was her world. What had happened in the last three weeks was another world. A world she knew she didn't belong in.

"I've never known you to be a wallflower."

She swung around in the swivel chair. Alex. Her heart began to pound, even though she willed it to stop. Maybe altogether. Paula gripped the armrests tightly. Her mouth felt suddenly dry. "How long have you been standing there?"

"A couple of minutes. I went to the party first. You weren't there."

"No, I wasn't."

He walked in, and she rose to her feet, suddenly feeling vulnerable. "You forgot these last night." He held her shoes aloft.

Paula snatched them back, then, embarrassed, let them drop to the floor. "I forgot a lot of things last night."

"Like?"

She raised her head, keeping emotion from her voice. "Like who and what I am."

"Why didn't you ask me? I know exactly who and what you are."

"Alex—"

He held up his hand before she could go on. "I've been doing a lot of thinking since last night."

"So have I." She saw that he was about to say something. "Don't stop me because my courage is going to run out if I don't say this all at once."

He nodded, wondering what he was in for, knowing that whatever she said didn't matter. He had made up his mind. "Go ahead."

Paula began to unconsciously pace as she talked. "I want to talk to Diana and fix things up for you."

Diana? What had she to do with anything? Alex crossed his arms before his chest. "Oh you do, do you? And just what is it you plan to fix now?"

She didn't care for the sarcasm. This time, it hurt her rather than goaded her on to make a retort. "Your future," you big idiot, she added silently.

"With Diana," he repeated, as if trying to make some kind of sense out of her words.

What was wrong with him? Had he suddenly been struck stupid? This was all he wanted, right? "With Diana," she gestured vaguely, impatiently, in the air, "with her father, with the firm."

A touch of humor began to rise in his eyes. "Sounds a little crowded to me."

"Don't make jokes, Alex," she snapped, fighting to keep the tears out of her voice. "That's my department." Her voice softened. "I couldn't stand the guilt of messing up your life, your career. I know how important it is to you, how much energy and time you've put into it. I'll go see Diana and tell her that what she saw that night was all part of a charade."

He looked at her for a long, silent moment. She thought she was going to scream. "Was it?" he finally asked, his voice low.

"Weren't you paying attention?" she demanded. "Of course it was a charade." She stopped pacing in front of him. Something in his eyes made her stop. "Wasn't it a charade to you?"

"I don't know." He looked at her thoughtfully. Didn't she know? Of course she did. For some reason, it frightened her. He couldn't picture that, Paula frightened. It made him feel protective. "Maybe everything before that was the charade."

A small nugget of hope began to build in her soul. A smile rose to her lips. "Alex, you're babbling."

He gathered her in his arms. It felt so good just to hold her, to take in that fragrance that was hers alone. "I always seem to do that around you," he said, repeating the words he had said to her only three weeks ago in an entirely different frame of mind. He leaned his forehead against hers. "Why do you suppose that is?"

"I don't know." She echoed her own response. "I'd like to believe that I bring out the best in you."

"You do. It took me a hell of a long time to realize that, but you do." He leaned back a little, to get a better look at her face. "As for what's important to me, I don't think you have the faintest idea what's important to me."

He kissed her then, long and hard. There was no mistaking the passion or the promise. Paula's heart leapt up. Oh God, she had been so miserable without this. She threaded her fingers through his hair, pressing him even closer as her tongue touched his, sending electric sparks through both of them. When he stopped kissing her, they were both breathless. And misunderstandings, hurt feelings and pain were beginning to fade.

"Does this mean you care?" It was hard not to sigh the words.

"No." Alex almost laughed out loud at the perplexed look that flashed across her face. "That means I love you, the for-better-or-for-worse kind of love." He kept his arms around her. "That means I can't seem to function without you anymore, even though I tried to talk myself into it. I tried to talk myself into a lot of things along the way, like that I was happy doing what I was doing."

"You weren't?" Though she had often teased him about it, she had thought that he was content at least in his way of life. To hear otherwise surprised her. And gave her added hope.

He shook his head. "I wasn't happy, I wasn't unhappy. I wasn't anything," he grinned, "except around you."

"Then you were angry."

"Then I was alive," he corrected. "*You* made me alive. You made me think and feel and want." Slowly he ran his hands up and down her sides. "Oh God, did you ever make me want."

"Really?"

He kissed the corners of her mouth. "Really."

The feeling, she thought, was mutual. Very, very mutual. She curved her body into his. "Even when you were putting me down?"

"Most especially when I was putting you down. You got under my skin. I didn't know how to handle that. You represented everything I thought I didn't want." He let several kisses flutter across her face. He loved the way she closed her eyes and sighed. "Everything I really did want. You made me discover that stability isn't a place, a situation, it's an inner peace that you carry around inside. No matter how crazy you appeared at times, you always seemed to have that." He had to stop himself or else he would be tempted to separate her from her sweater and skirt. "And I didn't."

She didn't want him to step away. There was laughter in her eyes as she took a step forward, melting their distance and his restraint as she pressed her body up against his and this time threaded her hands around him. "But you had a lot of other things going for you."

"Oh, like what?" he asked, amused.

"You're dependable." She saw him raise his brow.

"Very exciting description."

"I *like* the fact that I can depend on you, that you come through for me, even against your better judgment. From where I stand, a little stability would be rather nice right about now."

He framed her face in his hands. "Well, you're not getting it. I want those pinwheels of yours, those rockets and that wild ride in the eye of the hurricane." His mouth covered hers in a short, almost savage kiss that drained her. "You're my hurricane, Paula. Don't ever stop being you. Say you'll marry me, Paula. I need you." His voice lowered. "I love you." To his surprise, he saw tears gather in her eyes.

"Are you sure?"

A tear trickled down her face. He kissed it away. "Never more sure of anything in my life."

"Really, really sure?"

"Really, really sure."

She grinned at him. "It's about time you figured that out." Oh God, she loved him so much. Then she became serious again. "But what about your job? Won't things be rather difficult for you now that you've spurned the boss's daughter?"

"No," he assured her, "not difficult at all."

That didn't make any sense. She had seen the anger in Diana's eyes that night she saw them together. "How can you be so sure?"

"Because I quit this morning."

If he had told her that he had sprouted wings and could fly, she wouldn't have been more stunned. She gripped his shoulders and rose on her toes, as if to emphasize her surprise. "You did *what*?"

"I quit. I had to." Alex stroked her hair. He loved the silken texture. "Corbett walked into my office this morning, wanting to discuss the 'wild oats' I was sowing. And yes, to answer that question I see rising up in your eyes, he was putting a lot of pressure on me to see my way clear to marrying his daughter. But while he was giving me his latest 'talk,' I suddenly realized that if you were 'wild oats' I never wanted to sample any other kind ever again.'' Alex smiled broadly as he remembered. ''That didn't sit very well with him.''

''I can imagine.''

''So I quit.''

Paula bit her lower lip. ''Alex, you're giving up an awful lot for me.''

''You were just willing to give up a lot, too,'' he reminded her.

''Me? What was I giving up?''

''Me.'' He kissed her forehead so tenderly, Paula's limbs were in danger of dissolving right then and there. ''For my own good, I gather.''

Paula rested her hands on his chest. Now that she noticed, his tie was undone. It was a nice touch. ''You've picked up my father's modesty.''

''I'd rather pick up your father's daughter.''

''You have her, Alex. Maybe you've always had her.'' She wrapped her arms around his neck. ''Do you think we'll ever stop arguing?''

His hands about her waist, he drew her close again. ''God, I hope not. I couldn't think of anything more boring.''

Paula laughed, delighted. ''You're learning, Alex. You're learning.''

''I have a great teacher.'' He leaned to kiss her, but Paula pulled away.

''What are you planning to do?''

He kept his eyes on her lips. ''Kiss you until my mouth turns numb.''

Amusement lit up her face. ''No, I meant about your future.''

He took a small nip out of her bottom lip. ''That *is* my future.''

A shard of pleasure slashed through her. ''I mean your career.'' Words were becoming increasingly difficult to form.

''Oh, that.''

''Yes, that.''

"I was thinking of striking out on my own, actually. A little risk, a little daring. But I feel confident. It might be just what I need. *After* the honeymoon, of course." He leaned forward to kiss her again, but she had turned her head.

"Wait. Here." She picked up the tickets that she had dropped on her desk and placed them in his hand.

Alex looked down at his hand. "What're these?"

"Tickets to Las Vegas. My father gave to me so that I could get away. Want to get away with me?"

"Now that's the best idea you've ever had." His gaze skimmed her body, and she moved forward into his arms. "Well, maybe the second best idea." He lowered his mouth to hers, but she backed away again, although only slightly. He looked at her quizzically. Now what?

"We have an audience." She nodded toward the opened door.

Wally and Paul were standing in the hallway, grinning broadly. They had seen Alex leaving the party and had guessed at his destination.

"Don't mind us," Wally laughed heartily.

"Don't worry," Alex promised, nudging the door closed with his elbow. "We won't."

Through the closed door, they heard her father say, "Great idea I had."

"What do you mean, *you* had? It was my idea," Paul protested.

"They're at it again," Alex murmured.

"This time they're going to have to settle their own problems. I'm busy."

"How busy?"

She drew up on her toes, her body molding against his. "Very, very busy," she whispered against his mouth.

She didn't have a chance to verbally elaborate. But then, she thought, they'd done enough talking for one day.

* * * * *

Harlequin Romance ®

Delightful

Affectionate

Romantic

Emotional

Tender

Original

Daring

Riveting

Enchanting

Adventurous

Moving

Harlequin Romance—the
series that has it all!

HROM-G

HARLEQUIN PRESENTS®

HARLEQUIN PRESENTS
men you won't be able to resist falling in love with...

HARLEQUIN PRESENTS
women who have feelings just like your own...

HARLEQUIN PRESENTS
powerful passion in exotic international settings...

HARLEQUIN PRESENTS
intense, dramatic stories that will keep you turning
to the very last page...

HARLEQUIN PRESENTS
The world's bestselling romance series!

Harlequin® Historical

HARLEQUIN®

I N T R I G U E®

THAT'S INTRIGUE—DYNAMIC ROMANCE AT ITS BEST!

Harlequin Intrigue is now bringing you more—more men and mystery, more desire and danger. If you've been looking for thrilling tales of contemporary passion and sensuous love stories with taut, edge-of-the-seat suspense—then you'll *love* Harlequin Intrigue!

Every month, you'll meet four new heroes who are guaranteed to make your spine tingle and your pulse pound. With them you'll enter into the exciting world of Harlequin Intrigue—where your life is on the line and so is your heart!

Harlequin Intrigue—we'll leave you breathless!

INT-GEN

Lucille Ball
and
Desi Arnaz

The day Desi Arnaz proposed to Lucille Ball she had just completed an interview for an article titled Why I Will Always Be A Bachelor Girl. Despite her doubts that the marriage would last more than six weeks, Lucy exchanged vows—and wedding rings purchased from Woolworth's—with Desi at the Byre River Beagle Country Club in Greenwich, Connecticut. It was 1941.

Their marriage produced a boy and a girl and lasted nineteen years before it ended in divorce. Together they made the "I Love Lucy" show one of the most celebrated television programs of all time.

B-LUCY